every little thing she bakes is magic

Carrie Hope Fletcher

all that she can see

sphere

SPHERE

First published in Great Britain in 2017 by Sphere
This paperback edition published in 2018 by Sphere

7 9 10 8 6

A CIP catalogue record for this book
is available from the British Library.

ISBN 978-0-7515-6320-7

Typeset in Sabon by M Rules
Printed and bound in Great Britain by
Clays Ltd, Elcograf S.p.A.

Papers used by Sphere are from well-managed forests
and other responsible sources.

Sphere
An imprint of
Little, Brown Book Group
Carmelite House
50 Victoria Embankment
London EC4Y 0DZ

An Hachette UK Company
www.hachette.co.uk

www.littlebrown.co.uk

To the voices in our heads that tell us
we aren't good enough: do be quiet.

The Hermit

'See the good in people and help them.'

Gandhi

Prologue

Always Welcome

An elegant hand flipped an old-fashioned lever and, with a satisfying sizzle, six lightbulbs flickered into life above six long tables. Cherry looked around at her almost-finished bakery. The wood of the tables was a warm, autumnal colour and there was an old, brassy till on the counter with buttons that *clickity clacked*. It had cost her a small fortune, but the sound of the *ding* when it opened made it worth every penny. Though she had wondered whether the room was *too* old-fashioned, the black slate floor, giant chalkboard and gold and turquoise wallpaper gave it a modern twist. Before Cherry opened the bakery doors to the town, it needed to be finished to her liking and she couldn't wait for the glass cabinet by the till to be filled with sweet treats for people to come in and enjoy.

It was ten o'clock at night. Cherry had an early start in the morning so had been tucked up in bed with her book, reading the same paragraph over and over again, her mind on tomorrow, when a familiar tingle in the back of her head and a faint moaning had brought her downstairs to the bakery. It wasn't the sound of someone hurt or in pain, nor did it sound sad. It didn't even sound like a person. It sounded like Loneliness – a sound Cherry knew only too well. Someone, somewhere, was feeling alone.

Rain was steadily falling from dark, night-time clouds in thick drops that could soak you to the bone in moments. The beginning of a storm. The sea didn't help as the waves mischievously whipped up, spraying over the railings and onto Margie as she walked home to her cramped and empty flat. A strong gale pulled furiously at her drab clothes and wrinkled skin. She nuzzled into her fur-lined coat collar, imagining warm arms surrounding her, hugging away the cold. Margie kept a dress shop in the village a little down the road from her house on the seafront, but business was bad. Money was tight and life behind the counter was as lonely and unfulfilling as life at home but she persevered nonetheless, staying later and later each night making dress after dress after dress. Margie didn't feel like life was one step forwards and two steps back, she simply felt like all her steps were backwards, no matter how hard she pushed. So one day she had stopped pushing and let the tide of life carry her wherever it desired instead.

Little did Margie know that the reason she felt so empty and unfulfilled was because every step she took a shadow crept a few feet behind her. It was a tall, looming creature with a devilish grin, big black eyes, and the silver fur around its neck glimmered. Its long, spindly fingers were pierced through the hem of Margie's soul, like pins through fabric. It wiggled its digits and Margie shivered. Its name was Loneliness and it was mean.

Margie was no exception, of course. We're all followed by ... something. It's not the poisonous voices that creep into our heads as we're drifting into sleep, or that prickling feeling we get when we think we're being watched. No, the things that follow us are literal; they're actual, and they're made up of entirely bad feeling. Loneliness, Anxiety, Aggression, Depression, Disappointment, Sadness, Hopelessness, Uselessness, Regret and many, *many* more make up the ranks of creatures that we mistakenly befriend. Unwittingly, we invite them to attach themselves to our souls, allowing them to dictate our lives, like a dreary puppet show in which we are the puppets and they are the puppet masters.

They're intelligent, too. When thousands of people across the planet feel the same awful feeling at the same awful moment, that creature splits and multiplies and attaches itself to each person experiencing that feeling. With every split, they become stronger. They can't be seen and their voices can only be heard as our own voices in the back of our minds. Most people don't know their souls are being controlled by something else. The only way to get rid of them is to let light and love and happiness destroy them – as we feel better, they feel worse, and will shrink and shrink until there's nothing left. If only we could see these beings in their true form, with their soulless black eyes and the peculiar way they sit on their haunches ready to pounce – then we would try our hardest to be optimistic and look to the light, even when life has turned bleak. Instead, we ignore our bad feelings and inner demons because it's *easier*, which leaves these beings free to pull on the puppet strings.

Margie's soul had been lost to her ever since her husband had passed away thirteen years ago. At first, Grief took its hold, but Grief is temporary so Margie didn't dance with that particular feeling for long. Loneliness, though, lingers and it found a fast friend in Margie.

When she wanted to talk to those around her, it pinched her lips closed and whispered in her ear, telling her that no one cared about what she had to say. When Margie found herself by the phone, wanting to call someone just to hear another person's voice, Loneliness held her hands against her sides. It found ways to keep her to itself, and slowly but surely she'd stopped resisting altogether.

Margie didn't know she was fighting Loneliness; she couldn't see it, and she had no idea it was controlling her every move. She had, in human terms, simply given up, just like everyone whose soul is no longer their own eventually does.

As a sob was about to escape Margie's throat, a noise cut through the whistle of the wind and she snapped her head around towards a light in the doorway to her right. The light hit Loneliness, burning it like a white-hot branding iron. In pain and panic, it lifted its hands to shield itself from the light and in doing so its fingers slid out of Margie's soul, tearing the fabric a little.

'You there!' called a voice above the gush of the sea.

'Me?' whimpered Margie, pointing to herself with a red raw hand.

'Come in!' The young lady in the doorway reached inside and pulled up the blind in the front window, revealing a warmly lit coffee shop with a bakery counter and lovely wooden furniture. Margie looked towards her journey home, grey and miserable, much like the evening she'd find when she got there, and hesitated.

'Quickly!' the woman shouted, looking over Margie's shoulder as though she had seen something in the darkness. Margie undeniably felt danger somewhere in the shadows and before she, and Loneliness, knew it, her feet were moving her towards the light.

Once Margie was safely inside, the young lady quickly closed the door and offered to take her coat. Margie guessed that she couldn't have been more than twenty-five, almost half her own age, and she seemed to be wearing pyjamas under an oversized knitted burgundy jumper with grey slippers on her feet. She had a kind, heart-shaped face and her Afro hair was secured in bunches on the top of her head. The lady helped Margie out of her dripping coat and as she did Margie noticed how grey and blotched her own skin looked next to the lady's warm, dark arm. The young lady shook the worst of the rain from the coat and hung it on the coat stand next to the counter.

'Now,' said the lady, smiling. 'What can I get you? On the house.'

Margie didn't know what to say. She was sure she didn't know this young woman and yet she was talking to Margie like they were old friends.

'Erm . . .'

'Wait, don't tell me.' The woman held up a finger and scrunched her eyes closed. Margie looked down at her sodden shoes and the wet footprints she'd left on the wooden floor and wondered if maybe she should take them off but when she looked up, the woman had disappeared. Margie could hear the clattering of plates and the tinkle of cutlery towards the back of the shop.

'You . . . you really don't need to go to any trouble,' Margie called weakly towards the noise. She had found her voice but it was too feeble to be heard from wherever the woman had gone to.

Margie looked around and realised that the shop was only half finished. Cans of paint sat on the floor next to stripped skirting boards and the wires for the lighting were exposed. Margie felt awkward and out of place so before she made an even bigger fool of herself she dashed to the coat stand and grabbed her coat – putting her right arm through the left hole in a mad panic, but it didn't matter. She just needed to leave. She opened the door quickly, not noticing the old-fashioned bell above it, which rang out loudly.

'WAIT!' called the lady, reappearing with a small plate in one hand and a steaming mug in the other. 'Please don't go. I just ... I want to help.'

Loneliness was sitting outside the shop – with its back against the wall, it was poised, ready to latch itself back onto Margie like a barnacle on the bottom of a ship the minute she walked outside. Standing on the threshold, Margie thought again of her pokey, cold flat and wondered what exactly it was she was running back to. The door swung shut.

'Sorry,' Margie said. 'I'm not very good with ... people.' She shrugged off her coat again, which the lady hung back on the coat stand. She gently manoeuvred Margie by the shoulders to the table where she'd placed the plate and the mug. There was a large chunk of cake on the plate. *Marble, by the looks of it*, Margie thought.

'I wasn't very good with people either until recently,' said the lady, taking a seat across from Margie and handing her a fork. Margie took it and separated a delicate sliver of the cake. 'Turns out I just wasn't very good with myself.'

That sentence bounced around the pit of Margie's stomach and settled with a rumble. She looked down at the fluffy morsel on her fork and took a bite. The cake was moist but dense, and chocolate and vanilla flavours burst in her mouth. When Margie swallowed she could feel it warm her from the inside out, the kind of warm you feel when you snuggle into bed on a cold night with a hot water bottle tucked between the sheets. Margie took another bite. And another. And another. It wasn't until she went to have yet another mouthful that she saw there were just crumbs left and she'd eaten the whole slice.

'That may be the best cake I've ever had,' Margie sighed. Then she chuckled and, remembering how good it felt, chuckled at the feeling of chuckling until Margie was laughing so hard she thought she'd never stop. The lady sat and laughed with her, seemingly enjoying the feeling of making someone happy. Eventually Margie wiped tears from her eyes and said tentatively, unsure of how to make conversation, 'Are you new here?'

The lady nodded. 'I am.'

'Are you staying?' Margie asked, gesturing to the shop that was clearly midway through renovation.

'I am. I thought this town could do with a bakery.'

'Oh ... we already have one,' said Margie quietly, torn between not wanting this lady to leave town but also not wanting the bakery in the village to lose business. The townspeople were very fond of their spectacular Belgian buns.

'Not one like mine,' the lady said, smiling as she took the plate and placed it on the shop counter.

'No, I suppose not,' Margie said, still feeling warm.

A silence fell over them, one that didn't feel awkward or that needed filling. It was a content silence that friends often share.

'I suppose I should get home,' Margie finally said, without moving.

'All right,' said the lady, reaching for Margie's coat and holding it open for Margie to put her arms through. When her coat was on and she was at the open door, Margie turned without warning and hugged the lady, who hugged her back just as hard.

'Thank you.'

'Go on. Get yourself home before it gets too late.' The lady gave her a gentle push out of the door.

As soon as Margie's feet touched the ground outside, Loneliness hopped towards her but was surprised to find it was shorter than when Margie had entered the shop. It still latched its fingers onto Margie's soul but as its fingers were smaller than before, they didn't fit the holes it had made as well any more – it had a harder time keeping hold of her. Margie walked to the road, but before the shop door closed she turned in panic.

'Wait! I didn't catch your name!'

The lady was now only a silhouette against the warm yellow light. 'It's Cherry. Cherry Redgrave.'

'Nice to meet you, Cherry. I'm Margie.'

As she started to walk on, Cherry called, 'Margie?'

She turned to look again at Cherry and even though she was still just a silhouette, Margie was sure she was smiling.

'You're always welcome here.'

1

The Usuals

Cherry had never wanted to be a baker. As a child, she had wanted to be a firefighter. She had dreams of gushing water from snake-like hoses, pouring onto burning, crumbling houses; of reuniting children with their mothers after carrying them from the flames and sometimes of rescuing dogs from wells and kittens from trees. But baking? Never. However, as life often does, it dragged Cherry off in a direction she hadn't expected and she now found herself standing in her very own bakery, and it wasn't even her first one. It may not have been her childhood aspiration, but she couldn't imagine herself doing anything else now. When she unlocked the door at eight every morning, when she flipped the sign from CLOSED to OPEN and when her first customer of the day made the bell above the door jingle, something deep within her hummed, *This is where you're meant to be.* Letting go of her firefighting dreams didn't seem all that painful when she'd found she had an inexplicable talent in something so delightfully delicious.

After meeting Margie, it had taken Cherry another two weeks to get her bakery by the seafront in working order. There was no sign outside, nothing to signify this was a place to buy cake and sip tea, yet Cherry knew people would come. They always did.

This was Cherry's eighth stop on what she called her 'Flour Power Tour'. She would move to a small town, find a shop with cheap rent and set to work. Once she felt her task was done, that she'd done all the good she could do, she would move on to somewhere else and do the same all over again.

Some visits were shorter than others. The longest had been a year and a half, surprisingly in the smallest town she'd visited. Cherry had found that the smaller the town the bigger the issues, and had a feeling that maybe this latest stop might be one of her longest stays yet.

Merely days into her stay, she knew this would be a difficult place to leave. Each morning, she came downstairs from her flat above the bakery, wearing a freshly ironed pair of pyjamas, ready for a busy day ahead. Cherry always wore pyjamas – she didn't understand why everybody didn't. When a previous next door neighbour had insisted she get dressed into something a little more appropriate she had replied, 'They're the comfiest item of clothing known to man. Why anyone would choose to wear dresses you can't breathe in and high heels you can't walk in when pyjamas and slippers are readily available to everyone ... well, it's beyond me!'

So she tied her hair into two Minnie Mouse-esque bunches, donned a pair of flannel pyjamas, skidded across the shop floor in her matching slippers and unlatched the door. Within moments, her Usuals started to arrive.

Sally Lightbody, aged seventy-two and retired, was always the first person to show up. She'd breeze in at 8:15 every morning, swathed in layers of floaty silk. Her silver hair was tangled and matted into dreadlocks which she tied tight above her head with a purple and green patchwork scarf, a scarf that perfectly matched the satchel in which she kept a black box of Tarot cards. Sally had been drawn to Cherry's shop one day not by fate but by a desperate need to relieve her bladder.

'Go on,' Sally had said, waving her box of cards at Cherry until she nodded. Sally shuffled and drew the first card, and her lips curled at the corners. Immediately, she swept her cards back into their black box and sipped her tea. Sally refused to tell Cherry what the card had revealed, but every day since, she arrived at 8:15 and would sit in her usual spot by the window until closing time. Throughout the day, customers would come to Sally to have their fortunes and futures laid out before them. She never asked for money for her services and she always bought her first slice of cake herself, but it had become customary to buy Sally a slice of something sweet in return for a reading. Her usual treat(ment) was a Will-Power Walnut Whip first thing, and from then on Cherry served her Victoria sponge, Sally's favourite.

Sally looked calm but beneath the bundles of silk and crystal necklaces, she had an obsessive streak. She'd had many fixations over the years: food, alcohol, Dickens, Laurel and Hardy, obscure inventions no one ever heard about and now fortune-telling. One by one, each thing had consumed her and she would live, sleep and breathe them until there was nothing more of them to consume. Fortune-telling had kept her obsessed for almost thirty years now, however, and when Cherry asked why she'd stuck with it for so long, Sally had replied, 'It's the future, love. It's always changing.'

At 10:30 Margie would pop in for a chunk of marble cake to keep her going in her empty shop, and then at 12:45 George Partridge, the thirty-four-year-old miserable librarian, would show up for a coffee. George's mother had been the town's librarian; her mother in turn had been a librarian, and her mother before *her* had also been a librarian, but George hated reading. Growing up with books shoved into his hands, being forced to recite prose and quizzed on great writers had instilled in George a resentment for all kinds of literature.

And then at five o'clock on the dot, Cherry's final Usual of the day would arrive.

'The usual please, Miss Redgrave,' said a voice.

Cherry couldn't see its owner but she knew exactly who it belonged to. 'And which usual would that be today, Bruce?' she said, wiping her hands on a tea towel as Bruce clambered onto a tall stool at the counter. His hands grasped the brown leather seat and as he heaved himself up, his size-four feet came off the ground. He swung his legs around like a gymnast on a pommel horse and with a breath of relief he replied, 'Whatever you say it is.'

Cherry gave him a smile but as she ducked to reach for his treat in the display counter, her eyes welled with tears. Her gaze drifted past the cakes to the large front windows of the shop and there, standing with its forehead slumped against the glass, peering in with its long drooping eyes and gangly limbs hanging lifeless by its sides . . . was Worthlessness.

Cherry looked around the tables, at all her usual customers sitting in their usual spots with their usual orders on their usual plates, wearing their usual masks in an attempt to hide what Cherry could plainly see: their bad feelings. The feelings formed a disorderly queue outside the bakery when their souls were inside, grumbling and gurgling, writhing and wrestling: Sally's Obsessiveness, Margie's Loneliness, George's Depression, Orla's Exhaustion and Bruce's Worthlessness.

17

They howled and moaned to be let inside, to take control of their humans once more, but Cherry's bakery was a safe place for her Usuals. She didn't know why but she had realised a long time ago that no matter where she opened up her bakeries, some kind of line was always drawn at the doorway, a line that no bad feeling could cross. Maybe it was because of all the good feeling she'd contained inside her shop. But they would still thump against the woodwork and bang on the windows, unheard by the townspeople and desperate to get in.

Cherry's bakery was a safe haven, a place where people could forget their troubles for an hour or two. And when their bad feelings latched back onto them as they left, Cherry noticed that their troubles seemed a little smaller than before.

2

Meddlums

From the moment she was born, Cherry Redgrave saw things other children didn't. She spoke of frightening figures that were swathed in scales, of gaunt goblins with shiny skin, and of ferocious faces with jabbering jaws. And most frighteningly of all, for every adult she saw she also saw a monster, a shadow, standing close by. As a child she thought this was a normal part of life, and she wasn't aware that no one else could see all that she could see, so when she was caught staring curiously over people's shoulders and babbled about invisible shadowed figures, adults thought she was mad and taught their children to stay away from her. Parents wondered when she would grow out of imaginary friends but Cherry wondered when parents would admit to seeing what was clearly right behind them. And then, on one ordinary day at primary school, tiny four-year-old Cherry finally realised the truth – that she was the only one who could see them.

The teacher had asked all the children in Cherry's class to form a line, starting with the shortest. Cherry had pointed to the creature at her teacher's shoulder and asked, 'What about him?'

'Who?' Mr Harrison asked, looking behind him and seeing nothing at all.

'Your monster! He's taller than all of us! He should stand at the end of the line.'

Cherry had tried to explain how the creature often waved at the class and that his smile was so wide it wrapped around his entire face and met in the middle at the back of his head. Cherry soon found herself in the headmistress's office trying to explain herself. While her teachers were terrified that the school had been infiltrated by an odd man trying to lure children away, what Cherry had actually seen was far more worthy of their concern – but nobody believed it to be real.

'It was a *monster*! Like that one in the corner!' Cherry had insisted. Her continued disturbing behaviour resulted in a change of schools and several trips to a nice lady with a comfy couch who had puppets whom she made ask Cherry questions about what she saw. And all the while Cherry couldn't stop watching the gremlin on the therapist's shoulder who kept pulling at her hair.

Cherry's new school was much nicer, she thought. She'd learnt not to talk about what she saw and only pulled faces at the monsters occasionally when she knew there weren't any adults looking. She muddled through the school years, keeping herself to herself and it was only when there was a commotion in the playground one day that seven-year-old Cherry realised she wasn't alone after all.

Kids are usually carefree and too busy spilling jam down their fronts or spinning in circles to adopt the heavy troubles of the world that manifest themselves into these beings. However, one child, a bully by the name of Maddison Flint, had developed a squat troll called Neglect that mimicked her every movement, which often made Cherry laugh out loud. Maddison was not a slender or elegant girl. She had more muscles than most weightlifters, a neck that puffed like a bullfrog when she shouted and two long brown plaits that looked as though they hadn't been unravelled since she had hair long enough to braid. To Cherry, Maddison and her troll looked one and the same.

On this day in particular, however, it seemed that Cherry wasn't the only one trying to stifle laughter. A ring of Maddison's cronies had formed around her, penning in a small boy whom Cherry recognised as the new pupil that had joined her year the week before. Cherry hadn't given much thought to how he was fitting in but given that Maddison was holding him a few inches off the pale-blue hopscotch lines by the scruff of his school shirt, Cherry figured badly.

'What d'you say?!' Maddison yelled, spraying spit in his face. The troll opened and closed its mouth in time with Maddison's but if Cherry hadn't known better she would've sworn that this only amused the boy further, and he only half-stifled his laughter. Maddison shook him roughly until his laughter stopped.

'I said, what d'you say?' she hissed, holding the small boy close to her puce and sweaty face.

'I said,' the boy giggled, apparently deliriously transfixed by something over Maddison's shoulder, 'you look like your troll!' and he was lost to laughter once more.

'Troll?! You calling me a troll?!' Maddison dropped him to the playground tarmac and kicked him in his side but before she could cause any more damage, a whistle blew and a teacher ran over to break up the ruckus. Maddison and her posse dispersed, running in several different directions, while the teacher consoled the spluttering boy she'd rescued.

'Ah, here's a helping hand,' the teacher said, spotting Cherry standing nearby. 'Cherry, dear, could you take Peter to the welfare room? There's a good girl.' She helped Peter up and wrapped his arm around Cherry's shoulders so she could take his weight, but as soon as the teacher had disappeared to sort out another playground misdemeanour, Peter snatched his arm away and wiped it on his shirt.

'Did you see it too?' he asked, rubbing his eyes. Cherry noticed the deep purple semi-circles underneath them and wondered if Maddison had hit him in the face too.

'Did I see what?' Cherry said slowly.

Peter's face fell and he balled up his hands. 'Why does no one see them?!' he shouted, his small face furious. 'Some of them are HUGE!'

'See what?' Cherry asked cautiously, trying not to look at Frustration who had hold of Peter's shoulders and was rocking him rapidly back and forth as Peter aimlessly bounced his fists around.

'They're monsters! Bogeymen! Meddlums!'

'Meddlums?' Cherry was struck by the word. She'd never heard it before.

'Monsters! You know how girls are made up of sugar and spice and everything nice?' He started to circle her, his wide eyes never leaving her face.

'Yeah ... '

'Well, Meddlums are made up of ... ' His eyes bore into hers and he nodded for her to continue the rhyme.

' ... slugs and snails and puppy dog tails?' she said.

'No-wer!' he exclaimed. 'That's what boys are made up of! Meddlums are made up of tears and sad and everything bad!' He spat when he talked. Cherry wiped her face.

'Oh. Well ... I knew that. I just didn't know the rhyme.'

'That's because I made it up.' He hooked his thumbs into his pockets and puffed out his chest, smiling proudly.

Then he stopped abruptly. 'Wait ... you know? How do you know?' Peter took her by the shoulders and started shaking her. Cherry looked into his eyes, so full of frustration, and suddenly all she wanted was to help him.

'Because I can see them too,' she whispered.

'You can?'

Cherry nodded.

'Prove it.' Peter let her go with a little shove. 'Who's that behind Maddison?'

'Neglect,' Cherry replied without skipping a beat.

'And behind her?' Peter pointed to a little girl playing hopscotch with Grief holding onto her ankle.

'Grief. She lost her auntie a couple of weeks ago,' Cherry said.

Peter's face broke into a smile and suddenly Frustration didn't have quite so tight a hold on him. He stepped forward and stood very close to Cherry as he asked, 'We're best friends now, right?'

'I suppose so.' Cherry shrugged, stepping back. 'But that means you have to tell me why you call them—'

'Meddlums,' Peter finished.

'Meddlums,' Cherry repeated, enjoying the taste of the word.

'D'ya know why?'

Peter was standing very close to Cherry again. She wanted to run away but he knew something that she didn't and she needed to find out what it was. Cherry wondered if anyone was watching them but a quick glance around the playground showed her that even if they were looking, no one cared what they were up to.

'Why?' she whispered.

'You know your good feelings?' Peter asked, and Cherry nodded. 'They meddle 'em all up until you feel horrible inside and they keep you feeling that way for ever and ever until you *die*.' Peter made a horrible squelching noise as he drove a make-believe dagger into his stomach.

'Meddlums.' Cherry repeated, rolling the name around her mouth. Yes, that felt like the right thing to call them.

'Meddlums,' Peter said with a final nod.

Cherry would always remember that day. The day she put a name to the grotesque faces that had haunted her and the people she loved since she could remember. The day she made a friend. Having someone to finally share her secret with, someone to make faces at the Meddlums with, someone to cry to when one was particularly frightening, was comforting. It was the kind of comfort Cherry hadn't realised she needed until it was there. Other children thought Cherry and Peter were odd but other children had *always* thought they were odd so the fact they were suddenly sitting next to each other at lunch and playing together in the playground didn't make them any more odd than they were before. If anything, it made sense.

'What do your parents think about what you can see?' Peter asked her during lunchtime one day.

'My dads say I'm special,' Cherry said, smiling.

Samuel Redgrave knew his daughter could see things others couldn't and whether it was in her mind or whether it was real, he loved and accepted her for the child she was – nothing more, nothing less. Her other father, Lucas, loved her too, of course, but he was also scared of their adopted daughter, especially since she'd described his own Meddlum to him: a foaming, gnashing wolf-like creature, with a large tongue that lolled from its mouth and roaming eyes that rolled in their sockets. Lucas worried what the future may hold for his child who had either an all-consuming imagination or a mental defect that caused constant hallucinations. Samuel pulled Cherry closer when she started to talk about what she could see, but Lucas couldn't help taking a subtle step away.

'What do *your* parents think?' Cherry asked Peter now.

'Mum left. Dad hates me,' he said matter-of-factly, between bites of his ham sandwich.

Cherry was speechless. Knowing this about Peter's parents now, she found it odd that he didn't have more Meddlums tormenting him. Frustration had melted away, little by little, since Cherry and Peter's friendship had begun. At first it'd left muddy slush over Peter's home-work but after a couple of weeks, Frustration had become a mere puddle in the bottom of his schoolbag. At that moment, Cherry swore a playground oath to always be there for Peter and to do her best to fend off Frustration should it ever appear behind Peter's shoulders again.

Cherry thought her friendship with Peter was lifelong, that they'd always have one another to lean on, but there was one other day Cherry would remember that put paid to that.

That day, Peter came to school looking like a Meddlum himself. His skin was deathly pale, making the hand-shaped bruises on his arms look even angrier than they would have otherwise. The purple semi-circles under his eyes were darker than ever before.

'Did ... did a Meddlum do that to you?' Cherry asked, nodding towards his arm. She so wanted to hug him – she knew they'd be the talk of the playground if she did, but holding back caused her eyes to sting and water. She couldn't bear to see her friend in such a state. She peered over Peter's shoulder and there, clutching the back of his collar, was a lump of coal, burning red under its black surface. It turned its face towards Cherry and grinned, flames in its mouth where there should have been teeth. Cherry gasped. She'd never seen Hatred before.

'No. Not a Meddlum. Just a monster,' Peter said quietly, wiping his eyes with the back of his hand before he cried in front of everyone.

That was the last time Cherry spoke to Peter. When the bell rang, they went their separate ways to their separate classes. Weeks passed and she tried to get Peter's attention but he looked through her like he didn't know her, like they hadn't been the closest of friends all this time. She left notes in his backpack when he wasn't looking. She even went as far as sneaking out of her own classroom and banging on the window of his to try to get his attention but his teacher noticed first and it only landed her in trouble.

The final time she saw Peter was from a distance. He was being dragged from school, kicking and screaming, by a man whom Cherry assumed was his father. Teachers and pupils followed them to the school gates, only to watch helplessly as a couple of other men Cherry didn't recognise wrangled Peter into an odd cream jacket that was covered in buckles and with sleeves too long for his scrawny arms. They bundled him into the back of a blue van that Cherry didn't think belonged to Peter's father, who was now standing motionless on the pavement, the expression on his face unreadable. He didn't wave or cry as the van drove off with his son in the back. Cherry couldn't read the black writing on the side of the windowless van but she knew for certain that she wouldn't ever see Peter again.

3

Loneliness and Flour

After Peter, her only friend, was taken away, Cherry had never felt more alone and that was the first time Cherry developed a Meddlum of her own: Loneliness. Often people try to avoid Loneliness by seeing friends and family and avoiding long periods of isolation but it was persistent. It wanted in, to insert itself into people's lives and do its worst. It would knock on doors with its long, spindly fingers, waiting to enter their homes and wrap those fingers around their lives and squeeze until the poor person was gasping for breath. And Cherry Redgrave soon became Loneliness's fondest victim.

One day, shortly after Peter had been taken away, the most popular girl in Cherry's class handed each pupil an invitation to her birthday party. Everyone, that was, except for Cherry. Before Peter, Cherry had been used to being left out of games. She was used to being in her own company and had even found that she enjoyed the solitude. After Peter, however, after getting used to his friendship, after knowing what it was like to have someone to share things with and the feeling of not being so alone, she felt the sting of being left out so much more than she ever had before. She swore she wouldn't cry and she was doing so well until she felt two strong bony hands on her shoulders. When Cherry looked up, she saw Loneliness for the first time and as it grinned maliciously down at her, two long spools of drool landed on her face and ran down her cheeks.

Most children invent imaginary friends to cope with feeling sad or lonely, except Cherry didn't invent hers and he may have been invisible to everyone else but he certainly wasn't imaginary. Peter had been taken away from her so suddenly and Loneliness had stepped in just when she needed someone the most and so she clung to that constant presence by her side. Loneliness was all she had needed when the other kids never invited her to play games in the playground. It was all she needed when a teacher left her behind 'by accident' on a school trip. Loneliness was all she needed when her father, Lucas, left without so much as an explanation or a goodbye. One day he was there and the next day he was just ... gone. Cherry was only eight years old. Most children are spared from being privy to their parents' innermost fears and feelings but not Cherry. She watched Sadness grow around Samuel like mould and there was nothing she could do to stop it.

After Lucas left, the children at Cherry's school would either tease her from afar or stay away from her completely, not just because they found her strange but because her single-minded peers, who had been raised by traditional single-minded parents, didn't understand why she had been raised by two men. And so she gripped Loneliness's hand even tighter and it happily held her closer. But Loneliness's grip wasn't as tight as it would've liked because despite all of this, Cherry still had her other father, her hero, and he was the strongest man she'd ever known.

Samuel Redgrave was a baker and owned a small bakery not far from where they lived. He smelled of cakes and flour and fruit fillings – smells that Cherry would relate to home for evermore. On the days when the other children had been exceptionally cruel, Samuel would lift his daughter up onto the counter and treat her to a slice of the day's 'special'. Cherry would eat through her sobs but would always leave the last mouthful for Loneliness – she couldn't help it. But it was the day that Samuel taught her to make cherry pie that she remembers most vividly. Maybe because it was the day he not only stopped her from crying but taught her how to stop herself from crying. Whatever the reason, Cherry would always remember that day as the day she truly fell in love with baking for the first time. Her father patiently showed her how to roll the pastry, not too thick and not too thin. He taught her how to destone cherries and then let her mix them in with the lemon, sugar, vanilla and cornflour, before playfully dabbing a blob of dough on her cheeks. Cherry was certain no pie would ever taste as good as the first pie she ever made.

Over time, Cherry found comfort at home with her father and in baking but Loneliness still remained and by the time she was in secondary school, she had grown accustomed to keeping her head down and her voice quiet. She slipped silently through the corridors, dodging the many, *many* Meddlums of her teenage peers, and with Loneliness cloaking her from the world, she went by completely and utterly unnoticed.

Samuel died suddenly when the aneurysm that he didn't know was in his brain had burst and no one took it harder than eighteen-year-old Cherry. Her whole world collapsed around her and Loneliness finally had her all to itself. It held her back from reaching out to those around her who had offered their help and it stopped her from opening the front door whenever the doorbell rang so that Cherry's only choice was to stay in bed. Grief showed up under her pillow one morning, cold and whimpering. Cherry curled herself around it and cried until her chest hurt and her eyes were sore. The more pain Cherry expelled, the warmer Grief became, and Loneliness watched on, feeling stronger than ever before.

It was only when the smell of pastry started to fade from the house that Cherry slid from the sheets and walked into the kitchen. If it hadn't been for Mrs Overfield, her generous if slightly nosey next door neighbour, leaving bags of groceries on her doorstep she would have starved. She had made a note to pay her back when things looked clearer but for now, she pulled ingredients for a cherry pie from the fridge. Loneliness worried she was trying to leave the house but it was relieved when she only made it as far as the kitchen. Still, it stood close by and watched her bake.

Cherry cranked the spoon in the batter, her tears falling into the mixture as she stirred and stirred and stirred. When the crust had glazed in the oven, and the fruit was bubbling and the smell had seeped into every pore of the house, Cherry felt ready to eat the pie that reminded her so much of her father. She delicately slid the fork between the lattice, gathering herself a bite. Cherry knew she couldn't bake as well as her father but she hoped the pie's familiar taste would loosen the knot in her stomach, even only momentarily. However, as soon as the pastry and the soft cherries passed her lips she felt instantaneously worse. It tasted heavy and solid and chalky. She'd never tasted Grief before but somehow Cherry knew that was exactly what she could taste: Grief.

Confused, Cherry set about baking another pie, and another, and another. Each pie tasted less and less like Grief, but her strange palette detected more and more odd flavours with each one, flavours she'd never tasted before but knew instinctively what they were. The second pie tasted like Confusion, the third tasted of Curiosity, the fourth like Astonishment, the fifth was Amusement ... Cherry didn't know how it was possible but she couldn't come up with another conclusion other than each and every pie tasted of what she was feeling. Loneliness relaxed, misinterpreting Cherry's repetitive baking as a bid to distract herself from Grief, and felt safe in the knowledge that she wouldn't be leaving for some time.

Cherry took out a notebook and a pencil from a drawer and noted how each feeling tasted:

Confusion: Clementines and mandarins.
Curiosity: Mushed banana, cat hair and mint.
Astonishment: Rosemary and silver.
Amusement: Fizzy raspberries, salt and phlegm.

Cherry stared at the list. But it couldn't be ... could it? Could she really taste what she was *feeling*? How was this even possible? Whatever was happening, Cherry knew there was likely to be more to this talent that she needed to discover. And so she baked. And baked. And baked. She attempted to concentrate certain emotions into cakes, muffins, pies and brownies and then she ate them, waiting to see if her suspicions were confirmed and each time they were – she really could taste her feelings. Sometimes it was the faintest of tastes, and other times her taste buds couldn't handle the intensity of flavour but she knew she had to keep practising.

Cherry was so preoccupied, frantically tasting and jotting everything down, that she hadn't heard Mrs Overfield enter the house. Not having seen Cherry emerge for weeks and fearing something awful had happened, Mrs Overfield had taken it upon herself to come in using the spare key she knew Samuel had kept under the doormat.

'Cherry, m'love?' Mrs Overfield called as she walked tentatively into the kitchen, stopping abruptly at the sight that greeted her. Cherry's black hair and dark skin were almost entirely white with flour, every surface was covered with cracked eggshells, batter, dough and baked goods still warm in their tins. As Mrs Overfield walked further into the kitchen, so did her Meddlum and with it, Cherry made her next great discovery.

Cherry had never known why she'd been cursed with the peculiar power to see everyone's inner darkness, the very worst of what they were feeling. Mrs Overfield's 'worst' was Worry. Worry was a large body that resembled a bundle of tangled grey wool, and it often reached down and vigorously shook Mrs Overfield's hands. Cherry was watching this exact thing happening now and suddenly she felt a jolt in her brain as a connection was made. *If I can see people's bad feelings and put my own good feelings into food*, she thought excitedly, *maybe my food can help make people happier again*. Before Cherry could acknowledge the responsibility she was taking on or how it might impact her life and her own happiness, she was darting from worktop to worktop. This could all go miserably wrong. Just because she could taste her feelings didn't mean that other people would be able to. But she had to try.

'Give me an hour and I'll have something for you. Just give me an hour,' Cherry said, without looking up. She scrambled around, collecting ingredients together. Mrs Overfield followed Cherry from fridge to cupboard, from chopping board and back, trying to find the perfect moment to interject so that she could have a proper conversation with her, but when she saw the concentration on Cherry's face, her tongue sticking out the side of her mouth, Mrs Overfield realised maybe this preoccupation was exactly what Cherry needed. After all, she was out of bed and doing *something*.

Worry was busy massaging Mrs Overfield's head and whispering little troublesome thoughts into her ear. Cherry couldn't hear what it was saying but she assumed none of it was good, so she concentrated all the Calmness and Serenity she could muster into a Bakewell Tart and just over an hour later, she presented a slice of it to Mrs Overfield.

'Cherry, is everything OK?' Mrs Overfield asked gently. 'It's completely natural to grieve but you've got to talk to the people that care about you. You can talk to me.' Worry had a firm grip on her head to ensure she kept her gaze fixed on Cherry so she hadn't yet looked at the Bakewell Tart. Mrs Overfield took in eighteen-year-old Cherry. Cherry looked like she hadn't slept in days, she'd lost weight and Mrs Overfield was sure she hadn't showered for a while either. Cherry had even lost count of the days. Worry tightened its grip on Mrs Overfield, in full control of its prey. Loneliness, on the other hand, had become complacent while Cherry had been baking, so when Cherry reached out to take Mrs Overfield's hand it was taken by surprise. It lunged for Cherry but was too late.

'Mrs O?' Cherry squeezed her fingers and instantly Worry's throat tightened and its whisperings were muted. Cherry turned Mrs O's hand and placed the plate in her upturned palm. 'Eat this. Please?' Cherry said, holding the small fork out to her.

'All right ...'

With Worry quieter and calmer than before, Mrs O plunged the fork into the icing, through the crust and then daintily nibbled at the morsel. Cherry watched in wonder as every muscle in Mrs O's body visibly relaxed and then in horror as her eyes rolled to the back of her head and she slumped backwards onto the sofa, squashing Worry in an instant. She was out cold. Cherry ran to Mrs O and thrust her fingers to her neck, trying frantically to find a pulse. Once that gentle *thump thump* beat beneath her fingertips she pulled away and it was then that she saw Worry slip and tumble off of Mrs O's shoulder and into her lap. Its arms were shrinking and then with a great pop its body deflated until it was just half the size it was before. Cherry's moment of panic passed and had now been replaced by a feeling of happiness and contentment. Cherry leaned over and kissed Mrs O on her forehead, careful not to touch Worry's twitching fingers. She ran upstairs to take a shower, not even realising Grief had disappeared from her bed, the only sign it had been there the black tear stains on her bed sheets. Loneliness lingered, but with a new sense of foreboding that something had shifted.

Over the next few months, Cherry honed her talent. The act of channelling her feelings into her baking provided her with a small amount of peace. Loneliness still clung to her clothes but its fingers often slipped. After her breakthrough with Mrs O (who woke up hours later, claiming she'd had the best sleep of her life), Cherry realised she'd put too much Relaxation into the tart, resulting in Mrs O's swift fall into deep sleep. Like all ingredients, her feelings had to be measured. Cherry also realised that trying to force herself to feel certain things when she wanted to include them in her recipes was impossible. She had to find a way to 'collect' them so she had a supply for the future. If she could do that, maybe she'd feel ready to re-enter the world and see if she could help more people after she'd helped Mrs O. She watched one feel-good movie after another and cried Happy Tears into a jar. She slept with fresh fruit in her bed to infuse them with a Good Night's Sleep. Cherry even spent hours cuddling a chocolate bar so it absorbed her Tender Loving Care. She found ways to build up her supplies and she tested her recipes on an unsuspecting Mrs Overfield to whom Cherry had given the spare key, much to Loneliness's horror. It found itself a little shorter and the fur around its neck was beginning to thin out.

Mrs Overfield's Worry, while not as visible as it once was, still remained. Cherry soon realised though that Mrs Overfield was carrying plenty of emotional baggage that she could tailor her baking to in order to get rid of Worry once and for all. When Mrs O complained how she never felt brave enough to call the television company when her signal cut out, Cherry whipped up some Confidence Crème Caramel. When Mrs O's cat died, Cherry made a batch of Comfort Cookies. And when Mrs O applied for a new job as a part-time cleaner and worried they would never take her on because of her tender age of sixty-four, Cherry baked her a Que Sera Cake. Once she started eating Cherry's baking, Mrs O was never out of balance for long again.

It took Cherry a year of baking and spending time with Mrs O to feel ready to leave the house for more than a few minutes at a time. Up until then, she'd relied on Mrs O to get her groceries but Cherry knew it was time to re-enter the world. She lived in a small English village by the sea so her world was small – but for someone who hadn't left her house very much in the past year, it felt huge.

Loneliness had never been far away during that time and in a funny way had been quite a close friend to Cherry but love from Loneliness isn't really love at all and Cherry knew it was time to start life afresh.

'You *can* do this,' Mrs O said to Cherry.

Cherry was stood in the doorway to her house. She tilted her head back towards the sky and the sun gently smiled down on her face. 'I don't think I can,' she replied.

'*I don't think you should*,' Loneliness said, reaching out a shadowy hand as Cherry took a tentative step forwards, but the sun singed its knuckles slightly and it pulled it back in shock.

The light was trying to claim Cherry as its own.

'OK. OK. OK,' Cherry said between shaky breaths. Having recovered itself, Loneliness followed, squinting against the painful light.

'I'm right here, Cherry,' Mrs O said. 'And I can't walk very fast anyway so the only way to take this is slowly.' They walked arm-in-arm towards the village. *Towards people*, Cherry thought.

They were approaching the high street, and suddenly Cherry had to pause. She could see the townsfolk milling about in the distance but, also, there were Meddlums everywhere. Each person had at least two or three and all of them looked happy and hungry – and stronger than her. The thought of attempting to rid just one of these people of their bad feeling, let alone the whole town, suddenly seemed impossible and Cherry doubled over, her head cloudy.

'Cherry?' Mrs O said in concern. 'Is everything all right?'

Cherry thought about how she'd felt useless her whole life. She'd felt useless when Peter was taken away, she'd felt useless when Lucas had left, and she'd felt useless when her father had died. And then Cherry thought of her own Meddlum and how much she wished someone would burn it off her like a wart, would help free her from its clutches. A feeling of purpose spread through her, then. She refused to be useless any longer.

'Yes.' Cherry straightened up and brushed down her skirt. 'Everything's fine. Let's go.' And she pulled Mrs O towards the sea of Meddlums.

The village was so small that everyone knew everyone, and no one's business was their own. The things that were considered a scandal here would easily be overlooked in a larger city. If Cherry had lived somewhere bigger, chances are no one would have noticed she hadn't been seen in a year but here, she was a household name because of it. *What a shame*, people would mutter as they walked past her father's house, looking up at the windows, imagining Cherry curled up in a ball, riddled with grief. Cherry had lost count of the number of times Pity had rung the doorbell and ran away. Cherry's knuckles grew whiter as she gripped Mrs O's arm tighter. It wasn't being among people and feeling their stares that she couldn't stand. It was all of the Meddlums.

Mrs Brewer's Anxiety and Boredom had their limbs tangled, feet in faces, hands in hair, wildly trying to untie themselves. Mr Datta's three Meddlums were a mess – Insecurity kept treading on Arrogance's toes and apologising, while Greed watched on, rubbing its hands together so hard its palms were almost worn away. Miss Kightley's Meddlum was directly behind her, its forehead against the small of her back and its long fingers prodding, poking and pushing her forwards. Impatience didn't like it when she slowed down.

Cherry was sure the town hadn't been this unhappy before her father had died. She couldn't understand how all these people had all these bad feelings and yet were doing nothing to help themselves. Cherry tried to slow her breathing but her brain was ticking too fast. She moved to a nearby bench, pulling Mrs O along, and sat down heavily. She delved into her bag and pulled out the scrunched-up notepad that contained her shopping list. She flipped to a fresh page and began jotting down each Meddlum and its owner.

Mrs O noticed the slightly crazed look in Cherry's eyes. She clutched the cross around her neck and sent up a silent prayer for her friend. She laid a comforting palm on Cherry's shoulder. 'Cherry, people are starting to notice you're out and about again.' Mrs O kept her voice as cheerful as she could. 'Let's carry on as normal, shall we?' Mrs Overfield wanted so much to help her but she feared Cherry might need professional help. She couldn't deny, though, that Cherry was an entirely different person to the flour-covered one she'd discovered a year ago. Even so, Cherry had a long way to go before she was back to what society considered 'normal'.

Cherry got to the bottom of the page and stopped to count: twenty-eight Meddlums for fifteen people. A thrill rippled through her, bringing her to her feet, her goal clear. 'And we're off!' she exclaimed, sweeping a surprised-looking Mrs Overfield down the road with her.

An hour or so later, Cherry and Mrs O were walking back up the high street when Cherry saw the shadow of a Meddlum. Its darkness engulfed one side of the street almost entirely and as it came lumbering around the corner she saw the young girl, tiny against the black fur of a Meddlum Cherry didn't recognise. The girl looked about seventeen, and wore a school uniform. Cherry dropped Mrs O's arm and ran across the road, only just missing the bonnet of a car and oblivious to the angry driver honking the horn in one long blast.

You!' she shouted at the girl, stumbling to a stop in front of her. 'What are you feeling right now?' Cherry had never seen this Meddlum before, and certainly not one this big or this obvious. It was tall and round with white tendrils of hair that were thick and matted against its scalp. Its face was long with a protruding nose and tiny half-moon spectacles were balanced right on the tip of it. It sniffed haughtily and made a particularly strong effort to look down on Cherry.

'What?' the girl said, clutching her stylish over-the-shoulder satchel closer to her body.

'How do you feel?' Cherry pushed impatiently, stepping closer and forcing the girl to step backwards. The girl turned and began hurriedly walking away but Cherry pursued, fixed entirely on finding out what this Meddlum was.

'Leave me alone,' the girl called over her shoulder, raising her voice.

'Cherry!' Mrs O had only just caught up with her. 'Leave that poor girl *alone*. You can't go chasing after people you don't know!' Mrs O was trying to keep her voice down to avoid alerting passers-by to Cherry's strange behaviour, but the slight commotion had already been noticed and several curtains were twitching.

Please,' Cherry begged, ignoring Mrs O. She ran around in front of the girl, causing her to stop dead in her tracks. She even placed her hands on the girl's shoulders. 'I just need to know exactly what you're feeling at this precise moment.'

The girl looked at Mrs O, frantic but seemingly harmless, and then at Cherry, kooky but clearly kind. 'Look.' The young girl flipped her sheen of brown hair over her shoulders, facing Cherry square on. 'I've had a really bad day. I've failed most of my exams and now I have to go home and tell my parents what a disappointment I am. They're going to kill me.' The girl was about to sob but she composed herself quickly before continuing. 'And then David Prime told someone in the year above, who told my friend Hannah, who told me that he was going to ask me out after school today and ... and he didn't. So the last thing I need is some weirdo following me down the street, OK?' The girl's eyes shone with tears. She turned on her heel and ran in the opposite direction, desperate to get away from Cherry.

'Disappointment?' Cherry said. 'It's disappointment?'

The Meddlum looked over its shoulder and winked at Cherry.

'DISAPPOINTMENT!' she yelled.

Mrs O reached over and cupped Cherry's hands in hers, squeezing them tightly. 'I think it's time to go home,' she said gently.

'Vanilla pods. I just need vanilla pods,' Cherry said distractedly as she scribbled the nameless girl and her Meddlum onto her list.

'Vanilla pods. Then home.' Mrs O led Cherry carefully towards the shops, pretending not to notice the stares from the townspeople.

A short while later, Cherry and Mrs O were back at Cherry's house. Cherry looked at her now very long list of townspeople and their Meddlums. At the top was Mrs Brewer. Cherry knew that Mrs Brewer loved tea, and was kind to people who were not kind in return.

Mrs Brewer: Anxious and Bored.

'Let's start with the Anxiety,' Cherry muttered. 'Tranquillity Teacakes, maybe.' She wrote her choice beside Mrs Brewer's name.

'What was that, dear?' Mrs O asked, looking up from where she was making tea.

'Teacakes,' Cherry said. 'I'm going to make some for Mrs Brewer.'

'How sweet of you!' Mrs O beamed. 'You seem very calm, Cherry. It's lovely. It's ... well, it's *unusual.*' She eyed Cherry, suddenly worried she was up to something.

'I'm always calm when I'm baking.' Cherry smiled for the first time in a long time. 'It makes me feel ...' Cherry breathed in the scent of pastry and with it the memory of her father struck her, '... less alone.'

And with that, Loneliness, who usually stood tall, shrank by two inches.

4

Proof in the Pudding

Cherry's self-expression had always been minimal. As a child she'd worn what her father had clothed her in, without question. She read the books she was told to read at school, nothing more, and she rarely watched television. She didn't sing along to the radio and she certainly didn't write or draw or play an instrument. She hadn't changed much as she grew older, except that she chose to wear, almost exclusively, pyjamas and slippers. But now that she'd found baking, everything had changed. It was the best form of self-expression she could've hoped for, maybe more literally than even she realised.

The Tranquillity Teacakes went down a treat. Mrs Brewer's Anxiety melted a little more with each bite she took. It didn't disappear entirely, but its limbs became thinner, shorter and less entwined with Boredom than they had been before. So, with less anxiety about going outside and with more drive to cure her boredom, Mrs Brewer left the house more often than she used to. She now felt more able to stand up for herself when the grumpy woman in the corner shop tried to short-change her. Usually, Mrs Brewer was so eaten up with angst that she would have just left without a word and beaten herself up later on about not saying anything. Instead, this time, Mrs Brewer took a breath and said, 'Excuse me, but this isn't right. You've short-changed me by fifty pence.'

'And?' sniffed the grumpy woman.

Mrs Brewer walked up to the counter and looked her in the eyes. '*And*, I'm not leaving until that fifty-pence piece is in my hand.'

Several people in the shop looked over in astonishment and the grumpy woman (not wanting an uprising among the elderly whom she often short-changed), reluctantly opened the till drawer and slammed the fifty-pence piece down on the counter with a grunt.

Mrs Brewer couldn't have known that it was the teacakes making her feel less anxious but something in her steady heart told her she should order some more. She turned up on Cherry's doorstep a few days later with a five-pound note in her hand, asking if Cherry wouldn't mind making her some more.

The Humble Pie that Cherry made for Mr Datta changed him for the better too, and the other residents noticed the difference in him. Mr Datta had always considered himself a very big fish in a very small pond. He was a tailor by trade and owned an elegant shop on the high street. Each morning he slicked back his hair, donned his hand-made suit and walked to his shop, his journey twice as long as it should've been because he couldn't help but stop to admire himself in shopfront windows several times. Although he was an incredibly talented tailor, no one entered his shop unless they really had to because they couldn't bear to hear any more about his latest female conquests or the offers to travel abroad to work with the most top-end designers, nor could they stand to watch him admiring himself in the mirror, combing his hair and licking his teeth.

Cherry left the pie on Mr Datta's doorstep with a note from a 'secret admirer', knowing he wouldn't be able to resist. The *i*s dotted with hearts would massage his ego enough to convince him to eat it. Two days later, Cherry smiled to herself as Mrs O recounted, with some astonishment, how Mr Datta had walked down the entire length of the high street without stopping to look at his reflection. Not even once. It was a good start but Cherry made a note to up the dosage a little in the next pie.

Cherry didn't know Miss Kightley very well but they lived three doors down from each other so Cherry thought it wouldn't be too odd if she popped over with her Patience Profiteroles. Impatience was constantly prodding the small of Miss Kightley's back so she came across as tightly wound but she had a good soul. Cherry had seen her wheel Cherry's bins to the front of her drive when Cherry had forgotten it was collection day, and she was always grateful for these small acts of kindness.

Miss Kightley was in her late forties and was happily unmarried. She'd had several partners over the years but she just didn't enjoy long-term companionship. 'The men I find only end up getting in the way,' Cherry had once heard her say to Samuel.

She owned the local florist, and because she was a clever woman who knew how powerful a tool the internet was, she now ran most of her business online and had employed Felicity and Fawn Seymour to run the store itself. Felicity and Fawn were a married couple whose front garden was full of colour and wildlife, and they were the perfect people for Miss Kightley to entrust with her livelihood. Their valuable help left Miss Kightley free to spend most of the year in Spain, and work from there, and when she did return to the town, she returned with glamour and her kind heart. But Impatience was never far behind either.

One evening, Cherry rang the bell after dinner and knowing that Miss Kightley didn't like to be kept waiting, she kept her delivery short and sweet. 'Profiteroles. For you. Just ... because.' Cherry handed Miss Kightley the bowl. 'And thank you,' she called over her shoulder as she quickly left, not giving Impatience the time to get riled.

'Thank *you*,' Miss Kightley said, eyeing the profiteroles keenly through the cling film. She had just been berating herself for not getting any afters while she'd been at the supermarket earlier so Cherry's appearance couldn't have been better timed.

She pierced the cling film with her fingernail, speared it straight into a profiterole, which she then popped into her mouth. As the cream oozed out of the sides and melted on her tongue, Impatience's prodding fingers began melting until they were nothing more than tiny little stumps.

Cherry had never felt so *alive*. She was helping people, really helping them. Perhaps now was the time to help herself, too.

'Are you OK?' Mrs O asked one evening, noticing that Cherry's hands were twitching and shaking. 'A little bit of calm would do your jitters some good.'

Mrs O was right. She needed some calmness. Cherry hopped off the sofa without a word, poked a hole in the foil that was covering the next batch of Mrs Brewer's teacakes and took a bite out of the smallest one. Would it help her? She chewed and swirled the sweet bread around her mouth, hoping to get a hit of serenity, but it was no use. It wasn't working. She could taste lavender and the beauty of the cold side of the pillow but her hands still shook and every nerve ending was crackling. She had thought it might be too good to be true. Cherry could help everyone but herself. Although she was happy to have a purpose, a reason to wake up each morning, this felt like a cruel twist to her strange gift. She had hoped that in helping other people reach their full potential, she would eventually feel like she was reaching her own – but curing her own ills with her gift wasn't going to be the way to do it.

When Cherry woke up the next morning, Mrs O had a surprise for her.

'Come on, you,' she said when Cherry opened the front door. 'Put something nice on. I'm taking you some-where.'

Cherry groaned but her curiosity over what Mrs O was up to got the better of her so she put on a new pair of blue and purple striped pyjamas and her usual grey slippers.

'Cherry Redgrave, you get back upstairs and put on something more appropriate for leaving this house!' Mrs O said, laughing but only half-joking. She was worried about Cherry's constant need to wear pyjamas. She had been so much better recently but refusing to get dressed seemed like the symptom of something else, something Mrs O couldn't fix.

'They're the comfiest clothes known to man,' Cherry insisted. 'Why anyone would choose to wear dresses you can't breathe in and high heels you can't walk in when pyjamas and slippers are readily available to everyone ... well, it's beyond me!'

Mrs O could see the determination in Cherry's eyes and

didn't have the energy to fight her. Not after she'd spent her morning planning the surprise.

Mrs O signed. 'Fine. At least your hair looks lovely,' she conceded. And it did. The purple scarf Cherry had tied around her head pulled her black Afro hair off her face into a curly explosion at the back of her head, bar a few curls she'd pulled through to the front.

Mrs Overfield led Cherry along a familiar route through the town, with Loneliness and Worry trudging not far behind. After a few minutes they entered the village and Cherry's steps started to slow so much that Loneliness almost stumbled into her.

'Please don't take me there,' Cherry said quietly. 'I'm not ready.' She could see the familiar outline of her father's bakery, silhouetted against the sun. On one side was Sew & Sew, the arts and crafts shop, and on the other was a second-hand bookshop, imaginatively named The Second-Hand Book Shop. Cherry stared at the bakery. It was still so full of character. Cherry had chosen the fire-engine-red paint on the window frames and door when she was a child and her father had gladly obliged. The sign above the entrance used to read *Samuel's* but the paint was cheap and now, a year after her father had died, it said *S mue 's*. Cherry couldn't bear it.

'Cherry, my dear. How long can you shut yourself away for? I mean, really?' Mrs O said gently, looping her arm through Cherry's. 'I know it's painful but ... don't you think the best way to mourn your father is to honour his memory? I've tasted your baking and it's just as good as, if not better than, Sam's.'

Cherry stared at the sign above the door and was hit with a sudden feeling of having let her father down. She thought of all that time she had wasted under her bed-sheets, indulging in Loneliness's game, when she could have been looking after her father's legacy. They continued walking and as they got closer, Cherry spotted the makeshift sign pinned to the top of the door frame. On a large piece of cardboard, someone (Mrs O probably) had added the words *and Daughter* underneath what was left of Samuel's name.

Cherry rolled up her sleeves, literally and figuratively, an idea beginning to take shape in her mind. 'You're right,' she said.

It's time I take what I can do seriously, she thought. She started to think about which types of treats she would bake first, how she would rearrange the tables and chairs and how she'd make use of that large kitchen in the back. This was the purpose she'd been looking for.

'And I know you're stubborn and you probably don't want to ... wait, what did you just say?' Mrs O spun to face her.

'I said, you're right,' Cherry sniffed. 'It's been long enough and Dad wouldn't have wanted me to spend the rest of my life ... alone.' She glanced behind her and saw Loneliness shrink into her shadow. 'I am a baker. I've always been a baker. It's time I started acting like one.'

Mrs O had done more than just put up a scruffy sign. While the outside needed a lick of paint, the inside had been restored to its former glory and Mrs O explained how the townspeople had all chipped in. Miss Kightley had paid the rent on the building for the next year on the condition that Cherry always had profiteroles on hand. Mrs Brewer and Mrs Overfield had bought her the missing bits of equipment they couldn't find in her father's old things and they'd replaced anything that was broken with new things. And Felicity and Fawn had guaranteed her fresh flowers for every table, to be delivered weekly for the next six months.

'It's wonderful.' Cherry couldn't help but stifle a sob as she walked through the door and saw all her donors, her friends, standing in a line at the counter. They'd all been loyal customers of her father's when the shop had belonged to him and now they were showing her the same support. She would stand behind the counter proudly, not only because she wanted to be there but because her father's friends wanted to see her there too. That meant more to her than they could possibly know.

'We know you'll turn this place into something magical. Just like your father did.' Mrs Kightley wasn't the emotional type but Cherry was sure she heard the thickness of a lump in her throat.

Cherry looked over at the OPEN/CLOSED sign on the door. She'd always hated it. It was old-fashioned and made of tin that had turned rusty over the years. She couldn't understand why her dad wouldn't replace it and she'd always avoided touching it if she could. But now that the shop was hers, the sign was also hers and she couldn't bring herself to see it go. It was only small but it was a piece of her father and so it had to stay.

Cherry shook her head to clear her thoughts. 'First things first.' She turned to her friends. 'The menu.'

5

Too Much Of A Good Thing

The day Cherry officially opened 'Samuel and Daughter' was a roaring success. She had never seen so many people in one room – nor had she ever seen so many Meddlums. They had all tried to crush through the doors at once but something had blocked them and so they'd had to settle for standing at the threshold. They cowered, resorting to waiting outside, like dogs for their owners, yowling impatiently, and each time someone took a bite of cake, one of the Meddlums shrunk and the doorway started to clear. They even threw their crooked limbs around each other in fear.

Even those who insisted they didn't have a sweet enough tooth for Cherry's delights were soon won over when even just the whiff of a Contentment Cookie had them smiling. No one left that day feeling like their problems were unmanageable. Every person had a sudden new zest for life and everyone returned the following day. And the day after that. And the one after that. By the end of the month, Cherry had shrunk seven Meddlums to the size of spiders and the rest weren't far behind. *What happens if they all disappear?* Cherry thought. She now worried that if she continued to serve them good feeling, her friends might start to swing in the other direction. A town filled with the obsessively overjoyed with no worries to keep them balanced sounded almost as scary as the town she had started with. *Can you have too much of a good thing?* she thought.

Cherry soon had her answer in the form of the biggest Meddlum she had ever seen. It was so big that it didn't fit in its owner's house any more. Instead, it sat in the front garden, shivering and unimpressed. It belonged to Terrance Figgis. Terrance was having issues writing his latest novel so Cherry had served him a Motivation Muffin every time he'd come into the bakery.

'Five hundred and eighty-six words. That's it! Can you believe that? Something else is always just ... more important.' Terrance put his head in his hands in despair. Cherry slid a muffin under his nose.

'I always find a muffin helps me get my brain in gear,' Cherry said with a smirk. It turned out, however, that too much Motivation keeps you up for hours on end, working and working and working. In Terrance's quest to find Motivation, he had found Exhaustion instead and it was now sitting in his garden, getting larger by the day. Balance, Cherry had realised then, was of the utmost importance. From then, she tried to make her customers' usual orders without the extra added feeling but they soon noticed the difference and returned to ask, 'Have you changed the recipe?' or, 'Why doesn't it taste the same as before?' Cherry started to panic. She couldn't go on, filling everyone up with so much good feeling that it spilled out, creating new problems. It would leave them worse than before. Cherry had to do something.

'I'm moving,' Cherry announced. The whole bakery fell silent. She hadn't quite meant to declare it so bluntly but her brain had been whirring and clunking over the idea for weeks and she couldn't keep it to herself any longer. 'I'm ... moving.' She said again, a little more gently this time.

'But ... why?' Mrs Overfield said, a sob catching in her throat. 'Everything's so perfect,' she whispered.

'A little ... too perfect,' Cherry said, looking around the shop at all the faces she'd grown so fond of in the three months since the bakery had been open.

'Cherry, you can't leave. We need you here,' Miss Kightley sounded matter-of-fact but her eyes were creasing at the edges. Cherry wondered if it was her Softening Soufflé that was causing Miss Kightley to be a little gentler than usual.

'I don't think you do,' Cherry said slowly. 'For a while, we all needed each other but things are different now. I mean, I didn't know any of you before I opened this bakery. Not *really*. And now look at us. We see each other and talk every day. I know your children's names,' Cherry said to Mrs Brewer. 'You know my favourite flowers,' she said to Felicity and Fawn. 'I know how each and every one of you takes your tea!' Cherry felt a lump form in her throat as she realised just how far she'd come. 'This has all escalated so quickly and I feel like my job here is ... kind of ... done.' She shrugged, not knowing what else to say without giving herself away.

'But Cherry ... you can't just quit. This is a brilliant business. How will you live?' Mrs O came over and took Cherry's hand in hers.

'Oh, I'm not quitting! Never!' Cherry laughed. 'It's just that I feel like I've helped a lot of people here. With my baking. Right?' Everyone in the shop nodding enthusiastically and murmured their appreciation. Mr Datta even raised his plate of Humble Pie and bobbed his head in agreement. 'Who's to say there aren't more people who need a little pick-me-up too?' Cherry trailed off, wondering if she was being over-ambitious. She thought everyone's silence was confirmation that yes, that's exactly what she was being, until Mrs Brewer stood and said, 'You're absolutely right, my dear. How selfish of us to try to keep you here!' She walked over at quite a pace and planted a big wet kiss on Cherry's cheek, leaving a thick, red lipstick stain behind.

'Yes, completely right, Mrs B,' said Mr Datta who barrelled over and hugged Cherry so hard, her feet came off the ground. Cherry had changed Mr Datta more than most. Her pie had given him a whole new lease of life. The less he cared about his hair, about his unfulfilling conquests and about how he wanted everyone else to perceive him, the more room he had in his life to care about the things that really mattered. Like being personable. Like his business and livelihood. Like the child he hadn't planned on having; a child he'd only spent a handful of hours with since he'd been born ten months ago, a child that Mr Datta hadn't told anyone about because he was ashamed, and a child he'd often considered a nuisance, a weight that dragged him down. Now, because of the humility Cherry's pie had given him, his eyes had been opened. Now, he adored his son and wore the bed-head hair and the sick-stained shirts like a badge of honour. They told the world he was a father and he couldn't be prouder. In turn, the townsfolk couldn't be prouder of *him* and his shop was now a friendly, welcoming place where people enjoyed listening to his stories, not of his imaginary adventures, but of his child and his life as a father.

'We'll really miss you, Cherry,' Felicity said, shaking Cherry's right hand.

'You should still expect deliveries!' Fawn added, taking Cherry's left hand.

'That's so lovely of you,' Cherry said, 'but I'm not entirely sure where I'll end up! I've not really thought this through.'

'Well, it's a good job you've got a businesswoman on your side, isn't it?' Miss Kightley said, looking up from her phone. She'd been tapping on it for the last few minutes. 'I've just contacted a friend of mine in Cardiff. He's lost a tenant in one of his properties. It's a very small little shop. Used to be an ice-cream bar but strangely it didn't do too well in Wales. There's a one bedroom flat above the shop. This is the rent. How does that sound?' She turned her phone to show Cherry the details from her friend. She registered the monthly rent with interest and a growing sense of excitement – she could definitely afford that, for a while at least. Suddenly, moving away was all very real.

'That sounds ... that sounds ...' Cherry looked around at the smiling faces of everyone she'd come to love. Then her gaze drifted past them to the window. There was nothing obstructing the view and she could see the trees swaying in the wind and the spray of the sea in the air. There were a few tiny Meddlums scuttling around on the pavement, but they seemed much more manageable now. There really was nothing tying her to the seaside town – her work here was done. She thought of her inheritance and the money her father's bakery would fetch. She thought of the freedom of being able to travel wherever she wanted to and of having a purpose.

Cherry turned to face her friends, a happy smile on her face. 'That sounds marvellous. I'm in.'

CHERRY'S FLOUR POWER TOUR

Brighton: 3 months
Cardiff: 7 months
Newcastle: 2 months (Not enough Meddlums!)
Aberdeen: 1 year 6 months (Too many Meddlums!)
Gloucester: 5 months
Reading: 8 months
Sheffield: 1 year
Plymouth:

6

Cherry Online

Four years and seven months after Cherry had first decided to move on and said goodbye to her father's bakery and their family home, she found herself by the seaside once more. One night, as she lay in bed above her bakery in Sheffield, it called out to her. She could hear seagulls and felt the waves crash against the walls of her mind. It was too soon to return back home so she boarded a train and travelled four hours to Plymouth. Another twenty minutes in a cab took her to Royal William Yard where a little pop-up shop was waiting for her. Cherry knew it was too small for a lengthy stay but it would do for a while, just to be close to the sea. And once again, Loneliness wasn't able to cross the threshold. It often tried to, but each time it burnt its rubbery skin on the invisible barrier. It persevered though and kept running and jumping at the door. Cherry sat and watched for a while, enjoying that wherever she went, Loneliness was never able to enter her bakeries.

After a lot of organising, redecorating and a huge amount of baking, she opened the doors to her new bakery. The benches were polished wood, the walls were papered in gold and turquoise and she'd purchased the old-fashioned cashier till from an antique store. Although Cherry had invited Margie into her bakery before it had been ready, no one visited on the first day. An elderly couple did look into the window, as did their two-headed Meddlum, but they continued on. A group of school children also lingered in the doorway for a minute or two on the second day with their Meddlums, each of them far larger than their owners, all pushing each other out of the way to get a better look, but they didn't buy anything. Cherry wondered what she was going to do, and then it struck her. She knew just the right person who could help her drum up business in a heartbeat.

'Miss ... Miss Kightley?' Although Cherry was now used to interacting with people and being talkative and social, she still found Miss Kightley intimidating and at her heart, Cherry was naturally timid.

'Hello? Who is this?' Miss Kightley said.

'It's Cherry. Cherry Redgrave?' There was silence on the other end and then Cherry heard Miss Kightley sigh.

'We thought we'd lost you, dear. Fallen off the planet. It's so good to hear your voice. How are you?'

'Fine! I think. Maybe.' Cherry perched on the shop counter, watching potential customers only glance through the windows and then waltz past on their merry way. 'Maybe not.'

'It sounds like seeing a bit of the world has done you good, though.'

'The world? My Flour Power Tour hasn't made it past the British border! This country is enough to keep me busy for now. Seeing the world is an ambitious idea. Maybe one day.' Cherry twirled the black cord on her old-fashioned rotary dial phone.

'Flour Power Tour?' Miss Kightley chuckled. 'Well, you sound happy. Now, I take it there's a reason for this unexpected call? Anything I can do for you?'

'Just need a bit of advice, really. I've just opened a new bakery in Plymouth but no one's even coming in, let alone buying anything.'

'Hmm. Why not hold a launch event? Start spreading the word that you're open for business that way.'

'Maybe,' Cherry said. 'But why would anyone come?'

'Out of curiosity?' Miss Kightley suggested. 'You just need to get a few people there to kick things off. If you sent out the invite to your Facebook followers I'm sure a couple of people would show up, at least!'

'F . . . Facebook?'

'Oh, Cherry. Please tell me you're on social media? Facebook? Twitter? Instagram? How have you had *any* business without it?'

'I . . . well . . . I . . .'

'The internet can be the making of a business. It's a miracle you've survived this long in this day and age without it. I'll create the pages and send you all the details in an email. Usernames, passwords, links, you name it, I'll send it over. What's your email address?'

Cherry was stunned. 'Um . . .'

'Oh, Cherry.' Miss Kightley sighed, yet there was a trace of excitement in her voice. Miss Kightley thrived on this kind of thing. 'Not to worry. I'll take care of everything. Don't you worry!' And with a click, she was gone.

'The internet,' Cherry said to herself. She opened the drawer under the counter and rummaged around until she found her old Nokia 3310 that she'd bought when she was a teenager. She'd never bothered upgrading. She hadn't used it all that much but it was still working, although after she charged it and clicked through various buttons and menus, she realised it didn't come with in-built internet usage. Not like the fancy touch-screen phones she saw everyone glued to. 'Really? The internet.'

Cherry didn't even own a laptop. She'd never had the need for one and she thought they were for authors and editors, photographers and celebrities. She had never dreamed it would benefit her and her business in any way.

Word of mouth had always been her biggest ally and that had been enough to get her bakeries going in the past. But that clearly wasn't going to work this time. Her bakery had never been this hidden away before. Usually enough people wandered past so that at least two or three would have their interest piqued and would come in during the first few days of her being open. They would then tell their friends and their friends would tell their friends and soon her bakery would be full of customers every day. She hadn't realised how quiet and out of the way Royal William Yard would be when she accepted the tenancy. She was worried, but she also trusted Miss Kightley, who was a successful businesswoman and managed everything online. She knew what she was talking about. Cherry just needed to listen to her. 'I've ventured this far outside of my comfort zone . . . ' Cherry dropped her Nokia into the bin.

The following day, Cherry opened her bakery later than usual so she could go and purchase a laptop and mobile phone. She charged them for the recommended amount of time while tapping her feet impatiently and keeping an eye on the door, hoping someone would come in and save her the trouble of having to get to grips with all of this unfamiliar technology. But no one came. By the end of yet another completely unsuccessful day, Cherry grabbed a muffin from the display and took a bite out of the top. She wiped her hands on her pyjama bottoms, tentatively opened up the laptop and gingerly pressed the power button with the tip of her finger. The start-up noise made her jump and she closed the lid immediately. A hysterical laugh escaped her lips.

'Come on, Cherry. You can do this.' She opened up the laptop once more, this time much more determined and confident, and followed the on-screen instructions. Once that was done, Cherry rang Miss Kightley to ask for her email address and log-in details, and quickly logged into her brand new email account.

DING. The email from Miss Kightley containing all the information about her new social media profiles landed in her inbox. Cherry opened it, a thrill of excitement running through her. She was beginning to understand why people spent so much time online.

@FlourPowerTour

Password: SamuelWouldBeProud

Cherry's throat squeezed shut for a moment. She gathered herself, took a deep breath and logged into Twitter. Miss Kightley had already sent out a few tweets on her behalf but the account only had one lone follower: Miss Kightley. When Cherry checked her Facebook page she saw that Miss Kightley had already sent out an event invitation for the bakery's official opening on 13 January. That gave her only five days to prepare and she had a lot of work to do before then. She was determined to make this opening a success.

Her phone vibrated with a text from Miss Kightley. *Pictures*, it said. It vibrated again. *People like pictures.*

Cherry unhooked her phone and ran out the door. The January sun had started to set but it had turned the sky orange which looked lovely against the white of the bakery's shopfront. Even though the shop had no sign, the towering cakes and trays of muffins and scones in the window made it clear this was a bakery. Cherry flipped the camera around and moved to stand in front of the window.

'Here goes nothing,' she said as she smiled and took her first selfie.

Cherry took that Sunday to explore a part of Plymouth called The Barbican. There was a little ferry that would take her there. It only cost a pound a ticket, took fifteen minutes and it left from Royal William Yard. She stuffed her bag full of the flyers she'd had printed for the opening, with the address of the bakery and the date of the event in big bold black letters against 'cupcake-frosting pink' paper. (Cherry didn't realise such a colour existed but the woman in the printing shop assured her it was legitimate. After hearing all about Cherry's bakery, of course.) She hopped off the boat with the only other two passengers who had taken the trip over. They were looking at her and her striped pyjama bottoms with disdain, even though she was wearing a coat over the top and her nice slippers with the reinforced soles. Cherry couldn't help but feel a little lost. Although she was so much better at social interaction these days and didn't feel as awkward around people as she once did, new places still made her feel uneasy. This was ironic considering she moved around so much, but the truth was that Cherry liked comfort and once she'd come to know a place she'd rarely venture further than a mile from her bakery. All she needed was to get through the initial trepidation of being somewhere unfamiliar and then she would finally relax.

'Oh, I almost forgot.' Cherry turned back to the boat driver and handed him a slightly creased flyer. 'My bakery. It's in Royal William Yard. Officially opens on the thirteenth. Please come? Lots of free samples.' The driver took the flyer with a smile and nodded his thanks. Satisfied that at least one person might show up out of interest, Cherry turned on her heels and headed for the quaint shops up the little hill.

Cherry pulled out her phone and started taking pictures of the lights above the streets and the old shuttered windows, and sent them to Miss Kightley. *I love it here!* she wrote and smiled at the 'boop' noise the phone made as the message whizzed off. Cherry was staring at her phone, contemplating exactly how the message was transported from one place to another, when someone crashed into her. His sunglasses came clean off his face and his coffee sloshed over the side of his cup and onto his expensive-looking shoes.

The man turned on Cherry. 'WHAT is your PROBLEM?!' His face was a livid shade of red.

'I'm so sorry! I should have been looking where I was going!' Cherry said, mortified. She bent down to pick up the glasses.

'Give them to me,' he snapped.

Cherry was about to hand them over when the man snatched them from her fingers and she was sure she heard one of the temples crack. 'Stupid little girl,' he spat, opening his palm and seeing the clearly broken pieces of his glasses come apart in his hand. He looked at her, the expression on his face one of absolute fury. 'Look what you've done! Skipping about like the whole world is at your beck and call. Not giving a moment's thought to those around you.'

Cherry took in his young, wrinkle-free face, his thick dark brown hair, only slightly speckled with grey, his trendy, long, tan coat and faded jeans and she wondered how old he must be to have called her 'little girl'. She was twenty-four and he didn't look all that much older than her – two or three years at the most, although his eyes seemed far older. The man continued to berate her and as she wasn't used to dealing with conflict, she would normally have tried to find a way out of the conversation as quickly as possible. Yet he didn't seem to be looking at Cherry. He was looking past her, at something behind her. She glanced over her shoulder and saw only Loneliness peeking out from behind a lamp post, clearly not used

73

to dealing with conflict either, but there was nothing else of interest. She turned back to the man and something over his shoulder caught *her* eye. There, holding hands in an unusually neat line were Frustration, Cynicism and Mischief. Cherry had learned over the years that the more orderly and organised the Meddlums behaved, the longer they had been attached to their owner. These three had clearly been around one another so long that they were completely in sync, each of them enabling the others' bad habits. Frustration stood in between Cynicism and Mischief, squeezing their warped and broken hands. Its green skin was bubbling like boiling water, blistering and bursting. The other two were gazing at it with what looked like adoration. The sight turned Cherry's stomach.

'Are you even listening to me?' the stranger demanded, catching Cherry's disengaged eyes and glancing over his own shoulder.

'I think I'd better be going,' Cherry said, circling the man whose red cheeks were now returning to a normal hue. 'Oh, but here.' Cherry dug into her bag. Although unpleasant to talk to, he was clearly troubled. Exactly the kind of person she should be helping. 'Just ... come along. I think it might help.' Cherry fled before the stranger could say another word.

It took a little bit of time and a lot of deep breaths to shake away the ugly feeling the angry stranger had left her with. At times like these she wished she was back in her father's house, in her old room, with the door bolted shut. Things had been less complicated before she'd re-engaged with the world. Loneliness reached around her shoulders and gave her an uncomforting hug and whispered, 'But you're not there. You're here. Alone.' Cherry shrugged off its arms but the words kept running through her mind, repeating themselves over and over in her own familiar voice.

Cherry knew there was a famous gin distillery in Plymouth. Gin was one of the very few alcoholic drinks that Cherry actually liked. It was her father, Lucas's, favourite and he had let her try some of his gin and tonic one Christmas when she was small. It had tasted dry and bitter but the fizz of the tonic and buzz of the gin made her feel like she was swallowing a lightning bolt and right now all she wanted was to feel that sensation again. She quickly googled the distillery's location (she was getting the hang of this internet thing) and seeing that it was only a short distance away, she began walking in its direction. After a few minutes, she turned a corner and could see the white-painted building ahead with its blue trimmings. However, something else caught her eye and snatched her attention away. On the right-hand side of the road was a bright red and yellow shop. White window stickers in the shape of crystal balls, open palms with lines zig-zagging across them and several constellations were scattered across the glass. The window display was made up of crushed velvet red cloth and a real crystal ball. From a distance it looked as though the crystal ball was hovering magically in mid-air but when Cherry got closer she could see that there were strings holding it up. Behind the ball was a photo display of, Cherry guessed, some of the shop's clientele. Some faces looked excited, beaming at the camera. Others wore slightly more reserved smiles. Above the shop, in intricate white writing, were the words PSYCHIC SISTERS. The door opened and the bell above it rang out, startling Cherry.

'Coming in, sweetheart?' A woman wearing a beautiful orange headscarf poked her head out of the door, a cloud of smoke wafting around her. Her make-up had been applied with precision, giving her face a doll-like appearance. Purple eyeshadow had been blended all the way up to her eyebrows and a beauty spot had been painted on her left cheek. As she tapped the cigarette holder in her hands, making the burnt ash fall to the ground, Cherry noticed the little brown liver spots on her hands and was astounded at how well the make-up was concealing her age.

'Erm ... no. Not today. I'm new here. Just looking around,' Cherry said, trying to smile.

'It's all right. You'll be back.' The woman grinned, revealing a large gap between her two centre teeth. There was a smear of red lipstick on them.

'Right,' Cherry said, nonplussed. 'Um, could I ask a favour though?' She pulled out one of her flyers and held it out to the woman. 'Would you be able to put this up in your shop, please?'

The woman took the flyer, gave it a quick once over and bobbed her head. 'We have a notice board inside. Consider it done.' Cherry thanked her and then went on her way once the woman had disappeared inside the shop.

Despite her own abilities, Cherry couldn't help but doubt fortune tellers. In all her life she'd only met one other person who could see what she could see and she still felt sad every time she thought of Peter's fate. Being openly vocal about his gift had resulted in Peter being taken away and Cherry had never heard from him again. Surely it was best to do what she did in private and keep it to herself? It meant she was able to use her gifts subtly, without anyone seeing madness in it. How many people were out there who were *really* like her and shouted about it to the world? Very few, she thought. It's the people who have no idea what it's like to truly be different who *do* scream about it. If they really knew what it was like, to feel so isolated because of that difference, they wouldn't wish it upon themselves.

Loneliness reached out and interlinked its fingers with hers, sending a shiver through her.

Cherry purchased a bottle of sloe gin from the distillery and a bottle of tonic water from the supermarket before she got on the boat back to Royal William Yard. She thought about the day on the journey back and just as the boat docked, her phone buzzed. It was Miss Kightley again. Her text said, *Check your Facebook page.*

Cherry raced as fast as she could back to her tiny bedsit above the bakery, the cold stopping her frozen feet from getting there any faster. She put the bottles down on the counter, flipped her laptop open and fumbled over the password three times before successfully logging in. Once Facebook was open her eyes darted about, still not used to the interface, so she wasn't sure what Miss Kightley's text had been about or what she was supposed to be looking for. It was then that she saw the number next to the word 'Follows'.

'A hundred and two?!' she squealed. She snatched up her phone and shot a text off to Miss Kightley. *A hundred and two?! How?!*

A moment later the reply came back: *Welcome to the internet.* Cherry grinned and sent a quick reply back. *It's bloody marvellous.*

7

The Big Day

Cherry hadn't laid out a single baked good. How could she when her baking was so personal? Each item had to be hand-selected for its recipient otherwise she'd be handing out Chocolate Charms to already charming Charlies and doling out Don't Doubt Yourself Danishes to undoubtedly independent Danielles! Cherry's bakery was unique because of her personal, intimate touch and there was no way to know what particular feeling a person might need in their own special piece of Victoria sponge until she had met them – and their Meddlum.

Cherry was pacing around the bakery in her gold silk pyjamas. She'd thought that matching the wallpaper would be a nice touch, and she'd even strung up some black and gold balloons around the place and on the door so people knew that they had the right place. At 8 a.m., she pulled the black ties around her bunches tight, unlatched the door and turned her father's old sign that she'd hung up last night from CLOSED to OPEN. There was no one waiting outside but Cherry hadn't expected there to be. She was hoping that people would arrive later on, after work maybe. She was planning to stay open until 7 p.m., just in case there was a post-work rush. *I hope people come*, she thought. She turned back to her counter, ready to send out another Facebook post to let everyone know the bakery was open, when the bell above the door rang out. Cherry turned to see an elderly woman with silvery dreadlocks, dressed in purple and green patchwork and reams of silk. She was also hopping from foot to foot.

'Hi there,' Cherry said. 'Welcome! I'm Cherry. How can I help you?'

The woman smiled. 'Hello. I'm Sally. Sally Lightbody.'

Cherry had been practising smiles in the mirror for the past few days but she now found she needn't have bothered. She was so excited to share her treats with the townspeople that she was practically beaming at Sally until . . .

'You don't have a loo, do you?' Sally asked apologetically.

'Oh. Um. Yes! Yes, of course! It's just around this corner. First door on the left.'

'I will buy something when I come back out, I promise.

It's just me and me old age. Can't walk five minutes out of my own house before I'm busting again!' Sally waddled past Cherry, who couldn't help notice that Sally's patchwork bag had a similar crystal ball embroidered onto it to the one she'd seen in the window of the fortune tellers in The Barbican. Interesting.

While Sally was in the bathroom Cherry checked the display counter and fiddled with all the labels that she had purposefully placed to face her so she could make the correct choice for the customer once she'd seen what they needed. She glanced out of the window and noticed that Loneliness had made two friends. An odd-looking ball with tiny stumpy arms and legs was sat on Loneliness's shoulders. Its oversized hands were pressed flat against the glass. On top of it sat a smaller but just as ugly Meddlum that looked utterly bored. Its arms were folded and it kept rolling its eyes, over and over. Cherry frowned at them all and the ball-like Meddlum started to shake, as though crying. It made it harder for Loneliness to maintain its balance and it began to wobble. Guilt on top of Obsessiveness on top of Loneliness. *At least only the Loneliness is mine*, Cherry thought.

'Rightio, then,' Sally said, reappearing, 'let's see what we've got 'ere.' She wiggled her half-moon glasses, peering into the display case. 'Got any Belgian buns? I love a Belgian bun.'

'No Belgian buns, I'm afraid,' Cherry said politely.

'Wha—no Belgian ... well! What sort of baker are

you, then?' Sally said, sitting on one of the brown leather stools and swinging her bag onto the counter.

'One that's very interested in the symbol on your bag. I've seen it before, just the other day actually. I passed by a shop in The Barbican. It was ... um ... what's it called ... ?'

'Psychic Sisters?' Sally offered.

'Yes, that's the one! I saw one just like it in the window.'

Sally looked down at the embroidered crystal ball on her bag. 'I bought this bag from Psychic Sisters but it was years ago and I've not been back there in a long time. I only used to go to see if my own readings were accurate. Can't seem to part with the bag, though.' Sally reached into the bag and pulled out a rectangular box. She slid the lid off and Cherry could see that inside lay a deck of black cards. Cherry looked at them, curious.

'Go on.' Sally's lips curled into a slow smile. 'Shuffle 'em.'

'I thought you weren't supposed to touch other people's Tarot cards?'

'Oh, you are a bright one! Nah, I don't believe in that. It's not like sharing underwear! Besides, this is your reading. You should touch the cards.' Sally pushed the box towards her. Cherry picked up the deck and started to shuffle. Once she was satisfied that they were thoroughly shuffled, she placed them face down in front of Sally.

'Here we go then.' Sally turned over the first card, left to right, but held it up facing away from Cherry.

'Well? Am I doomed?' Cherry asked.

'No, m'love,' Sally said, returning the card to the deck and then putting the cards back into the box.

'That's it?' Cherry said, surprised.

'One card is all I need.' Sally winked. 'Now. Why no Belgian buns?' She leaned her chin on the back of her hand.

'How about this? In an apology for my lack of Belgian buns and in return for the reading, I'll give you something else to eat, on the house?'

'I never say no to free cake!' Sally said, her youthful eyes lighting up.

'Great. But first, I have a question. How did you fall into fortune telling?' Cherry had a feeling the answer would tell her all she needed to know about Sally's Meddlums.

Sally looked thoughtful for a moment. 'It sort of chose me, really. I get obsessed with things, y'see? I go through phases of loving something so bloody much that I can't get enough of it. Then one day I wake up and realise I know everything there is to know and poof! I'm cured! Never think about it again. But I haven't had that with fortune telling yet. Nothing's lasted as long as this has.' Sally gestured to her bag and laughed fondly.

'How long has your obsession been fortune telling?' Cherry asked, watching Loneliness scratch its claws at the front window. Sally clicked her tongue, racking up the time in her brain.

'Oh, it must be around thirty years or so now.'

'Wow! That *is* a long time. Why is fortune telling different from the rest of things you've been obsessed with?'

'It's the future, love. It's always changing.' Sally put the cards back into her bag. 'Well, now. Where's my cake, then?'

'All right, all right.' Cherry laughed. 'I've got just the thing for you, but it's in the kitchen. I'll be back in a minute.' She ducked into the back where she'd lined up trays and trays of cakes, muffins, biscuits and cookies, each containing a different feeling.

'Obsessiveness ... obsessiveness,' Cherry muttered to herself. She turned to the book that was full of her own special and secret recipes, and flipped through the alphabetical pages until she got to the Os. 'Obedience, Obnoxiousness, ah, Obsessiveness. I knew I'd treated this before.'

Contentment Cake: To keep the customer calm and at peace with what they've already got, no matter the amount or size.
Tastes like: Tea and mandarins
Indifference Icing: To try to balance their overly keen interest.
Tastes like: Marmite

Cherry always made a note of how every emotion tasted on her tongue, even though she never knew if it tasted the same to other people or if that taste was unique to her. Did contentment taste like tea and mandarins because those were the things that made her feel most content? Did indifference taste like Marmite because she was seemingly the only person in the world who didn't love it or hate it? She doubted that she'd ever know how things tasted to those she helped. Her hands worked quickly, cutting a generous slice of Contentment Cake and expertly squeezing out the blue icing from its piping bag into the shape of a crystal ball.

'Voila!' Cherry said as she walked back into the bakery with the plate held proudly in front of her. She presented it to Sally with a flourish.

'This looks delicious! A little bit of friendly advice though, m'love; you may want to serve your customers a bit quicker or this queue will get even longer!' Sally gestured behind her and Cherry looked around, noticing for the first time that there were seven other elderly customers shuffling about.

'Amazing what a quick text can do, isn't it?' Sally held up her phone and gave Cherry a cheeky smile. Cherry forgot herself for a moment and pushed herself up and across the counter to plant a giant kiss on Sally's cheek.

'Oh! You're quite a funny one.' Sally gasped in surprise but she laughed good-naturedly too. 'Well, what are you waiting for? You've got customers!'

'Right, then!' Cherry called out to the people waiting. 'Come on up and tell me a little bit about yourselves!'

Cherry didn't charge anyone for their cakes but she did place a donation jar on the counter which seemed to fill up at a considerable rate. By late afternoon every table was full, coats were falling off the stand and her stock of baked goods was over halfway gone. Cherry smiled at the background noise of people talking, forks tinkling against plates and teacups clattering. She closed her eyes for just a moment, enjoying the buzz and finally feeling at home for the first time since she'd arrived in Plymouth.

'You haven't got a slice of that marble cake left, have you?' said a feeble voice, breaking Cherry out of her reverie. She opened her eyes and saw two familiar faces in the doorway. One she was pleased to see, and the other, she may not have wanted to see at all but was pleased to see it was smaller at least.

'Of *course*, Margie! Come on in!'

Margie excitedly bounded into the shop but her Meddlum, her own Loneliness, sat outside with the rest of them. Cherry noticed that a second Meddlum, a tiny one about the size of a Chihuahua that Cherry recognised as Anxiety, was clinging to Margie's Loneliness. Cherry realised then that Margie had probably always had Anxiety but because of how neatly it had moulded itself to her Loneliness, it had been camouflaged when she had met Margie for the first time all those weeks ago.

'Pyjamas?' Margie asked, pointing at Cherry's gold number.

'Yup. I . . . er . . . never wear anything else,' Cherry said.

'You look lovely,' Margie said kindly.

'Why don't you have a seat and then we can chat? I won't be a moment.' Cherry popped into the kitchen and cut Margie a slice of 'Me, Myself and Everyone Else' Marble Cake. It was the treatment she would have eaten herself were she able to reap the benefits of her own abilities. She added three Tranquillity-soaked cherries on top and dusted them with Hope-infused edible golden glitter. When Cherry returned with the cake, Margie was still standing in the same place, her coat tugged even tighter around her shoulders.

'Would you . . . like to take it away?' Cherry said, not able to keep the edge of disappointment out of her voice.

Maggie hesitated and then nodded. 'Could I?' She looked nervously at the busy tables and Cherry understood immediately.

'Of course, Margie. Anything.' Cherry boxed up the cake and its trimmings and Margie dropped three pound coins in the donations jar. With a timid smile, she quickly left but not before Anxiety gave Cherry the finger through the window. Cherry had only looked away for a moment when—

'WHAT is your PROBLEM?!'

Cherry looked up and saw the same man she'd bumped into on the day she'd gone to The Barbican. Frustration, Cynicism and Mischief were right behind him. She ran to the doorway.

'Are you OK?' she asked Margie, who nodded, her eyes welling up. She quickly backed away and scuttled off down the street before Cherry could say anything else.

The man spun round to face Cherry. 'What's it got to do with you, Miss Full-Of-Hope-And-Wonder?' he snapped. Cherry couldn't hold back the shocked laugh that spluttered out of her mouth.

'I'm sorry?'

'Yeah, you should be. I shouldn't have bothered coming here in the first place. You and your bloody free cake.' Cynicism leaned over and whispered something in his ear. 'Bet it's not even free. Bet you've got a tip jar that I'll be guilt-tripped into filling.'

Cherry took a quiet, deep breath before speaking. 'Come inside. Please. I think I've got exactly what you need and I *promise*,' she crossed her heart, 'that you won't have to pay a penny.'

The man eyed her through his badly repaired glasses that now sat slightly skewed on his face. He gave a slight nod that was so quick Cherry almost missed it.

'*Wonderful!* In you come!' Cherry bounded into the bakery once more and saw him notice that she was wearing pyjamas. The smallest of smiles flickered across his full lips. 'Were you on your way here when you bumped into Margie?' she asked.

When he didn't reply, Cherry looked over her shoulder. He was still standing in the doorway and all of Cherry's customers were staring openly at him, their conversations stalling mid-sentence. Without looking at any of the people watching him, he walked purposefully towards Cherry. Every pair of eyes was watching him intently.

'I'm Cherry.' She held out her hand.

'I'm Chase.' Chase looked at her hand but didn't shake it. Cherry shrugged and put it back in her apron pocket.

'You're not allergic to nuts, are you?' Cherry asked, watching Frustration, Mischief and Cynicism waddling around in wide circles outside, knitted more closely together than they'd been the other day.

'No. Why?' he replied.

'Just checking. I'll be back in a bit. Wait there.'

'You haven't taken my order!' he called out as she walked into the kitchen.

'I already know what you need!' she called back. She quickly found what she was looking for: a rather large Optimism oatmeal cookie, drizzled in milk chocolate with Acceptance almonds scattered haphazardly on top.

'This is guaranteed to make you smile before you leave here, I promise. Will you try it?'

Chase looked at the plate, his nose upturned, but Cherry gently nudged it towards him and hesitantly, he picked the cookie up and nibbled the edge. Instantly, his face changed, but it wasn't a smile on his face. It was a grimace.

'What have you put in this?' he demanded.

'What ... what do you mean?' Cherry's stomach flipped. 'It's just an oatmeal and almond cookie.' She let out a high-pitched laugh that sounded fake, even to her ears. It certainly wasn't the nonchalant tone she was aiming for.

'No it's not. I know it's not.' Chase shoved the plate back towards her. 'You're tampering with the food,' he said, raising his voice so everyone could hear him.

'I don't know what you're talking about,' Cherry insisted. 'But talk like that can ruin a business.'

Chase stood up and leaned across the counter, threateningly close to her face, and hissed his next words. 'Then you need to stop what you're doing.'

'I don't know what you think I'm doing but I can assure you that—'

'Look, you can try to fix this town's problems and make everyone here feel better with your spiked cookies but if there's one person you're not going to get to, it's me. What was that, anyway?' He picked up the cookie and took a bigger bite, swirling it around his mouth with this tongue, chewing loudly. 'Optimism?' He swiped his finger across the plate scooping up the melted chocolate and almonds. 'And ... Obedience?'

Cherry was stunned. '... Acceptance, actually. But how ... how do you ... ?'

'Oh, did little Mary Berry think she was special? Well, you're not, so listen to me and listen well.' Chase walked behind the counter spitting out each syllable. 'You can't change people. No matter how much you try to make them feel better or worse—'

'Worse?' Cherry shook her head. 'I'd never—'

'People don't change.'

Everyone was watching the exchange in silence. No one moved, apart from Sally who was shuffling her Tarot cards furiously.

'That's not true,' Cherry said, holding her ground and his gaze. 'I choose to see the good in people,' she hissed.

Chase smiled tightly and laughed a laugh so full of malice that Cherry wished she'd never invited him into her safe haven.

'You think I don't see the good? That's *all* I see,' he said.

A tear rolled down Cherry's cheek as she realised what he meant. 'You're like me,' she whispered and her Loneliness halved in height immediately.

Chase stared at her. Then, without another word, he pushed the plate off the counter so it crashed to the floor with a clatter and left. Frustration was standing a little taller than before as it followed Chase down the road and away.

'Are you all right, Miss?' a kind voice asked.

Cherry looked around but couldn't see who had spoken until she caught Sally's eye. Cherry moved her gaze downwards and saw a very short man standing at the counter. He had a round face with kind blue eyes and a faded pink beanie hat that Cherry liked very much.

'Yes,' Cherry said, walking out from behind the counter, pulling out a stool with a shaky hand and sitting down. 'Yes, I am thank you, sir.'

'Bruce,' he said holding out his hand. 'Don't mind Chase. Lived here all his life and he's never been any different. Always bitter and feeling like the world owes him something.' Bruce pulled himself onto the stool beside her and leaned across to take her hand once more. 'I wouldn't give him a second thought.'

'No, you're right. I won't,' Cherry lied as another tear escaped.

'And don't you shed another tear because of him,' Bruce said squeezing her fingers, mistaking her tears for sad ones. How could she explain that the tears she was crying were happy ones?

As everyone returned to their conversations and she saw that Bruce was looking after Cherry, Sally calmly turned over the top card of the deck, from left to right.

8

The Magician Reversed

Chase Masters was the son of Madame Velina, a local palm reader, and had lived in Plymouth all his life. His mother was a charlatan who had come from a long line of charlatans. Not that they'd ever admit that, of course. Nor did they really believe that's what they were. They believed they had a connection to worlds beyond ours so if they needed a bit of help here and there (steaming open mail, hacking into email inboxes, the odd bit of eavesdropping), and it was in the name of helping people, where was the harm? Velina and his aunt, Danior, thought they were doing good by charging punters twenty pounds a pop for their guesswork and gut feelings but Chase knew better because he really *was* as different as his family claimed to be.

Chase could see the good in people. Well, the good they felt. Everyone is taught to see the good in people, metaphorically, but Chase had the ability from birth and to him these good feelings were physical beings. He was always able to give everyone the benefit of the doubt, to forgive them and give them a chance at redemption and as a child who knew no better, Chase found this easy. It was short-lived, however, because children can be cruel and can find happiness in the most dubious of places. Watching Joy float around the heads of the school kids as they laughed at him lying bloodied and aching on the ground was a tough lesson for Chase to learn. As he caught sight of Awe applauding just before he passed out, he realised that those who felt good things weren't always good people. He could see whatever glorious things the other children felt, skipping about like anti-angels watching over the monstrous habits their owners enjoyed. Very few lessons are so hard learnt and can make a child so untrusting but from those fateful school days Chase began to mistrust his own sight and steered clear of overly happy people.

Chase decided early on not to tell his family what he could see. As soon as he realised his abilities were real and unlike anything his mother claimed to be able to do, he knew that telling them the truth would be a mistake. He saw two possible outcomes:

1. They would be overjoyed, ecstatic and annoyingly elated. They'd ask hundreds of questions to make him

prove it was true. They would constantly ask him what they were feeling and they would make him work in the shop.

2. They'd ask, 'what took you so long?' They'd think he was finally accepting his place in their family of fraudsters, who all believed they had this connection to the beyond, and he was no different ... and they would *make him work in the shop*.

Working in the shop would be his worst nightmare realised. He couldn't bring himself to endorse the family business by helping them run it. That would be too hypocritical. He may have hated the world and its inhabitants but he hated it because of people like this mother and aunt – he didn't want to take advantage of anyone and that's what would happen if he confessed what he could see. Telling them simply wasn't an option. He was happier being the black sheep who thought it was all a bunch of hocus pocus. Life was hard enough for him as it was.

Seeing the best in people was exhausting. What use was it when some people weren't necessarily good, just feeling positive things? For the most part, those who felt good things deserved to feel them – but Chase began to hate this even more. Over the years, his gift turned into a curse and he became bitter. He could see that the world was a wonderful place, so why wasn't he happier? He could see couples in Love saunter past in a lovesick daze but he was all alone. He saw people with Ambition and Motivation strive towards success from sunrise to sunset and yet he still hadn't found his purpose in life. He met people who had nothing but who still had Hope for their future and yet he could barely get himself out of bed every morning. Chase wasn't a bad person but sometimes he couldn't help winding people up just to see their Joy shrink. He'd push their buttons and touch their nerves, just a little, and it made him feel better for a few seconds before he felt sour again. The world was a beautiful and wondrous thing and it frustrated Chase no end. Many people long to travel the world but not Chase. He didn't need to see Joy and Happiness on the other side of the world. His hometown was more than enough for him and so he'd never left. Instead he'd spent his years trying to get countless businesses off the ground, each one failing harder than the last because he insisted on doing everything alone. He refused to work with other people. Each time everything came crashing down, he'd sink into an alcohol-induced stupor until the next crazy idea came along.

Despite all his Cynicism, Frustration and occasional Mischief, Patience and Resilience had quietly stayed beside him since he was sixteen. They had interlinked their fingers with his and rarely let go. They were the only things in the world he cherished. Patience made him breathe when Frustration poked at his back, and Resilience pushed him onwards when Cynicism tripped him up. It was the pair of them working together, gently pressing their warm hands against his shoulders, who took him back to Cherry's bakery the day after he'd behaved so badly at her opening. As soon as he'd laid eyes on her, he knew she wasn't normal. Not like everyone else in the town, who grated on his nerves each and every day. From the way she glared over his shoulder, as he so often did himself to passers-by, he knew she had a secret that closely resembled his own. He knew others like him existed in the world. Research on the deep internet had led him to cryptic forums filled with people claiming they could do what he could do, but it was hard to weed out those who were genuine and those who were trying so hard to make their lives more exciting than they were.

It was 5 p.m. and Chase had hoped the bakery would be emptier than it was. Sally Lightbody, whom he thought was the biggest crackpot he'd ever met, was sat in the corner deftly shuffling her black deck of cards from palm to palm. A couple were canoodling at the table round the corner, presumably thinking that no one could see them, and Bruce Bunting was perched on a stool at the counter. He was nattering away to seemingly no one until Cherry came out from the kitchen in a pair of duck-egg-blue linen pyjamas and a matching dressing gown trimmed with fur. Her gaze flickered to the door and their eyes met. To his surprise, she smiled and beckoned him inside. *She's nuts*, he thought. *I wouldn't invite me inside.*

'How lovely to see you again, Chase.' Cherry smiled, draping a pink tea towel over her shoulder.

Sally quickly directed her cards at Chase and shuffled them once again, unnoticed by the others.

'Lovely? Are you mad?' Bruce said incredulously, refusing to look at Chase.

'Oh, Bruce.' Cherry swatted his arm playfully. 'I doubt anyone would return after a scene like yesterday's if they hadn't come to apologise, now would they, Mr . . . ?'

'Masters. Chase is fine, though,' he said, looking at the floor. 'And no. They wouldn't.'

'See, Bruce? Now what can I get you, Mr Masters? *Plain*, of course,' she added quietly, giving Chase a knowing look.

'Don't sell yourself short! Nothing you bake is plain! I've tried nearly everything you've got back there and it's all bursting with flavour.' Bruce swivelled his stool so that he was effectively blocking Chase from the conversation.

'I bet it is,' Chase sneered.

'That Cynicism has you under its thumb, doesn't it?' Cherry gestured towards the Meddlum, waiting outside. It was shooting her such a foul look that she looked away quickly, with a shudder.

Chase frowned. 'Eh? Cynicism? What are you talking about?' He turned to the window, but could only see the subtle yellow light emitting from Patience and Resilience, who were stood in the doorway. Their feet had stuck firmly to the pavement when they'd tried to follow Chase inside. Bruce looked from Cherry to Chase, from Chase to Cherry and then to the window, where he saw absolutely nothing.

'Maybe you have been putting something funny

in those cakes,' Bruce joked. 'You're both behaving strangely!' He laughed as he hopped off his stool. He was about to leave when Sally beckoned him over and made him join her, mischief etched into the wrinkles of her eyes.

Chase took Bruce's place at the counter as Cherry fetched him a plain slice of Victoria Sponge.

'What do *you* see when you look out the window?' Cherry asked, curious that he didn't seem to know Cynicism was attached to him.

'What do *you* see?' he countered.

'I asked first!' she insisted.

'Fine.' Chase turned back to the window and pointed. 'Patience and Resilience. They belong to me.'

'Really?' she said, remembering the way he'd yelled at her in the middle of the street after a rather small collision.

'You can't see them?'

'Nope.' Cherry looked away from the window and directly into Chase's eyes. 'Nothing good out there for me to see.'

'So you only see the bad in people.'

'And you only ever see the good. Lucky you,' Cherry said, watching Loneliness panting at the window.

'Gratitude has just arrived. Belongs to Bruce although looks to me like it's aimed at Sally.'

Cherry looked over at where Bruce and Sally were sitting and sure enough, Bruce was beaming at his dreadlocked companion as she pointed to each of the Tarot cards she'd drawn for him and explained what they meant.

'He's also got Understanding,' Chase continued, rolling his eyes. 'Contentment is Sally's. That's what you get when you retire, I suppose. I see a lot of elderly people with Contentment. She also has Acceptance and Nostalgia on her side. Apparently, she and her husband were madly in love, the whole town could see it. They were the human embodiment of true love. Sweet if you like that sort of thing.' He shrugged.

'Apparently?'

'He died long before I was born. Mum says a part of Sally died then too.'

Cherry looked over at Sally and she noticed something she'd never seen before. At the start of each of Sally's smiles there was a slight hesitation, a moment of questioning. Each time she felt the smallest flicker of happiness, she also felt like she shouldn't be smiling at all.

'I had no idea ... ' Cherry said, looking away as Sally's gaze fell on them both.

'There are two belonging to you out there as well but that *would* be telling.' Chase smirked and took another bite of his cake.

Cherry cocked her head at him. 'I guess you don't want to know what I see for you, then?'

'You'll tell me anyway,' Chase said without looking up. 'I think you're a bit of a show-off.'

'What do you mean?' Cherry narrowed her eyes as Chase gestured all around them.

'This bakery. You don't set something like this up if you don't want everyone to adore you and what you do for them.'

'That's not what this is,' Cherry said, taking her tea towel from her shoulder to wipe the sweat off of her hands. She looked around at everything she'd created. The top half of the chalkboard wall was a unique guest-book, full of positive messages from customers, and the bottom half was full of drawings from the younger customers. Everyone who was currently in the bakery looked content, unaware of what Cherry was doing for them. This place was a haven, a safe space not only for those who stumbled across it but for herself too. This was a place where bad feelings were left behind and good ones were created. What she was doing was no different than an anonymous donation to a charity, or leaving a five-pound note in a library book for the next person to buy themselves a coffee. An anonymous act of love and compassion. While her customers enjoyed Cherry's baking, they'd never quite know what she was doing for them and just how much she was helping them.

'Of course it is.' Chase's voice broke through Cherry's thought. 'And not only that but you're kind of exploiting everyone's pain too.'

'Now just a minute!' Cherry threw the tea towel down on the counter.

'No need to get flustered!' Chase smiled, pleased with himself. 'I'm just telling you how it is. You've come up with a way to make money off everyone's misery. It's quite impressive. Wish I'd thought of it.' He stuffed a large bite of cake into his mouth and chewed it loudly and sloppily.

'I *help* people!' Cherry said, her voice rising. Sally's eyes flickered in their direction and Cherry took a deep breath. The last thing she wanted was for Bruce to come barging in and getting defensive on her behalf. While she appreciated how much of a shine he'd taken to her and the bakery, this was a conversation she didn't want anyone to hear.

'Sure you do, sweetheart.' Chase put yet another forkful of cake into his mouth. Irritated, Cherry snatched the plate away and he laughed.

'This isn't much of an apology.' Cherry felt a heat race through her body and up to her face.

'No, I suppose it's not.' Chase held up his hands, still smiling. He looked at her steadily, the sneer on his face softening into something almost rueful. The knot in Cherry's stomach tightened. 'I really am sorry that I got so angry yesterday. I've never met anyone like me before and it took me by surprise. I didn't know how to react, so I didn't react well.'

'That's an understatement,' Cherry snapped. 'Quite a big understatement.'

'Maybe.' Chase shrugged. 'Either way, I'm sorry. I

shouldn't have behaved towards you like that. That being said, I do stand by what I've said here today. You are taking advantage of people and actually, it's given me a marvellous idea.'

'Idea? What idea?' A sense of unease spread through Cherry.

'Think of it as a gift. Better get baking, Mary Berry. You're not going to know what's hit you,' he said with a finality that chilled Cherry to the bone. He stood to leave.

'I don't see what you see,' Cherry said, catching his attention before he could leave. 'We've both been dealt very different hands from the same dealer and while you see the good in people, I see the worst. I'd think twice before trying to hurt someone who has seen the darkest side of you.'

'Everyone's seen the darkest side of me. I've never tried to hide it.' He laughed bitterly. 'I'm not trying to hurt you, Cherry. I'm trying to learn from you.' And with that, he left.

Bruce raced over to check that Cherry was OK but Sally remained where she was. She shuffled her cards for a final time and directed her energy towards Chase, watching him storm away. She flipped the top card from left to right and staring up at her was the The Magician, but reversed.

For the first time in his entire life Chase felt a fire in his belly. He'd always known he was special, that his abilities made him different from everyone else, but he'd shunned them in order to be less like his family, to distance himself from their fraudulent ways. Now, however, he had a plan to make life a little more interesting. Finally, he'd found a purpose not only to make his days worthwhile but to earn himself a decent living too.

Chase stood outside the Plymouth Gin Distillery and grinned.

Mischief wriggled in between Frustration and Cynicism, centre stage at last.

The Tower

'Those who look for the bad in
people will surely find it.'

Abraham Lincoln

9

The Rivalry Begins

Cherry had never had enemies. She had always been too reserved and too quiet to make friends, let alone have anyone notice her enough to actually turn on her. But now she was sure that she had an enemy in Chase and she already knew she didn't like it.

'What did he *mean*, he's trying to learn from me?' Cherry paced up and down the bakery later that evening once she'd closed up. 'What does that even mean? What is he going to try?'

Bruce and Sally had kindly offered to stay and chat for a while, to make sure Cherry was all right before they went home. Margie had seen their silhouettes on her way home from work and had come to investigate so she was helping Cherry wipe down the tables. Cherry loved that she'd made friends and had people to talk to but she had to tread carefully and be mindful of what she was saying. No one knew her secret. Except for Chase.

'I haven't the foggiest,' Bruce said, scratching his stubbled chin. 'He's always been an odd chap. Never managed to get any of his businesses off the ground.'

'Businesses?' Cherry asked.

'Yeah. He's made several attempts,' Bruce said with a wry smile. 'A delivery service, personalised Christmas decorations, he was even a driving instructor for a while but all his students kept crying. Even tried getting a normal job once, too, in the local pub, but he didn't make it easy for himself. He insisted on flair bartending. He was actually quite good and it would have gone well if he hadn't been such a wind-up merchant. After a few words from him, a brawl would always kick off.'

'"Flair bartending"? Never heard of it.' Cherry shook her head.

'It's where those show-offs who think they're clever take twenty minutes to pour you a drink because they're too busy flipping the bottles and glasses about. It's funny when they drop 'em though,' Bruce laughed.

'I always quite like watching it,' Margie said quietly. 'It's like Cirque du Soleil for alcohol.'

'I suppose it is.' Bruce smiled at Margie and she blushed. 'It's not the flair bartending so much as Chase himself. He's just not a pleasant sort. He's not like you,

Cherry.' Cherry batted the air like she was swatting away his compliment. 'I mean it. You're a breath of fresh air in this town. No one wants to work with Chase or help him and he's too proud to ask. Too arrogant, even. Thinks he doesn't need the help of people like us to succeed. Shame really. He's very bright. Just a bit . . . misguided.'

'I'm sure it's nothing to worry about, Cherry. He's a strange one – always has been,' Sally reassured her, but Cherry couldn't help but worry. Besides Peter, Cherry had never met anyone like her. As a child she'd dreamed of entire families who had the same ability she had, and who all used it to help those around them and do some good. She hoped that one day she would find a family of her own somewhere in among the people who saw the world as she did. Cherry had never expected there to be so few like her and she certainly never expected someone like Chase Masters to share her gift. He was too wild, too untamed. Cherry got the impression that he saw his ability as an affliction rather than something to hone and embrace and use to help others. Cherry worried about what that might mean for both of them, living in such close proximity, and already adversaries. It also made Cherry want to help him.

'What do you expect from the son of a palm reader! Oh – sorry, Sally. No offence intended,' Margie said, colouring in embarrassment at her faux pas.

'None taken, love. We're an odd sort of person and I'm

sure if I'd had children they'd be just as mad as me,' Sally said kindly.

'He's the son of a palm reader?' Cherry asked.

'Yes. His mother and aunt run that fortune-telling place in The Barbican together,' Sally said.

Cherry remembered the woman who had poked her head out of the shop on the day she'd visited The Barbican, the day she'd met Chase, and wondered if it had been his mother or his aunt. Sally was twirling one finger by the side of her head and crossing her eyes at Margie who couldn't help but snigger.

'You think they're mad?' Cherry asked, surprised. 'Aren't you all in the same profession?'

'It's one thing to entertain folk with your ideas of what their future could be, based on cards they draw. It's another to claim supernatural powers and charge people large sums of money for guesswork masquerading as fact!' Sally was talking quickly, her voice rising. 'Sorry. I'm sorry.'

Bruce put a calming hand on her shoulder. Cherry couldn't help but notice Margie's eyes flicking towards that affectionate touch and then looking quickly back down at her feet.

'I just get wound up by people who give others false hope,' Sally explained. 'I tell all the people I read for to take everything I say with a pinch of salt. Everyone's future is like a work of art. It can be interpreted in many ways and even then it will constantly change with every decision you make. Everything I say is factual at that moment in time but by the time you've made another decision, something as simple as having tea instead of coffee or ice cream instead of chocolate, you've started down another path that could lead to another future. A future that hasn't been read yet.'

'"It's the future, love. It's always changing."' Cherry repeated Sally's words back to her and Sally's smile widened, her expression full of affection for her friend.

'Exactly.'

'Do you have to book an appointment to see them?' Cherry asked.

'Who? Madame Velina?' Sally said, taking Bruce's hand in her own.

'Is that his mother?' Cherry asked.

'Yes,' Sally replied, tracing the lines on Bruce's palm with her fingertip. 'His aunt is Madame Danior. Their shop is usually pretty quiet so I'm sure you could just walk in and see them. Or book an appointment for later,' she added, her voice quiet.

'Oh, Sally. I'm not going for a reading,' Cherry reassured her, realising she must have been hurt by the idea of Cherry wanting to see her rivals. She knelt by Sally's chair and took her other hand. 'I'm going to talk to them about Chase. I want to find out more about him and maybe understand why he's suddenly got it in for me. You're the only fortune teller I need – you're the best one I know.'

'I'm a silly old fool,' Sally said, wiping away a tear. 'Just promise me you'll be careful with those two.'

'Are they really that terrible?' Cherry said.

'They both just like to ... push the boundaries.'

'The boundaries of what?' Cherry asked.

'Of what is morally right.'

10

Amateur

'Do you have anything with alcohol in it?'

If she'd had a brother, Cherry thought that he'd be a lot like George Partridge – except that George was white. But his character was playful and he had a lovely brotherly temperament that made her long for a family of her own and the two of them had a lot in common. Well, apart from Cherry's love for reading and George being possibly the only librarian in the world who hated books.

'It's only just lunchtime!' she scolded good-naturedly before fetching George's regular treat(ment) from the kitchen. She set the Encouraging Eclair before him, hoping it would help battle the Defeat that was banging its head repeatedly against the doorframe. She looked at him thoughtfully. 'Why are you a librarian, George? You have a new story every day about a visitor who's wound you up. Remember last week? That girl who asked you if you could tell her about a book she'd read once but couldn't remember the title *or* the author?'

'Yes, I remember. She got cross when I said I couldn't possibly know which book she was talking about. Threw a magazine at me,' George said.

'You did tell her to sling her hook,' Cherry reminded him.

'Maybe I deserved it. That man who calls up once a week and places his Chinese takeaway order called again yesterday. These days I just tell him it'll be forty-five minutes and hang up.'

'You don't?!' Cherry laughed.

'I do. It's just easier!' George chuckled.

'Why are you a librarian, George?' Cherry asked again.

'Because my mum's one. Her mum was one. Her mum was one. And so it goes on. That library essentially belongs to every generation of my family. It just means my life hasn't turned out anything like in the books I let everyone borrow.' George swept his blond hair back to reveal his sorrowful blue eyes. 'I wanted to be a vet. I love animals,' he sighed.

'I can tell.' Cherry smiled at his blue and cream knitted jumper that had cats all over it. 'So, why can't you become a vet? It's never too late, George.' Cherry tried to sound encouraging but she was going to have to let the eclair do its work. George's scrunched-up face told her he was very much done with talking about what might have been.

'I can't let Mum down like that. I just ... can't do it,' he said, taking a bite out of one end of his eclair, cream sloshing out of the other. 'Tell me, do you ever go out around here?'

'Erm ... I haven't. Not really. I mean, I don't often leave the ... well ... I *could* ... it's just ...' Cherry's cheeks started burning.

'Hey, now. No need to panic. I just never see you out anywhere other than in here and I thought you could do with a friend to show you around. Nothing more, nothing less.' George's face was kind. Beautiful but kind and Cherry hoped he felt that brotherly vibe towards her as much as she felt that sibling-like attachment to him. She took a breath.

'Actually, that sounds lovely.'

'Oh. So you wear pyjamas ... everywhere?' George said.

'You're one to talk. I don't think I've ever seen you wear anything other than an animal jumper.' She prodded him with one finger as she stepped out of the bakery, wearing a red cardigan and black pyjamas.

'Touché.'

'So where are we off to?'

'The Gin Distillery! Probably one of the most famous

things Plymouth has to offer, it's not too far away in case you decide it's too much and want to come home and apparently the cocktails in the bar are delicious. Thoughts?' He offered her his arm.

'I am rather partial to a gin and tonic. Let's go.'

But when they arrived, they couldn't even get near the distillery as the street was full of people bustling around, all waiting to get inside.

'What on Earth ... it's never like this! It's just a little distillery with a bar! Not that it's not worth seeing,' George said quickly, obviously worried that Cherry would think he'd brought her somewhere boring. 'Excuse me?' he called out as they neared the group. 'What's going on here? Is there some kind of ... free drinks promotion? Or a private event?'

'It's this new flair bartender they've got in,' a bloke near the door said. The woman he was with was craning her neck desperately to see inside each time the door opened. 'His flairing is good but it's his drinks that everyone's talking about. Apparently they're incredible. Trouble is, because of him, it's hard to even get inside.'

'Flair bartending?' The blood drained from Cherry's face.

Even tried getting a normal job once, too, in the local pub, but he didn't make it easy for himself. He insisted on flair bartending. He was actually quite good ...

'Cherry? Cherry!'

But she was gone, pushing through the crowd and

116

causing people to yell profanities at her as she shoved past them. George kept apologising on her behalf but he couldn't keep up with her and Cherry soon lost him in the crowd. There was no security on the door – they clearly weren't prepared for this level of custom – so Cherry ducked inside. It was completely rammed and the noise of people yelling their orders was deafening. Cherry saw Chase's Meddlums immediately. The three of them were sitting on one of the many shelves that were filled with bottles of gin. Frustration and Cynicism had their hands on Mischief's shoulders, cheering it on as it downed shot after shot of neat gin. As Cherry pushed in closer and closer, Chase came into view. He was behind the bar, twirling a silver cocktail shaker in one hand and pouring sloe gin into a glass with the other. As though he could sense her presence, he looked up and caught her eye. He grinned at her. Cherry didn't return his smile. He beckoned her forward and two well-dressed men in blue blazers let her past.

'What can I getcha, darling?' Chase asked, leaning towards her across the bar.

'An explanation. What are you doing?'

'Nothing you haven't already done.'

'Another Negroni when you're ready, mate!' another customer called.

'Coming right up, sir!' Chase's hands moved deftly, whipping up the order in no time at all. One part gin, one part Campari, one part sweet red vermouth.

'Watch this,' Chase said to Cherry, his expression innocent.

He bent down to the floor behind the bar, the customer's drink still in his hand. Cherry had to lean so far over the bar that her feet came off the ground but she could just about see Chase making a strange movement with his cheeks.

'Chase, stop playing around, what are you—?' Then he spat into the drink. 'CHASE!'

Quickly, he stirred it with a black plastic stirrer until all the saliva bubbles had disappeared. Chase straightened up and placed the drink on the bar.

'Here we go! Seven-fifty please, mate.'

Cherry watched the money exchange hands, horrified.

'How could you?' she hissed when he turned back to her, ignoring the endless rumble of shouted drink requests.

'Oh, come on. As if I'm going to spend my time infusing gin. I wouldn't know where to start. This is much more efficient.'

'You've not practised at all, have you? This has been six years of my life, perfecting this. The measurements are so exact, Chase. Too much of something and someone could get seriously hurt! You don't even have enough time with each person to get to know them or figure out what they need. You could be putting anything into their drinks!'

Cherry rarely raised her voice in anger and even though the noise levels meant it was impossible not to shout in this place, she had a feeling that she would have been yelling regardless of the noise.

'I know what these people need. Everyone wants love and happiness and comfort. I've seen it all my life. They're all the same.' He widened his eyes with his fingers. 'Even you, Cherry. Self-righteous, high and mighty Cherry. Fancy a drink while you're here?' He winked, and that was when Cherry saw red.

She didn't know what she was doing until it was done. The idea flitted into her head and by the time she'd fully processed it, she'd already pulled her fist back and her knuckles slammed against his face with a crunch. Chase's eyes widened in shock as he fell back into the wall of glasses and bottles behind him. The noise bubbled to a simmer until there was just a low hum. People were staring at Cherry. Her stomach churned but she took a deep breath, kept her eyes on the floor and said as clearly and steadily as she could, 'He spat in all your drinks.'

She turned on her heel and made her way out of the bar and onto the street where she found George. He was arguing with someone in the queue.

'I'm just trying to find my friend! She went in five minutes ago – please just ... wait, there she is!'

Cherry grabbed George by the hand and pulled him back in the direction they'd come, ignoring his calls for her to slow down. She didn't stop until she saw the familiar red and yellow shop.

'George, I'm so sorry tonight turned out like this.'

'Like what, Cherry? You're shaking! What happened in there?' George held her shoulders, trying to steady her.

'Nothing . . . I mean. Not nothing. I punched Chase in the face,' she admitted.

'You what?!' George laughed, a look of disbelief on his face.

'I know, I know. He wound me up and I rose to the bait. I've never hit anyone before. I'm so ashamed of myself, but—'

'No, that's great! I've wanted to hit that snarky bastard for years!' George held up his hand for a high five but Cherry took it in both her hands and pulled it back down to his side.

'I shouldn't have done it and I will apologise but right now . . .' Cherry heard a bell ring and there in the shop doorway were two faces, watching her with interest. 'But right now, I need to have my fortune told.' Purposefully, she strode towards the shop with the crystal ball in the window.

'Are you mad?' George asked.

'Absolutely,' she said. 'Isn't everyone?'

11

Family

'I knew you'd be back,' Madame Danior said, showing her lipstick-stained teeth. 'Didn't take you long at all.' She opened the door wide to let Cherry inside but Cherry's feet remained stuck to the pavement.

'Your nephew is Chase Masters?' Cherry asked.

'Mmm.' Danior rolled her eyes but Velina stepped into the dim light and hit her sister's arm with the back of her extravagantly ringed fingers. Velina's make-up was the same as her sister's; thick and colourful. However, her fake eyelashes had been stuck on almost half an inch above her real ones and her real eyebrows had been covered with porcelain foundation and harsh, angular black fake eyebrows had been drawn above them giving the impression that she wore a constant scowl on her face. She wasn't wearing any lipstick either so her lips were almost invisible. She had hidden any trace of natural expression, which made her incredibly hard to read. Her head was wrapped in a pink headscarf so there was no hair on show and Cherry wondered if she had any at all whereas Danior had pulled strands of her red hair, presumably dyed considering her age, out from under her orange headscarf. Danior was a good foot and a half taller than Velina but there was something about the way Velina held herself that made Cherry curl in on herself. Strangely, the only thing that gave Cherry some comfort were the two Meddlums fixedly staring at each other while sitting on one of the sofas. She watched through the shopfront window and saw that each Meddlum was mesmerised, scrutinising every inch of the other with puffy, narrow eyes. One belonged to Danior and one belonged to Velina, their rubbery skin tinged the same colour as their respective owners' headscarves but despite them belonging to different sisters, Cherry could identify that they were both, undoubtedly, Doubt. The sisters, while outwardly confident with their own fortune telling talents, very much doubted the other's ability. Cherry felt a little less intimidated knowing that they might not be as omniscient as they portrayed themselves to be.

'Careful, Danior. You don't want to put that sort of negativity out into the universe. Karma will bite back when you least expect it.' Velina took each end of her blue silk scarf in either hand and flung it from around her neck, over her head and then threw it over Cherry's head and around her neck with a flourish. 'No need to be afraid of us, dearie. We don't bite.' She tugged gently on the scarf and Cherry felt that she had no choice but to enter the shop.

The walls were covered in crushed red velvet from floor to ceiling, and purple sofas adorned with several throw pillows lined the room. Cherry guessed it was supposed to look plush and expensive but when she looked closer she could see that the sheets of fabric had been stapled to the walls and the sofas had many small cigarette burns which explained the faint smoky smell and the haze you could only see when you looked up at the badly fitted lights.

'Why have you come, child?' Velina batted her badly placed eyelashes.

Cherry smiled as sweetly as she could despite her mistrust. 'Why don't *you* tell *me*?' Her own confidence startled her and instantly she felt her stomach flip.

'We don't do readings for free.' Danior snapped.

'Now, now Dani. I'm sure we can make an exception. After all, my son isn't treating you with the respect you deserve, is he?' Velina walked to the back of the shop where there was a curtain of multi-coloured beads. She pushed it aside, making the beads clatter against each other and glint in the light. Just when Cherry thought she had disappeared, her hand pushed through the beads and she beckoned Cherry with curling fingers. The noise grated on Cherry and she clenched her teeth as she walked through the doorway before Danior, careful not to disturb more of the beads.

'Sit.' Velina said.

There were two blue wooden chairs that looked like they belonged in a nursery, and a small wooden table in between them. The table was full of scratches and dents and had red nail polish marks scattered across it from where the sister's nails skimmed the surface when they held customer's palms or turned card after card. Cherry took the seat opposite Velina, and Danior tutted when she realised she'd have to stand.

'Tea?' Velina asked, pouring herself a cup of steaming green liquid from the Chinese teapot that had been heating on a hot plate in a corner of the room.

'No, thanks.'

'I insist,' she said, pouring a second cup.

'Really, I'm fine,' Cherry said.

'*She insists*,' Danior said with a glare.

'Okay . . . ' Cherry took the cup from Velina. It smelled like normal green tea but when she took a sip it tasted exceedingly grassy, as though the tea leaves had been left to brew for too long. Cherry tried to turn her grimace into a smile but the gag that caught in her throat couldn't be stifled. She put the cup down, ignoring the disapproving look Danior gave her before she sank back into the shadows.

'Feeling better?' Velina asked.

Cherry didn't know what to say. Surely they hadn't spiked the tea? She felt normal but still, she nodded her head.

'Good,' Velina said and Danior's lips smacked as they cracked into a smile. 'Have you ever had your palm read before?' Velina looked her straight in the eyes.

'I can't say I have,' Cherry said, rubbing her cold yet sweaty hands together under the table.

Velina placed both her hands face up on the table and raised her faint, real eyebrows, the drawn ones fixed. Cherry's hands twitched as she hesitated.

'We haven't got all night,' Danior said from the shadowed corner of the room.

Reluctantly, Cherry placed her hands, palms up, in Velina's, and she was transfixed by the contrast of her dark skin against Velina's white skin. Their hands created a yin-yang of sorts.

'My, my, someone's nervous. Got something to hide?' Velina said, slipping her right hand out from underneath Cherry's, picking up the end of her blue scarf and wiping Cherry's palms down. Cherry tried to pull her hands away but Velina closed her fingers around her wrists.

'Definitely got something to hide.' Velina smiled with her invisible lips. Cherry unclenched her hands and Velina's fingers relaxed. 'Hmmm.' She hummed as she closed her eyes.

Cherry suddenly felt very exposed. She'd just wanted

125

to find out about Chase. She hadn't expected this kind of supernatural interrogation from the sisters.

'You've a strong aura, Miss Redgrave.'

'How do you know my last name?' Cherry asked, her heart starting to thump harder.

'Darling. Look around you,' Danior drawled in a bored voice.

'Oh, yes. I suppose that was a silly question,' Cherry said but it wasn't a silly question. She didn't believe in what Velina and Danior did. It wasn't real – it couldn't have been.

'Now. Let's see.' Velina finally looked at Cherry's palms. 'Oh ... oh, my dear. You're a mess.'

'No, I'm not,' Cherry said defensively. Velina looked up at her through her rows of eyelashes and Cherry met her gaze with her own steady one.

'According to all these broken lines on your left hand, you are.' She tutted. 'So sad.'

'Okay. Why am I a mess? What do the broken lines mean?' The more Velina went on the more Cherry fought the urge to roll her eyes. Velina sucked in a sharp breath.

'Your heart line is split perfectly in two. See? Right there?' She took her left hand out from underneath Cherry's right and pointed to a crack in the line that ran along the top of Cherry's left palm. 'You have a habit of putting other people's needs before yours. Your ... emotions sit on the back burner. You know how every-one else feels but they rarely get to know the *real* you in return – do they?' Velina didn't look up so Cherry took the opportunity to swallow. 'This line here,' Velina pointed to the next line down that swept in from an inch below her index finger and ran right through the centre of her palm but, yet again, was broken. 'You're a sensitive soul. You're so easily swayed by how other people feel. It's a long and deep line though, Cherry. You're a clear thinker. Focused. I've heard people appreciate that about you.'

Cherry had almost forgotten about Danior but suddenly she coughed and spluttered and Velina stole a glance in her direction. Cherry looked up and could only see the light glinting off Danior's jewellery but she was sure that cough wasn't anything to do with clearing her throat. It was a warning to Velina to tread carefully, Cherry was sure of it.

'What else have you "heard"?' Cherry asked, but Velina just stroked Cherry's palms.

'This line here is your life line.' Velina ignored the question and instead gestured to yet another broken line, this time in two places. 'Did something bad happen to you as a child, Cherry?'

'What does my hand say?' Cherry raised her palm a little.

'Each break represents a traumatic experience. There are two breaks – both are near the start of the line but there's a significant gap between them. Something bad happened as a child and then again later on, perhaps when you were in your late teens.' Cherry clenched her teeth as memories of one father leaving and one father dying ran through her mind. Velina closed Cherry's palm and stroked it with her pointed red talons. 'Not all just . . . *smoke and mirrors*, now is it?'

Danior coughed again, louder this time, and Cherry was now certain it was a tell. She was hinting to Velina to stop talking.

'How did you know I'd said—?'

'You best be off now. It's getting late.' Velina stood and Danior pushed herself off the wall and stepped forward, back into the light.

'No,' Cherry said, wiping her hands down her cardigan. 'No?'

'Did she just say no?' Danior hissed.

'I came here to ask you something. About Chase.'

'You can ask but it doesn't mean you'll get any answers.' Danior turned to leave the room but Velina caught her arm.

'Now, now Danior, now now.' She nodded at Cherry.

Cherry's mind was racing. Now that the moment was here, she wasn't sure how to ask the question. 'Is he . . . different? I mean . . . can he do anything like what you claim—' Danior scoffed and Cherry redirected the question, '—anything like what you *do* here?'

'No,' Velina said bluntly. 'Next?'

'Are you sure?' Cherry pushed.

'Extremely. Why, do you think we don't speak? He

thinks we're mad, we think he's plain, ordinary,' Danior said, yawning.

'I see. That's all, then.'

'You can see yourself out,' Danior said, brushing aside the beaded curtain to let Cherry through. Cherry ducked underneath Danior's arm but Velina and Danior's air of intimidation irked Cherry and made her feet pause and turn on the spot. 'Respect your elders' was something Cherry had been taught very early on in life, but as she grew up, she realised respect was something to be earned and sometimes wasn't relevant to age or experience. Velina and Danior certainly hadn't shown her anything closely resembling respect and so despite her wobbling knees, Cherry said,

'Actually ... I suppose there is one last thing.'

'What now?!' Danior stamped her foot.

'You might want to get that cough seen to, Danior. It really gives you away.' Danior's eyes widened. 'Oh, and learn how to make a decent cup of tea. Yours tastes like grass.'

12

Not Good Enough

Cherry had never liked mysteries. She was usually so full of anxiety that she often avoided anything full of suspense. However, now that she found herself inside of one, she found it far more intriguing than she thought it would be and far less worrying than when you're watching from the outside.

'They're fraudsters!' Cherry exclaimed when Sally came into the shop the next day. It was 12:45 p.m. and Sally was much later than usual. Margie had already been in at her usual time of 10:30 a.m. and Cherry had had to put some cling film over Sally's walnut whip. 'Where have you been?' Cherry asked.

'Nowhere special. Who are fraudsters, dear? Velina and Danior?'

'Yes! They *must* be! Velina somehow knew about things I'd said like ... like when I said what they did was just smoke and mirrors! She repeated the same phrase to me, like she wanted me to know that she knew, but then Danior coughed really hard and warned her off. Like this!' Cherry hacked up phlegm from the back of her throat.

'Lovely,' Sally said drily, moving her plate away from Cherry's coughing.

'Don't you see? Danior was coughing because Velina was getting too arrogant. She was giving away too much. She also said that she'd *heard* things about me. I bet you *anything* they've got this place bugged.'

'Bugged?'

'Yeah! Isn't that what it's called? When they hide those secret devices so they can record what everyone's saying?' Cherry had never watched much TV but with the internet now at her disposal, she'd found a love for crime shows. The thrill she got from fast car chases and close calls with death was far beyond anything she could ever imagine having in her own life.

'Yes, that is what it's called, but would they really go to that expense? Let alone that length?' Sally dismissed the idea with a wave of her hand and picked up her walnut whip with the other.

'Okay,' Cherry conceded. It *was* a bit far-fetched. 'Maybe they haven't bugged my shop but that doesn't mean there aren't other ways of listening.'

'Or maybe they really are just psychic?' Sally said, shrugging.

'You really think that?' Cherry was surprised. 'But yesterday you said that it was all guesswork masquerading as fact.'

'I know what I said!' Sally snapped, and then took a breath to calm herself. 'I'm sorry. I didn't mean to snap.' She looked around to make sure the shop was empty. 'They *are* fraudsters but you have to be very careful what you accuse them of, Cherry. Especially without any real evidence. They may be old but they're a vital part of this community. Been around for years. You've only just got here and with the influence they have over this tiny bit of town, they could wipe you out. It's best to just . . . leave them to it.' Sally didn't wait for Cherry to respond. She picked up her plate and went to her usual spot in the corner by the window.

'Sally . . .' Cherry said but Sally merely waved her attempt at an apology away. Cherry hadn't realised she'd been touching a nerve and wished she hadn't poked so hard. She made a mental note to whip her up something special to say a proper sorry later on. Now, however, she had other things to worry about. It was 12:50 p.m. and George hadn't shown up. He'd been in every day for over a week at exactly 12:45 on the dot. She'd thought they'd become good enough friends that he'd let her know if he wouldn't be visiting. *Maybe he's on his way and just bumped into a friend or something*, Cherry thought.

133

Cherry *hoped*. She hoped until 1:15 when the bell above the door rang and Cherry looked up eagerly but the face in the doorway wasn't George's.

'Hi,' said the rosy-cheeked woman from the doorway.

'Hello!' Cherry waved her tea towel at the elegant lady. She was very tall and wore a long, plain, formal black dress with a duck-egg blue coat that swished at the hem, and she was carrying a cello case like a rucksack.

'I'm Orla,' she said, struggling to get her cello through the door, tendrils of her blonde hair stuck to her sweaty forehead. Cherry ran to help her but then hesitated when she realised she wasn't sure how to help. 'I hate my seven-year-old self for choosing such a big instrument. Why couldn't I have picked the flute?' Orla went back outside, took off her instrument rucksack and pushed it through the doorway on its side.

'At least it's not a double bass!' Cherry said. She waited for Orla to get settled and then asked, 'Orla. Yes, you've been in before. I just didn't recognise you underneath that case! What can I get you?'

'Well, I've know you're good at picking for your customers so ... I guess I should ask what you think I need?'

Cherry stole a quick glance out of the window and there on the pavement was a gallumphing bear of a creature that yawned as she caught its eye. Cherry could spot Exhaustion anywhere.

'Here. Let me take that. I bet you're rather tired dragging that around everywhere. Are you part of a band?'

Cherry took the cello and was surprised at the weight of it. She couldn't imagine dragging it upstairs to her flat, let alone from shop to shop. She placed it behind the counter for safekeeping.

'An orchestra, actually. I'm playing with the new show that's on at the Theatre Royal. Only here for a week before we move on again.'

'Impressive! Bet it's a tiring business moving about so often.'

'Like you wouldn't believe,' Orla said, trying her hardest to stifle a yawn.

While Orla took a moment to rest, Cherry went into the kitchen to fetch a Sleepy Sticky Toffee Pudding. She put it in a takeaway box and sealed it shut with a gold star-shaped sticker.

'Here,' Cherry said, handing the box to Orla, 'but you can't eat it now, this is a treat you have to eat before bed. I know that sounds weird but just . . . trust me.'

Orla took it and nodded without question, stifling yet another yawn.

'Anything in particular you'd like to see while you're here?' Cherry asked. 'Although I'm new myself so I may not be the right person to ask for directions.'

'I really wanted to see Royal William Yard, The Barbican and the Gin Distillery and I've already seen them all! I went to the Gin Distillery last night and it was incredible. It was heaving, there were so many people but the cocktails were amazing. I've not had such a good night in a long, long time. I felt *awful* this morning though,' Orla said, clutching her head with one hand.

'I bet.' Cherry rolled her eyes.

'You don't like it there?' Orla asked, raising her eyebrows.

'Um ... not really. I just know one of the bartenders—'

'Chase?' Orla interrupted.

Cherry nodded. 'Yes. Do you know him?'

'I met him last night. He was flirting a lot. Should I be careful?' Orla's voice was tentative.

Yes, Cherry thought.

'No,' Cherry said. 'Maybe. To be honest, I don't really know.'

'Oh,' Orla said, fiddling with the side of the takeaway box.

'He's just a difficult person to get along with,' Cherry said carefully.

'He seems a good sight better than some of the people I work with. Well ... one person in particular. Theatre's a difficult job sometimes. People don't always know where the, er ... physical boundaries are.'

Cherry sensed she needed to tread carefully here. 'Or they do know where those boundaries are and ignore them anyway?' she asked kindly.

'Bingo. For the most part it's nice knowing you can go to work and get a hug when you need it but there are those select few who ...'

'... take it too far?'

Orla nodded and continued playing with the box absentmindedly.

'You're always welcome here if anything ever gets too much,' Cherry said. 'I know we've only just met but you're safe here. You gotta talk about this stuff, let it out.'

'I know, I know,' Orla said but Cherry got the feeling she didn't. 'Well, I'm going back to the bar again tonight. Another cast birthday! So I'll let you know if I find out anything more about that bartender.'

Cherry was about to decline when she realised just how interesting that might be. 'Thanks. I really appre—'

The bell above the door rang out with a clang as someone burst in. 'Cherry! You need to come quickly. It's George. He's asking for you.'

Without hesitation Cherry reached for her cardigan and then stopped. 'Wait! I can't leave the shop!'

'I'll watch the shop, Cherry,' Sally called from the corner, her gaze fixated at something outside. 'You won't be long.' She pointed with one of her cards to George, who had now come into view. He looked awful. There were vomit stains down his white T-shirt, his jacket was on inside out and he was only wearing one shoe. Cherry ran out into the chilly sea air.

'George? What on earth are you doing?' She took his arms in her hands to steady him as he lost his footing on a cobblestone. George's eyes took a moment to focus on her. 'Cherry! Oh, Cherry, you're here! You're you, and you're here!'

'Yes ... I'm me and I'm here. Why aren't you back at work?'

'Back at work? I've not been to work at all.'

'Why not, George?' Cherry's smile fell.

'I hate work. Gin is much better.' It was only then that Cherry realised George was drunk. She was a fool not to have seen it but Cherry hadn't been exposed to many drunken people in her life and she certainly hadn't expected it from George at one-thirty on a weekday afternoon. She noticed something else too: George's Meddlum was nowhere to be seen.

'You've been drinking,' Cherry said.

'Yup.'

'At the distillery bar?'

He burped. 'Yup.'

'With Chase?'

'You know what, Cherry, he's actually all right.'

'Is he now?' Cherry took his hand and started guiding him towards the shop.

'And his drinks! Wowzer!'

'How have they made you feel?' A car was slowly approaching and about to stop for them. She got him in through the door but he stumbled at the last moment and landed with a thump on the slate floor. He didn't seem to feel it though as he just sat himself up and leaned on one of the benches.

'I feel like I can do ... anything!' He waved his hands and wriggled his fingers. 'And I can do anything now because I quit my job at the library.'

'You did what?!' Sally stood up, her voice booming across the shop. George fiddled with the dirt under his nails.

'Why, George?' Cherry asked.

'Your mother is going to be devastated.' Sally was packing her cards into her bag. 'I've got some consoling to do. Mrs Partridge has been an old friend for years and you've never been grateful for what she's given you. Even so, I'm going to *beg* her to give you your job back. FOOL!' she shouted before marching out of the bakery. Cherry watched Sally sweep through the door, shocked at how her usually soft face had changed so quickly into one that made her shudder.

'George, I know being a librarian isn't what you want to do and I fully support your decision to quit and do something else but why have you got yourself into such a state?' Cherry asked.

'Cherry,' George said, wiping sweat off his forehead. 'You've got your life all figured out. This shop is your dream, right?' Cherry nodded: it was. 'I just want to live my dream too. I want to be vet . . . a veter . . . a . . .' Then George leaned his head between his knees and threw up on the slate floor. 'I've been sick on your dream,' he whimpered.

With a sigh, Cherry hauled George up onto a chair and brought over a bucket for him. She took a mop from the cleaning cupboard and started wiping up his mess. 'What did Chase have to say about all this?' she asked, trying not to breathe in the stench.

'He encouraged me to leave the library. Said I should grow a pair,' George hiccupped.

A figure appeared at the window. It was small with bowed legs and a hunched back, about the size of a cat which quickly grew to the size of a toddler. Guilt wailed like a toddler too, clawing at the skin on its own face.

'I didn't mean to make Mum cry. I don't want to make her sad, but making her happy means making me sad, and that's sad,' George said, hanging his head over the bucket, a forlorn look on his face.

'I'm sure she'll forgive you. If you want to be a vet there are ways to go back to school and get the qualifications,' Cherry reasoned.

'I have the qualifications. I trained. Five long years it took, and I have a veterinary degree but I'm a librarian because I love my mum. I couldn't disappoint her.'

'George, she's your mum. Surely all she wants is for you to be happy? Talk to her. Explain to her how you feel and I'm sure she'll come around.' He shrugged. He looked helpless and suddenly Cherry felt very small; just one person wading waist-deep in a lot of bad feeling. 'Want a slice of cake?' Cherry asked, wondering what types of regular cake she had left. George nodded, pushing at the last little bit of sick on the floor with the tip of his shoe.

Cherry moved into the kitchen and sank down onto the floor. *Deep breaths*, she thought, *deep breaths*.

'Chase can't do this,' she said to herself. 'He's going to ruin lives.'

Loneliness appeared at the back door and although it couldn't come in she could still hear its voice in her head.

You're just one person, Cherry. How can you stop him when you're all alone? He's stronger than you are. Willing to do more and take things further than you are.

'It's all about moderation. Measurements. I've spent years figuring this out,' she muttered. Her heart was pounding and she tried to steady her breathing but she no longer felt she was wading through bad feeling. She was drowning.

Yet he's already making more of an impact. He's already got rid of something you've been trying to fight for so long now.

'It takes time!' Her breathing wasn't slowing down. If anything, it was getting faster.

It took him no time at all. Face it, Cherry. You can't help them. You're not good enough or strong enough to help them, not on your own.

Cherry felt like the walls were closing in on her. Her fingers tingled, her ears started to ring and her vision blurred. *Oh no.*

'George,' she managed to call out. 'Help!' she yelled as the panic attack consumed her.

Once George had left, Cherry closed the shop and took the afternoon off to recover. She felt exhausted from the rush of panic that had consumed her and now her head swam with this predicament she found herself in. She tried to come up with a plan to handle Chase but her moral compass was strong and she was so set in her ways that she couldn't figure out what she should do differently to make the situation better.

The days that followed were difficult. George stopped coming to the bakery altogether, partly out of embarrassment but Cherry had seen him stumble past at least twice so she knew Chase had kept his custom, even if she hadn't. Orla still popped in for her Sticky Toffee Pudding to go but she always had tales of the night before, all of them involving Chase and his 'delicious' drinks. Sally, Margie and Bruce were old faithfuls and continued to come by as expected but aside from them, the bakery was dead. The odd customer popped in for a cupcake from time to time but they were few and far between and there were certainly fewer familiar faces. Cherry knew that some people associated feeling better with drinking alcohol but she hadn't expected things to change so drastically because of it. And yet she acknowledged that she never saw anyone eating their way through several slices of cake in the hope of finding enlightenment. Cherry's way of helping people had always been a gradual process. She had been building up friendships and trust, talking to her customers while building their good feeling bit by bit so they'd never be entirely reliant on her, and they would eventually find a way to help themselves and figure out a way to supply themselves with all the good feeling they needed and Cherry was just giving them a gentle push in the right direction. Chase, on the other hand, with his careless injection of feelings in his drinks compared to Cherry's careful measures, was giving them a quick fix and like anything that goes up, it must come down. Not only were Cherry's friends suffering from horrendous hangovers, but such high and immediate doses of good feeling didn't last for long. Their original Meddlums may have disappeared, but more often than not Cherry saw Guilt take their places the morning after the night before, a manifestation of the remorse they felt for their drunken actions. George had quit his job, and Orla had kissed the leading man of the show she was playing in. Cherry had counted twenty-four people with Guilt in tow in the last two days alone and she was sure that was the tip of the Chase iceberg.

'Mrs O, I'm fine, I promise,' Cherry said one evening as she was FaceTiming her old friend. 'It's just a minor setback.'

'What's happened?'

'Nothing ... bad,' Cherry replied, looking away from the camera, not wanting Mrs O to worry.

'Cherry ...' Mrs O peered at her through the screen.

'It's just a little ... unfriendly here. That's all.'

'Are the people of Plymouth not playing nice?'

'Most of them are. There's just one in particular who's being difficult.'

'Is it a person of the male persuasion?'

'It is, but his mother and aunt aren't much of a picnic either.' Cherry took a sip of water, still feeling shaky despite her panic attack happening days ago. 'Mrs O, what would you do if someone was doing what you do but making more progress?' Even though Mrs O was only on the screen she still couldn't make herself look Mrs O in the eye as she asked the question.

'What do you mean? I can't imagine someone baking better cakes than yours!' Mrs O's image wobbled and her microphone peaked as she waved her arms dramatically and accidentally hit the screen.

Cherry smiled, amused at this small moment of light relief. 'It's not the baking,' Cherry admitted. 'But it's something quite similar.'

'I'm not quite sure I know exactly what you mean, dear, but if someone is taking your business then you know what you have to do, don't you?' Mrs O said and Cherry raised an eyebrow. 'Bake yours even better.'

13

A Taste Of His Own Medicine

Over the next few days Cherry began to up the dosage in her baking. Only by a little, just to see what effect it might have, but nothing changed. Sally remained obsessive, Margie was still lonely and Orla was always exhausted. The only person it seemed to effect was Bruce, who was far more upbeat than Cherry had ever seen him after he'd eaten his first overly spiked Significance Sundae. Cherry wondered if this was because he was far shorter than her other customers and the increased amount of Significance she'd put in the sundae, even though it was only an incremental increase, made all the difference to Bruce. So Cherry kept his dosage the same the next time but continued to add a little more to the rest but there was still no detectable difference in any of her friends.

'What's with the thousand-yard stare?' Bruce said, pulling himself up onto his usual stool at the counter. 'Everything okay?'

'Oh. Yes. You know me,' Cherry said with an unconvincing smile.

'It's that Chase, isn't it? He's the reason this place is so bloody empty. Right bloomin' nuisance,' Bruce said and Cherry sighed. 'Hey, it's not all bad! I'll *never l*eave!' he gestured to himself and it made Cherry almost tearful to see how proud he looked of himself. That was a first.

Bruce Bunting was married but to a woman who had never been faithful to him. Bruce had caught her countless times sending various men inappropriate pictures and he had even found her in their own bed on two occasions with two different men. She was beautiful and intelligent, which was why Bruce stayed with her. He thought he'd never strike that lucky again. Had Cherry known why Bruce felt so worthless she would have tried to help in other ways, beyond her baking, but Bruce kept his cards very close to his chest. He thought that the only other person who knew was Margie, as she had once caught his wife red-handed too – but in truth, news within their community spread quickly and most of the townspeople knew about his marriage. This information in particular, however, hadn't yet reached Cherry.

Cherry covered her face with her hands, not because she wanted to cry but because she wanted to shut out the world for a moment. She wanted everything to just stop. She had never thought meeting someone who shared her gift would be so difficult, but she knew she had to keep her bakery and its customers safe from Chase and his dangerous and mindless behaviour. Even if that meant playing him at his own game for a little while.

'Right!' she said, slamming her hands down on the counter and making Bruce jump so hard he slid off his stool. 'Sorry, Bruce, but I have to do something about this. I can't just sit here.' Cherry pulled out her phone and opened up the Facebook app. She typed as fast as her unpractised fingers could go and in minutes she had a post ready to send.

'Ladies and gentlemen, and all those who have been so loyal to this bakery in the little time I've been here,' Cherry called out, as if addressing a crowd far larger than Sally, Bruce and the one woman in the corner sipping tea and reading her book. 'It's time to repay you all with another event. It may be short notice but this Friday, there shall be all the usual treats with no charge. Just a one pound entry fee at the door. I look forward to seeing you all then.' Cherry posted the details to her Facebook page and locked her phone with a flourish. Bruce applauded loudly, Sally simply nodded her approval from the corner and the one odd woman knocked back her tea, closed her book and left.

The event was a hit. While Cherry knew that some people turned to alcohol over cake in times of need, *free* cake was a different ball game altogether. *No one* could turn down free cake and Cherry made sure that the Eclairs were far more Encouraging, the Cake was more Consoling, the Cookies were overly Confident and the Pavlova was extremely Proud. Cherry hadn't held back on her measures on this occasion and she was confident her cakes would win her customers back. There were only so many drunken benders you could go on before the fun ran dry but cake never lost its charm (in her bakery, it was, quite literally, full of it). Unlike at her launch event, Cherry did lay her treats out on the tables this time. Her plan was to give her customers whatever they wanted, but in much bigger doses so that their overly positive feelings would convince them to come back to the bakery. Once they were visiting her regularly again she would remedy their overdosed happiness by still giving them what they actually needed but with more careful measures.

Laughter and chatter rang out from every corner and Cherry sighed with relief. This might just work. She looked over to the window. The number of Meddlums lining up outside was far less than the number of people inside, and the ones that were there were writhing in agony as they shrivelled and shrank. She looked around at the huge smiles on every single face and something twisted in the pit of her stomach. A voice in the back of her head that sounded like her own said, *This is going to end badly*, but she pushed the feeling and the voice into a far corner of her mind and ignored them.

'You can never have too much of a good thing,' she said to herself with a nod.

'You really think that's true?' Chase said, pushing his way to the counter past a group of three mums who had inexplicably started to dance, even though there was no music playing. Chase's left eye had a purple-blueish bruise around it and even though he was the last person Cherry wanted to see right now, she couldn't help but feel incredibly guilty that she'd hit him. She'd never had such an emotional outburst before. She doled out feelings to everyone else but she always kept her own under control. At least, she used to.

'Sorry,' she said quietly, gesturing to the bruise. 'I shouldn't have hit you.'

Chase rubbed the bruise with his fingertips but ignored her apology. 'So Mary Berry has finally upped her game. Looks like you've joined the dark side, after all.'

'That's not what's happening here,' she said, her expression serious.

'Really?' he scoffed. 'Look around! Do you see a single sad face in here?'

'Making people feel good isn't the dark side.' She fiddled with the fur trim on the sleeve of her pyjama top.

'No, I suppose you're right. Making people feel *too* good is the dark side,' Chase said, looking outside. The line-up of Meddlums he could see was at the other extreme to what Cherry saw. It was crowded and glowing, much like the inside of Cherry's bakery, but he felt that same tightening in his stomach that she had and he thought that this route may end up leading anywhere other than somewhere good.

'What do you mean?' Cherry said, wiping her hands down her flannel trousers.

'You said "you can't have too much of a good thing". I think that all depends on what each person decides is good for them,' Chase said, gesturing towards the window. 'See Bruce in the corner. Stood outside, waiting for him, is Understanding. It's that Understanding that keeps him going back to his cheating wife. That can't be good for him.' Cherry saw nothing and eyed Chase to try to gauge whether he was telling the truth. Even if he was lying to her what he was saying still made a lot of sense.

'So that's why he feels so Worthless all the time,' Cherry muttered, her heart starting to beat faster.

'Worthless?'

'Yes,' Cherry pointed out of the window but Worthlessness was nowhere to be seen. She dropped her hand and said, 'It's gone now. *I* got rid of it but his Meddlum was Worthlessness.'

'Meddlum?' Chase frowned. 'What's that?'

'It's what they're called. The things we see – they're Meddlums,' Cherry said, watching the monsters scream each time their owner wolfed down one of her treats.

'Meddlums,' Chase said, letting the word roll around

his mouth. 'Fine, Meddlums they are then.' He pointed to Orla. 'Her *Meddlums* are Ambition and Determination, and they're pretty huge. That's why she's always yawning. No matter what remedy you give her, she's the sort of person who will always find a way to overwork herself.'

A man with half-closed eyelids came over and wrapped his hands around Chase's shoulders. Chase looked at him in disgust.

'I see,' Cherry said. 'I guess the pudding I've been giving her hasn't been helping.'

'What did you lace them with?' Chase asked, prying the man's fingers off him.

'A Good Night's Sleep. It's in the toffee.'

'Nice!' Chase said, genuinely impressed. 'And Sally over there – well, Sally's an interesting one.'

'How so?'

'Ever since her husband died, Acceptance and Nostalgia have been her old faithfuls. But she's constantly in my mum's shop. Seeking out clairvoyants, fortune tellers and those who claim they can speak to the dead doesn't scream acceptance to me.'

'People do crazy things when they're desperate,' Cherry said.

'I guess. Anyone who turns to my mum and aunt for life advice must be absolutely mad.'

'You're not close?' Cherry asked. When Chase shook his head but didn't offer any further information, Cherry tried to change the subject and said, 'Well, if it makes you worry less, Sally told me she only used to see your mum and aunt to check that her own readings were accurate.'

'Oh, Sally never comes in for readings. They always just talk,' Chase said.

'She still goes?' That surprised Cherry.

'Once a week.'

Cherry wondered if Sally had been lying to her or if Chase was simply mistaken. He had just said that he and his family weren't close. *Easy mistake to make*, she thought, glancing over at Sally who was biting into a big walnut whip. Her two Meddlums outside popped out of existence.

'Sally's seventy-two, and her husband died when she was in her forties,' Chase went on. 'That's why she always keeps an eye out for Margie. Margie's fella died just after they got married. It was a real shock. He was only thirty-five and no one saw it coming, least of all Margie.'

'No wonder I was drawn here. There's just so much sadness.' Cherry wrapped her arms around herself.

'Margie's got a lot of Hope. Always has done and probably always will.'

'That's nice to know.' Cherry looked over at Margie, who had come to a social event where she knew there would be a lot of other people. *Progress*, Cherry thought.

'So. You can see the bad in people?' Chase asked and she nodded. 'Hmm. Can't imagine that's any worse than seeing the best in people.' Chase finally ducked out from under the man's looped arms and pushed him towards

152

the dancing mums, who gratefully accepted him into their group.

'Right. It must be awful seeing beauty and happiness and love and compassion everywhere you go.' Cherry rolled her eyes.

Chase narrowed his eyes at her. 'Yeah, it's wonderful seeing all of that, making you wonder why your life isn't the same. It's so good to feel worse about all the things you don't have and haven't done. People don't even know they're doing it!' Chase's fists were clenched.

'Doing what?' Cherry asked, confused.

'Rubbing it in my face!' He bashed his knuckles on the counter and Cherry's old fashioned till opened.

'Chase ... no one's out to get you,' Cherry said, pushing the till shut and glancing outside to see Frustration move in between Cynicism and Mischief. 'You have as much of a chance at a good life as anyone else.'

'It never feels that way.'

'Have you even given it a chance? Or do you see one good Meddlum and feel defeated once again? When was the last time you actually took a decent shot at something?'

Chase was quiet but she knew he had heard her. 'What would *you* know about it?' he said under his breath.

Cherry's jaw tensed. She felt a sudden urge to shake him by the shoulders to make him really listen to her but instead she leaned in close and said, 'Quite a bit, actually.' Chase looked up through his eyelashes, not wanting to acknowledge that he was no longer alone. He couldn't pretend that he hadn't met her and he couldn't ignore the undeniable evidence that someone else like him existed. 'Seeing the bad in people is just as hard. Do you think it's easy knowing how awful the world is? How badly everyone feels about themselves and each other all the time? I open my eyes every morning and there's Hatred, Depression and Obsession. Oh, and wait a minute, there's Confusion, Panic, Indifference, Jealousy, Guilt and Loneliness too. And that's just before breakfast! And the only way I can think to help is baking! CAKE! That's my solution. Cake. It's the *only* way I feel like I can help.'

'Why do you even *want* to help?' Chase said quietly, feebly.

'Because what else am I supposed to do? Everyone else manages to achieve their goals in spite of all the trouble that life throws at them so why should I be the only one without some kind of purpose? I've got this ridiculously inconvenient gift so I may as well use it. *Not* to be mischievous and to mess with people's emotional stability.' She looked Chase dead in the eye now that she could see he was really listening, 'but to be proud of something and to actually make some kind of a difference in this hard, beautiful, horrible, wonderful world. Chase? Are you even listening to me?'

As quickly as she'd had Chase's attention, it was gone again. He seemed to be focused on something else now. Cherry followed his gaze and realised he was focused on some*one* else: Orla. Orla was wiggling her fingers and flashing her teeth at him but Chase didn't look in the least bit interested. In fact his eyes widened and his mouth opened but Cherry couldn't make out what he was saying.

'Chase?'

'Cherry, call the police.'

'What? What are you talking about?'

'Call the police!' Chase pushed his way across the floor, roughly catching people's shoulders but no one shouted, everyone just laughed as he knocked them. Cherry stood up on the counter to get a better view of what was going on and she finally saw what Chase had seen. It had been impossible to see anything other than Orla's face through the crowd but Cherry now saw that there was a man behind her who had his hands firmly snaked around her and up her top. Orla didn't look distressed or scared, though; she was grinning from ear to ear. Before Cherry could even get down and to the phone, Chase had already reached them.

'Oi! Get off of her!' he yelled but neither Orla nor the man responded. Instead they just beamed back. 'I said, get your hands OFF!' Chase punched him hard on the jaw and his grip on her loosened as he stumbled backwards. He would have taken Orla with him had Chase not caught her and moved her aside. Chase straddled the man, whose face still held a crooked grin so Chase punched him again. 'It's people like you who make this world HELL!' They were next to the window and Chase could feel the heat of the man's Desire through the glass. He hit him again. 'STOP SMILING!'

'CHASE!' Cherry ran to Chase and tried to pull him off the man, whose nose was bleeding and quite possibly broken. 'Please, Chase. I've called the police – please don't make this worse.' Chase gave in to Cherry tugging at his shirt collar and got off the man and stood up. Orla was straightening her top still with a big smile on her face but even so, she collected her bag and coat and left.

'Fun's over!' Cherry yelled. 'Out! Put down the cake and OUT!'

No one complained. They simply gathered their belongings with plastic-looking smiles on their faces and filed out of the door in an orderly line.

'You heard her. Out.' Chase gave the man on the floor a rough nudge with his foot and gingerly he got up and stumbled out, leaving a few bloody fingerprints on the floor. Cherry locked the door behind them, turned the sign from OPEN to CLOSED and sank down to the floor, her fingers trembling as she pressed them to her eyes.

'She didn't even respond,' she sobbed. 'She didn't even react. To *anything*.'

Chase picked up one of the cookies. 'What did you put in these?' He licked it and instantly his face lit up. 'Blimey, Cherry.'

'Everything. Literally every good feeling you can think

of is in those cookies. Each one is a cocktail.' She couldn't bring herself to look at her bakery. She felt like she'd betrayed it and everything she'd set out to do.

'You didn't make them happy, you made them numb. This amount of happiness is like a ... a drug. Too much and the whole world disappears. Nothing holds any value any more.' Chase usually spoke with a harsh tone but this was the first time Cherry had heard any hint of compassion in his voice.

'I took it too far, didn't I?' Cherry hugged her legs in close and buried her face in her knees.

'Maybe a little.'

'I hated the fact that you were taking over something I'd spent years perfecting. And you were taking over so ... recklessly. And now look at me! This is recklessness at its finest!'

'I know. I guess I've never been good at taking my time with anything. I always want to be the best as soon as I begin.' Chase looked surprised at his confession. 'I don't know why I said that. Any truth serum in those cookies as well?' Chase laughed but Cherry looked up at him through tearful eyes and bit her lip.

'There is a little bit of Honesty in there, yeah.' She expected Chase to be cross but he just laughed harder.

'Of course there is!'

'But I haven't had any so at least you know I was being honest because I wanted to be,' Cherry said.

'True. But even so, I would have been honest anyway.

I can't seem to lie to you.' He knelt down by her side and nudged her knee. 'Look, we can fix this.'

'We?' Cherry sniffed.

'Well ... yeah. If you want?' Chase found that he couldn't look at her and that his palms had started to sweat.

'Why?' she asked, and the realisation hit him: it was because he didn't like being apart from her. Not only because she understood him in a way no one else ever had but also because he enjoyed the way she smiled. He liked the way she looked in pyjamas and he both loved and hated the way he never wanted to be anything but honest to her. All his life, other people's feelings had been thrust upon him but now his feelings for Cherry were all his own. 'I still want to be the best! If you give me lessons and make me better at ... whatever this is you do, we can put this town back together again. Shouldn't take too long!' Chase stood up and brushed the crumbs off his trousers. He held out a hand for her and she gratefully took it.

'On one condition,' she said. 'You have to wear pyjamas.'

'That had better be a joke,' Chase warned and just as Cherry parted her lips to tell him she was, in fact, being deadly serious, someone knocked at the door.

'The police! I totally forgot I'd called—' But when Cherry turned around and looked through the window, there was no policeman at the door. Instead, standing with immaculate posture and a stony face was a woman in a yellow sundress and a big circular blue floppy hat, with a brown briefcase by her side. Her hair was golden and plaited in one long fishbone plait down her back, the tip of which reached her waist.

'Hello?' Cherry opened the door.

'Hello,' she said.

'I'm ever so sorry, but we're closed,' Cherry said apologetically.

'I *can* read, dear. I'm not here for confectionary. I'm here for damage control.'

'Damage control?' Chase said coming to stand next to Cherry.

'Yes, dear. I'm Happy from the Guild of Feelers and thank whoever's watching over us that we've found you.'

14

A Meeting With Happiness

Happy wasn't happy. At least, nothing in her face gave away what she was thinking or feeling and Cherry wondered if she were to push Happy she would even flinch. She highly doubted it, although she would never dare try to find out.

In truth, Happy *was* happy. She had a loving husband, a son, a dog called Limbo and a wonderful job at the Guild of Feelers.

'So what exactly *is* the Guild of . . . what was it again?' Chase asked, sliding onto the bench at the table and sitting opposite Happy. Cherry came out from the kitchen with pot of tea, three mugs and a plate of cookies, and she sat down next to Chase.

'They're non-feeling, I promise,' she whispered, trying not to interrupt.

'I should hope so,' Happy said, pouring herself a mug of tea. 'The Guild of Feelers,' she repeated as though that was explanation enough. Cherry and Chase shared a blank look.

'Which is ... ?' Chase tried again.

'Sorry ... Happy,' Cherry said. 'I think you're going to have to start from the beginning.'

'You've not heard of us? Oh. That explains an awful lot.' Happy rattled her teaspoon against the inside of the mug, swishing the tea and three sugars she'd heaped in. 'The Guild of Feelers is an organisation for those of us who can see people's feelings. Some can see good, some can see bad, some get a fuzzy mixture of the two. We all see them differently. Colours and shapes for those with mild cases. Monsters, angels, animals and people for those in the more advanced stages of SF.'

'Advanced stages of ... what?' Chase asked.

'SF. Simply short for seeing feelings. We once had one girl who saw all feelings as different coloured cats. That's the better end of the deal.'

'What do *you* see?' Cherry said, trying to process all this, and stirring her tea so fast it sloshed over the sides.

'I used to see a haze of the two. They looked like ghosts and it was hard to decipher what was what.' Happy sipped her tea, her pinkie finger raised.

'Sorry, used to? You said *used to*.' Chase's heart started beating so quickly that Cherry could feel it through the bench they were sat on.

'I now have these.' Happy delicately put her index finger and thumb around her eye and stretched the socket open wide. Cherry looked closer and saw some kind of film, a lens, sitting over Happy's eyeball. It glinted a rainbow of colours as it caught the light. 'These lenses were specially designed by our paranormal science department. They can detect what's normal from what's *para*normal and filter out the feelings you don't want to see. Clear vision means a clear mind.' Happy flashed her hands across her deadpan face and wiggled her fingers. 'That's their slogan. Catchy, huh?'

'Filter out? How you can just get rid of something in someone's vision?' Cherry asked.

'We have software that detects feelings and places neutral images over them, blocking them from sight,' Happy explained.

'But surely it's impossible to keep track of that many people? And how can you possibly know what someone should or shouldn't see?' Cherry pushed.

Happy's face gave nothing away but she answered very quickly, without skipping a beat. Almost as if she'd said the words before. 'We've done numerous tests and we have some of the best minds on the planet ... overseeing the whole operation.'

'How can I get a pair?' Chase asked.

'There's a two-year waiting list but for special cases they make allowances. Each time a new pair is issued, it helps us. The lenses are linked to the Guild so we're able to see what you see. Just in case there are any glitches in the system or there's anything you're seeing that you *shouldn't* be seeing. I'll give you an application to fill out before I leave.'

'Oh, God. Thank you. *So* much,' Chase said with a big smile. He leaned across the table to shake Happy's hand. Cherry hoped the gesture was genuine and not a side effect from the cookie he'd licked earlier.

'Isn't that an invasion of privacy?' Cherry asked. 'Being able to see what we see through the lenses?'

'That all depends on whether you've got something to hide,' Happy said.

It really doesn't, thought Cherry.

'Sorry ... I have to ask,' Chase said, 'Happy? Is that your birth name?'

'No!' She laughed without smiling. 'I'm a Feeler – one of many. We are each assigned a specific feeling that we have to keep an eye on. Anytime a part of the world gets particularly ridden with our designated feeling, we have to take a visit to see what's going on and put it right. As I said, damage control.'

'I understand all of that,' Chase said. 'But is there a reason you don't ... *look* particularly happy?'

'Chase!' Cherry said through gritted teeth, jabbing him hard in the ribs with her elbow.

'It's okay. It's a valid question and I get it a lot. Feelings are my business. If my actual feelings were to get in the way, my judgement may be compromised when having to

164

make executive decisions on behalf of the Guild. What's right needs to come before what *feels* right.'

'Aren't they the same thing?' Cherry asked.

'Not always, no. What we feel can get in the way of our work so once every six months I have to undergo a minor procedure.'

'What kind of procedure?' Cherry asked warily. She didn't like the sound of this at all.

'Just a little bit of jiggery pokery. It used to be a little zap-zap here and a zap-zap there but that had far too many ... side effects. Now they have a much more efficient method of removing feelings. They burn them off like warts.'

Cherry frowned. 'But how? We can't ... touch them, so surely that's not possible?'

'The Guild have their ways. I've been with them for eight years and have yet to feel a thing,' Happy said matter-of-factly.

'That's because you literally. Can't. Feel. Anything,' Chase said very deliberately. 'I mean ... *removing* your feelings – that's ... that's—'

'Necessary,' Happy stated.

'I was going to say batshit crazy, but if you say so.'

Cherry jabbed Chase with her elbow again but this time a little softer as she couldn't help but agree with him.

Happy ignored him. 'Right. Down to business. Firstly, I need to speak to you about your little turf war.' Cherry and Chase suddenly found the wood of the table exceedingly detailed and were deeply fascinated by its visually intricate patterns. 'Hmm. Did things get a little competitive? Not the first time it's happened and won't be the last.'

'It isn't? It won't be?' Cherry said.

'Did you think you were *alone*?' Happy asked. Cherry and Chase nodded, wordlessly. 'Tut tut. There aren't many of us – a few hundred in the world at most – but we're here for you when you need us.'

'How have you only just found us?' Cherry asked, blinking hard and stealing a glance at Loneliness outside.

'How do you know whether someone is a serial killer until they've murdered six people? It's hard to spot until you make it noticeable. You see, those with SF are split up into Haunters and Flaunters. Most people are born with it but in some cases it lies dormant for years until one day, all of a sudden, there are monsters everywhere! Those ones are the easiest to spot. They make a big song and dance. They're Flaunters. The people who are born with the sight think it's normal. They deal with it from birth and more often than not just keep it quiet. It haunts them or they haunt other people with it by how they choose to deal with it. Sometimes individuals find ways to use their powers but again the *majority* keep it subtle. *Some* get rather boisterous.' Happy made her first facial expression since she'd arrived and raised her eyebrows at the pair, like a teacher berating her pupils. 'Nothing is ever too serious when the town is overrun by Happiness but when it swings the other way ... well ... let's not go into that. HERE!' She picked up her briefcase and slammed it onto the table, causing the porcelain mugs and teapot to rattle and a couple of cookies being lost to the floor. Happy stood up, spun the briefcase around to face Chase and Cherry and popped it open. The inside was lined with an obnoxiously yellow foam and at its centre was a small indentation in which lay a small glass bottle filled with tiny blue pills. 'It's Normality,' Happy said.

'There's nothing normal about that shade of yellow!' Chase said, squinting.

'Normality pills will restore your residents to their usual state of reality. Whatever their issues and joys were before you two started meddling will be reinstated.'

'I wouldn't say we were meddling—'

Happy held her hand up, cutting across Cherry's voice. 'Their bodies will be flushed of any feeling that isn't their own.'

'So, nothing I did before our ... "turf war" broke out ... none of that matters?' Cherry said, palms sweating. Were they really talking about undoing all of her work?

'I'm afraid not. That's not how this works, although we have been watching you for some time now, Miss Redgrave.'

'R-really?' Cherry wriggled her hands inside her sleeves and crossed her arms.

'We're very impressed with all you've been doing these

past few years and I actually have an offer to make you on behalf of the Guild. It's not often that those higher up are so impressed that they offer a place to a novice but ... we'd love to have you on board.'

'What? Work for you?' Cherry asked, incredulous.

'Mm-hmm, that's right.' Happy nodded.

'Would I have to ... give up my feelings?' Cherry's palms weren't the only things sweating now. The room had grown awfully warm all of a sudden. Cherry felt Chase shift closer to her.

'It's standard procedure when joining the Guild, but I guarantee you won't miss them.'

'How would she even know if she missed them or not?' Chase said. 'Taking away someone's feelings is like – like ... taking away a limb!'

'We'd never forcibly take away anyone's feelings, Mr Masters. No need to get *over-emotional*. Only those who willingly take jobs with us will be asked to undergo the procedure. I must warn you though that if you turn down this incredibly generous offer, you'd no longer be able to run your bakery because of what has taken place here today.'

'What?!' Chase raised his voice and their bench scooted back as he stood up abruptly. Cherry put a hand on his arm to soothe him and he slowly sat back down.

'Why wouldn't I be able to run the bakery?' Cherry said, blinking hard again.

'One day I'm sure you'd be able to reopen; however,

because of today's over-dosing on feelings you would be required to go on a two-year training course to learn the correct and proper ways to use your abilities. You'd then be able to pitch a proposal for your bakery to the Guild and explain how you would intend to use your abilities on the unwitting public in the future.' Happy paused for a moment. 'I'm pretty confident however that because of today's misdemeanour,' she tutted, 'you're unlikely to be approved.'

'Oh, God.' Cherry couldn't help it now. A few tears spilled over as she thought of losing her livelihood and everything she'd spent the last seven years building.

'You can't do this,' Chase said, putting his arm around the sobbing Cherry.

'I'm afraid we can. Don't think we don't have prisons of our own for people who misbehave on our territory.'

Cherry sobbed even harder.

'You really don't live up to your name do you, love.' Chase squeezed Cherry into him and she pressed her face into his shoulder.

'We'll give you a week to decide,' Happy said, removing the bottle of pills and placing them on the table. 'I trust you know what to do with these.' She closed the briefcase and walked to the door without waiting for an answer.

'What about me? Don't I get some kind of impossible offer?' Chase called after her.

'We've been watching you too, Mr Masters, and we know it was you who started all of this with your brash

169

and reckless behaviour. That reminds me.' Happy opened the briefcase once more, dug underneath the yellow foam and pulled out a few sheets of paper. 'Here is your application for the lenses. No doubt your special hatred for the world will bump you up to somewhere near the top of the list. You'll get your lenses and therefore what you've always wanted: to be normal.' She looked at Cherry then and said, 'Once you've made your decision, *we'll know.*'

The door clicked shut and an eerie silence followed. The bakery seemed cold and unfriendly. Something sinister lingered in the air.

Chase turned to Cherry and said, 'Well, she was a bundle of fun.'

15

Belonging and Honesty

They hadn't spoken to each other for so long that the silence had become a lullaby. Chase felt that it would be rude to interrupt such a comforting tune so he just listened to the slosh of water and the soft clink of cutlery against ceramic. Cherry was at the sink, scrubbing plates. She squeezed the washing-up liquid bottle and bubbles spurted into the air. She filled each one with a miserable thought and then popped them all, one by one, with a single finger.

Giving up on my shop. POP!

Disgracing the memory of my father. POP!

Going home and admitting defeat to everyone I know. POP!

Saying goodbye to Sally, George, Orla, Bruce, Margie ... and Chase. POP!

Never feeling anything again. POP!

She wished it was as easy as bursting a bubble. It felt satisfying to see her thoughts disappear with a pop but they didn't stay gone for long and grew back in her mind like weeds, their tendrils growing over all her happy thoughts until the happiness was near impossible to see.

'I've got to take the job,' Cherry said. It spurted out of her mouth like one of the bubbles, but it didn't pop. Even when Chase said, 'What?' and stopped drying the forks in his tea-towel-wrapped hand. 'That's a joke, right?'

'You heard that "Happy" woman. I can't carry on here, can I? I'm finished in the bakery business.'

'She said you could train! I know it seems unnecessary as you're already damn good at what you do but the alternative is ... barbaric! It's just madness!'

'Train? For what? To be turned down *years* down the line? Build up my hopes again only to have them dashed by some woman named after one of the seven dwarves? I'm not doing that. I'd rather—'

'Give up?'

'I know when I'm beaten!' Cherry turned to him with such a spin that water came sailing out of the sink in a tidal wave and the plate she'd been holding slipped out of her sodden hand and crashed to the floor, shattering on impact. Neither of them flinched. Chase held Cherry's sad stare while she held his determined one.

'I'm not going to sit here and let you get your feelings

sucked out of your brain. That's a sentence I never thought I'd ever say, but there it is,' Chase declared.

The ridiculousness of it all would have been funny to Cherry if the idea of having her mind messed with wasn't so horribly real. 'I won't even know what I'm missing,' she said, moving a piece of the broken plate around with her foot.

'*I'll* know. I'm not going to let you go through that . . . because of me.'

'Stop that,' Cherry chided gently. 'It wasn't *all* your fault, Chase. It takes two to tango.'

'Yeah, well.' He shrugged. 'I asked you to dance.'

Cherry wanted so badly to wish she'd never met Chase but in truth, despite his dismal outlook on life, his tendency to overreact and his desperation to be the best at everything, meeting him had been a pivotal moment in her life and she was ultimately grateful for it. Living your whole life thinking you'll never find someone who really understands you, that you'll always be carrying the weight of a secret, living a double life, was what had kept Cherry's Loneliness so strong, so healthy, so real. Since Cherry had met Chase, Loneliness hadn't grown at all. It had been kept in its place because no matter what, despite those irrational, habitual feelings that often crept up on her, Cherry knew she wasn't really alone, not any more. She reached into her cardigan pocket and pulled out the bottle of blue pills.

'I'm going to whip up a batch of cakes as a parting gift

for everyone in this town I've truly screwed over. Each containing a little bit of the Normality they deserve. That should do the trick. *If* they eat them, that is.' She rattled the bottle. 'I wouldn't if I were them. I once ate a bad kebab from a fish and chip shop in Sheffield and I've not eaten a kebab since, let alone one from that place.' She tried to laugh but it got strangled in her throat and died there so she turned back to popping her thoughts.

Silence reigned for the rest of the night until order had been restored to the bakery. As he was leaving, Chase didn't know how to say goodbye. He was unsure now about whether their relationship had shifted, so he just nodded – but when he turned to the street where the light had now faded and the street lamps were lit, he realised that when Happy referred to an incident, she wasn't just talking about Orla or what had happened inside the bakery.

'Oh my God.' Starting from the doorway of the shop, Chase took in the destruction that spread in several directions. Vomit, clothes, blood, cake boxes and half-eaten cookies were strewn as far as he could see. Some of the debris disappeared in the direction of the town centre, some led to the ferry that went to The Barbican and some of it was piled around sleeping bodies that lay in the middle of the street in various states of disarray. Cherry stood in the doorway, her fingers starting to tremble.

'It's all right, Cherry. We've been given a way to fix this. We can fix this. Cherry?'

Cherry's ears were full of the noise of her rapidly beating heart and her blood rushing violently through her body. Chase's voice was fading . . .

'Cherry? CHERRY!' Chase shouted as he caught her before she hit the floor.

I'll take care of it. x

Cherry read the sticky note stuck to the wall opposite her bed with bleary, half-asleep eyes. She reached inside her cardigan pocket and as she expected, the bottle of blue pills was missing. She looked down at herself to see that she had been perfectly enveloped in bed. Chase had literally tucked her in, the sheets sitting neatly around her frame. He'd even placed a glass of water at her bedside, which she immediately downed in a few gulps. Gingerly, she clambered out from under the sheets, changed into some fresh, clean pyjamas and went downstairs to her dark and empty bakery. The mess from the night before had been cleaned off the streets and whether that had been Chase or a kind neighbour, Cherry was grateful either way. (Although she did spot one lone pair of pink frilly knickers stuck to the windowsill of the art gallery opposite.) With her outside slippers on her feet, Cherry ventured out to find Chase.

The boat ride was colder than she'd ever experienced

and each time the boat hit a wave the sea sprayed into her face. She wiped the mist off her cheeks but Loneliness liked it so much that it leaned a little further over the side. Cherry disembarked at The Barbican and the eerie silence she was greeted with made her skin prickle. She'd only visited a handful of times but it had never been this quiet, especially at the weekend. Shops that should have been open were closed and people she thought she would've seen were clearly shut away indoors. She crossed to the other side of the road when she approached Velina and Danior's shop, not wanting to be seen by them and wanting to avoid her stomach churning the way it always did when she saw that red and yellow paint and those blasted white crystal ball stickers. But her curiosity got the better of her and, like slowing down and craning your neck to see a car crash on the side of the road, Cherry chanced a glance across the street. Velina and Danior were standing in the doorway, smoking their cigarettes out of long elegant holders. They watched her with hard, narrowed eyes and a chill ran down Cherry's spine. Her knees started to wobble but she ignored them and pushed herself forward, towards the gin distillery. As she rounded the bend in the road, she didn't need to look very hard for Chase. She didn't even need to enter the bar. He was outside the entrance, being held by the scruff of his shirt by a man in a navy blue suit. He was much shorter than Chase but Chase was holding his hands up like it was an arrest. She could only assume he was Chase's manager.

'It really isn't what you think, I swear,' Chase begged.

'You may have been good for business, Chase, but this?! This is unacceptable!' The man held up the bottle of blue pills which glinted in the sunlight.

'Oh no . . . ' Cherry said, realising what was happening.

'It's not what it looks like!' Chase pleaded again.

'It looked like you were . . . ' he looked around to see who was listening. Cherry pretended to look in a shop window. 'It looked like you were taking drugs! Right at the bar!'

'I swear that's not what I was doing. I was just—'

'THEY'RE MINE!' Cherry yelled, running over to them. She snatched the bottle out of the manager's hand but he didn't look surprised or impressed.

'And who are you? His accomplice? His dealer maybe, hmm?'

'No, I'm his friend. I asked Chase to take care of my medication for me because I often lose it and then forget to take it.'

Chase's manager wasn't buying it. 'Then why was he dividing the pills into little piles? Explain that!'

'Well . . . I wouldn't take a whole bottle of pills all at once, would I? Chase counts out how many I need a day to make sure I've got enough to last me until I can see a doctor again. Isn't that right, Chase?' Cherry jabbed him in the ribs. He nodded quickly.

'Yes that's exactly it. I'm a good friend.' He nodded more and more, resembling one of those plastic dogs that sit on the dashboard of a car. The manager regarded them both, looking them up and down, and shook his head.

'I'm sorry, it's just too risky. I can't keep you here. I have to fire you, Chase.' Chase closed his eyes and hung his head, turning away from them both. '*But*, I won't call the police. Just get those pills off my property.' The manager slipped back inside before Cherry had a chance to say a word.

'I'm so sorry, Chase.' Cherry's heart felt heavy.

'It's not your fault,' he said, squeezing her shoulder, and Loneliness shuddered. 'It was my idea – and I only took the job to annoy you anyway. It's just . . . well, now we've got to find another way to give this town a bit of Normality. I doubt anyone's going to eat your cakes, I can't get them in the alcohol and it seems everyone is keeping a low profile anyway. It's a ghost town out here!'

'I'd noticed,' Cherry said. 'Except for your mother and Danior. They weren't at the bakery yesterday and yet they still seem to be on full alert.'

'Oh!' Chase said.

'I know. They're just standing—'

'No! Cherry, you're a GENIUS!' He shouted this so loudly that a few seagulls nearby flapped into a frenzy. 'Come on.' Chase grabbed her by the arm and led her back down the street. When the red and yellow came into view Cherry's heart started racing again.

'Where are we going? I can't go back in there!' Cherry cried.

Chase stopped suddenly and Cherry stumbled into him. 'You've been to my mum's shop? Why?'

Cherry squeezed her eyes shut, not wanting to see his reaction. 'I went to go and find out if they knew about you. I had a suspicion they were ... well ... '

'Cheaters. Charlatans. Fraudsters. You name it, that's what they are.'

'They are? I *knew* it!' Cherry fist-bumped the air.

'I tell you that my mum and aunt are liars, cheating the population of Plymouth out of their hard-earned money, and you do this?' He mimicked her air-punch. 'Brilliant.'

'Sorry,' Cherry said sheepishly.

'You're mad,' Chase declared, smiling down at her.

'I know.'

'I love it.' Chase's eyes widened at his admission and then he started laughing.

'Me too.' Cherry smiled and broke into laughter too.

The street was empty, but if anyone had happened along at that moment they would've seen two happy, laughing people bent double, clinging to each other. Chase's hand found Cherry's and as the laughing subsided they were left smiling at each other and holding hands. For two people who had felt a lot of things and who had seen a lot of feelings, feeling whole because of finding a true connection with someone was something neither of them had experienced. Cherry felt like she'd found what she was looking for and Chase had found what he never knew he needed: someone. Not necessarily even someone to love. Just *someone*.

'So why are we going to visit your terrifying, lying mother and aunt?' Cherry asked once she'd managed to catch her breath.

'Shhh,' Chase said, knowing they might be listening from around the corner. He pulled her closer to the wall, further out of sight. 'When you met them, they offered you tea, didn't they?' Chase coughed out the last of his laughter.

'Practically forced it on me, yes.'

'Years ago they discovered the internet—'

'Marvellous, isn't it?!' Cherry said.

'—and they met another fortune teller on some forum. A clairvoyant, who claimed he could speak to the dead. Another lying bastard but far better at lying than my mum and aunt because he took them for a complete and utter ride. He sold them this green tea and told them it would make their customers far more susceptible to believing whatever they told them. It was all total bollocks, of course, but they bought it and have been giving it to their customers ever since.'

'It's just grass, isn't it?' Cherry said remembering the taste in the back of her throat.

'Grass in a glass.' Chase smiled. 'If they're that easily fooled and that desperate to get their customers believing . . . '

'You're a genius!' Cherry said and she kissed him hard on the cheek.

'Come on!' They rushed down the street hand in hand, Chase holding the bottle out before him. Velina and Danior were already waiting for them.

'Dani.' Chase nodded.

'*Boy*,' she said through gritted teeth. 'Come to visit your dear mother and aunt? We thought you'd gone for good this time.'

'Not this time.'

'Shame,' Danior sneered. 'You two seem awfully chipper,' she said, a cigarette holder balanced between her teeth, today's purple lipstick staining the rim and, yet again, her teeth.

'It's because we've discovered something,' Chase said.

'As soon as we heard about it we knew we had to come straight to you,' Cherry added. Chase held up the bottle. Velina and Danior's expressions shifted subtly from annoyance to intrigue. 'Can we come in?'

Danior roughly pulled them inside and Velina looked up and down the street, making sure nobody had seen them before closing the door. They followed Danior through the beaded curtain and into the back of the shop. She took up her usual spot in the corner and told Cherry and Chase to sit. Velina burst though the curtain with a flourish.

'Why the change of tune, dear son?'

'I thought you hated our ways, nephew dear.'

'I know. I know I've not been as supportive as I should have been but ... ' Chase's jaw tensed, 'I guess ... I've always felt like I've never had anything to contribute.'

'I think what Chase means to say is that he doesn't have the panache or ... or the intelligence that it takes to be a palm reader or an expert Tarot reader,' Cherry said. Chase caught her eye and without changing his expression he quickly winked at her.

'I knew you'd come around, that one day you'd see that what we do is in people's best interests,' Velina said, stroking her son's hair.

'What we do is give people hope,' Danior added. 'People don't often want truth. They just want someone to tell them things are going to be okay. Even if they're not.'

'I know,' he said and then with a little more conviction, 'I know! And that's why I want to help. This has been a few months in the making, but I have a friend – she's a clairvoyant too – and she does this amazing thing where she pretends the soul of someone departed has entered her and she speaks to her customers in different voices. She's a voice actress who's currently unemployed and she's making a killing in this field.'

'Interesting,' Velina said.

'But what does this have to do with us?' Danior spoke quickly, impatient.

'Well, my friend said she wouldn't have been half as successful if it wasn't for these.' Chase held up the pill bottle. 'Like you, she puts them in tea and serves it to her clients but they work differently to your tea. They're instant and *strong*. Really strong. One of these pills will make your client believe anything you say and, in her experience, the more generous you are about their future, the more generous they'll be too, if you catch my drift.' Chase rubbed his fingers against his thumb and Velina's eyes lit up.

'Are you certain?' she asked.

'One hundred per cent.'

'How do we know you're not lying?' Danior said, coming out of the shadows.

'Dani ...' Velina warned.

'I'm just saying ... prove it.'

'W ... what?' Cherry's palms became clammy.

'Prove it does what you say it does.' Danior placed both her hands on the table and leaned in towards Chase and Cherry. Cherry could smell her smoky breath.

'Okay, fine,' Chase said. He quickly opened the bottle of pills and shook one out into his palm.

'Chase. Don't,' Cherry whispered but it was too late. Chase knocked it back and swallowed it dry.

'Try me,' he said.

Danior's eyebrows flickered for a moment and her face cracked into the grin Cherry heard in her voice earlier but now that she saw it, it was worse than she feared.

'Did you know Velina isn't actually your mother?' Danior said, a swagger in her hips as she circled the table.

'What?'

'Oh yeah. We had a third sister.' Danior smiled.

'Dani,' Velina warned again.

'That's a joke . . . ' Cherry squeezed Chase's knee under the table. ' . . . isn't it?' Danior gave her sister a wide-eyed stare and Velina dropped her eyes and shook her head.

'So my mother is your other sister,' Chase said, wanting to ask questions, to deny it all but Cherry's trembling hand on his knee kept his focus on the task at hand. 'Where is she?' Chase's fists clenched as Excitement slowly came into the room, squatting on Danior's shoulders.

'She died,' Danior sighed. 'Killed herself. Dear Velina here stole her man and it was just too much for your poor mumsy to take.' Danior swiped a finger across her neck and let her tongue loll out the side of her wrinkled lips. Cherry dug her fingertips into Chase's thigh once more, silently begging him to go along with it. None of this was true, she was sure of it, they just needed to get them to believe the pills worked and then they could leave and forget about the horrible lies Danior was telling Chase.

'I've been searching for her ever since,' Velina said, gesturing upwards to the unknown, a tear trickling down her face making a clear path in her make-up.

'Why didn't you ever tell me?' Chase asked, looking at Danior, who in turn looked at Velina, whose head was hung in shame. 'Why?'

'Auntie Velina didn't want—'

Velina held up a hand to silence her sister. She sniffed

and finally lifted her eyes to meet Chase's gaze. 'I didn't want you to feel like you didn't have a family.' Velina threw her hands to her face and sobbed loudly and Chase knew instantly they were lying.

Velina and Danior changed their 'gift' every few years. They had gone from being psychics to mediums to clairvoyants and then to Tarot cards and palm reading. Back when Chase was a young boy, his mother claimed to be a medium, someone who had perfected the art of summoning the spirits of the dead and communicating with them through the realms. Velina was theatrical and tried to put on a show, pretending ghosts had possessed her by convulsing and flailing her limbs, knocking over anything in the way and then when she finally spoke, her voice was a low and rough growl. Although her imagination and acting abilities were very limited and somehow every ghost that entered her body had exactly the same voice as the last, her clients always seemed to recognise it as their loved one. The client's wishful thinking accounted for around eighty per cent of being a medium, which was half of the appeal for the sisters; it was quite easy. Chase would sit and watch Velina's every move and copy her actions and noises, and the one thing that Chase had perfected above all else was Velina's ability to cry on cue. She reserved it for special occasions when her clients weren't believing her straightaway or were asking too many questions that she wasn't able to answer. She would only ever be able to produce one tear that would slip silently down her cheek but from there she would throw her hands over her face, sob, wail and heave hard.

'I've seen things in the other realm. Things I never want to see again!' she would say.

'They tried to hurt me!' she'd wail.

'It's just ... too much,' she would cry.

It would cause her client to feel sorry for putting her through so much for their own selfish gains and be forced to come back again another day when she was more up to it – or at the very least, they would feel obliged to tip generously. Little Chase had learnt her tearful techniques and used them at home, at school, with his friends, in the few relationships he had had, in any situation that he wanted to get out of without getting caught or being penalised. It was manipulation at its finest and he'd learnt it from his own mother at a young and impressionable age.

Now when he looked at Velina, he saw himself. Selfish, shameless and a little heartless.

'Chase?' Cherry whispered. 'How do you feel?'

'I feel ... ' He looked at Velina, who was quieter now, still sniffing but he could see her eyes looking expectantly at him.

'I feel ... ' He looked at Danior, whose eyebrows were raised, her lipstick-stained teeth bared and her breath held.

'I feel ... ' Then he looked at Cherry, so full of hope and counting on him to say what they needed him to say.

'I feel so sad that no one told me the truth. You are my

family no matter what. Whether you're a mother or an aunt, you're still my family,' he said to Velina.

'Really?' she asked, wiping away her one single tear and smiling all too easily.

'Really.' Chase nodded, slipping his hand over Cherry's relaxed fingers, which were still resting on his thigh under the table.

'Wonderful!' Velina ran round the table and put her arms around his shoulders, planting a kiss on his cheek. Danior snatched up the bottle of little blue pills in her talons and started to unscrew the cap when Cherry said, 'So shall we talk about payment?'

Chase's heart stopped, Velina's smile vanished and Danior almost dropped the bottle.

'Payment? My dear, what on earth for?'

'The pills. I think it's only fair. Those pills will do wonders for your business so you should ... reward us.'

'You little—' Danior switched the bottle to her other hand and quickly raised her free hand but Velina quickly took it and placed it over her own heart.

'Now, now, Dani. Fair's fair. Cherry does make a good point. After all, we'd never do anything for free.' Velina disappeared through the beaded curtain and Cherry heard the till open, the rustle of money and the ding of the till being slammed shut. Chase hadn't said a word and when Cherry slid her eyes towards him, he was chewing the inside of his lip with great concentration.

'Here. Take it and leave.' Velina handed over a wad of

notes. Cherry took it quickly and put it in her pocket and stood to leave. When Chase didn't stand with her, she pulled at the shoulder of his jacket until he stood up.

'I suggest you hold an event and charge a little less per person than you normally would. Give them each a small mug of tea on arrival and they'll be putty in your hands. Guaranteed to keep returning,' Cherry said as she backed through the curtain and into the shop's waiting room, her sweaty hand clinging to Chase's shoulder as she dragged him to the exit. Velina and Danior herded them out, Danior still clutching the bottle in her red pointed nails.

'I hope you get all you deserve,' Chase said through gritted teeth and without so much as a goodbye, the door to the shop was closed in their faces. Cherry and Chase took a moment to exhale but then quickly made their way back to the port and onto the empty ferry boat that was leaving shortly. As soon as they sat down, the waves gently bobbing them up and down, Chase took Cherry's hand.

'You know they were lying, don't you?' she said, keeping her gaze fixed ahead of her on the waves, rising and breaking.

'Oh, I know,' he said, also looking forward.

She squeezed their interlinked fingers. 'I could see Danior's Deceit and Velina's Uncertainty.'

'And I could see my aunt's Glee and my mother's Excitement.'

'Even though they were doing something bad? You can still see the good?'

'It doesn't matter if they're good or bad people. I see what they feel. Bad people feel good about bad things.'

'Oh,' Cherry said, understanding.

They wore silence like a warm blanket around their cold shoulders all the way back to Royal William Yard. They walked hand in hand back to the bakery and once inside Chase went behind the counter, like it was the most natural thing to do, and flicked the kettle on. He busied himself making tea, rearranging Cherry's handwritten signs and dusting crumbs off the counter into his hand to put in the bin.

'Do you want to talk?' Cherry asked tentatively.

'No. Well, yes. But no.' He shrugged, stirring the tea hard.

'I know you've found it difficult. Seeing what everyone else has and wondering why you don't have it yourself, but ... I didn't really think about bad people getting pleasure from the bad things they do. That's got to be a hard thing to see,' Cherry said, edging her way towards him slowly.

'I don't trust *anyone*,' Chase admitted. 'I don't know how.'

'I understand that. But maybe ... maybe, the only person you need to trust is me?'

'What do you mean?'

'What if we stick together from now on? Team up? If

someone's bad, I'll know just by looking at their Meddlums and I can tell you about them so that you know, despite all the good things you might see.'

'... and if someone's good, I'll know just by looking at them too, despite all the bad things you see ...'

'It's perfect!' Cherry was at Chase's side now and she smiled up at him.

'It's not perfect, Cherry.'

'What? Why?'

'If you decide to leave, to ... join the Guild, you'll have your feelings removed. Your actual, literal feelings ... whatever they may be ...' he stirred his tea again, '... will evaporate. You won't be *you* any more.' His voice was sad and he reached out a hand and stroked her warm cheek with the back of his fingers. Once upon a time Cherry may have flinched, pulled away or maybe even left altogether at this kind of close contact. However, for the first time, she didn't want to move away. She welcomed it, because she'd finally found someone who understood the complexity of who and what she was, someone she could talk to freely without having to edit out the monsters.

'I don't know what to do.'

'What do you want to do? Stop listening to everyone else's feelings and listen to your own.'

So, instead of running, Cherry leaned into Chase's touch and closed her eyes and listened.

Chase hadn't touched anyone like this before. Relationships had always been a thing of passion but as quickly as a match is struck and fizzles out, so did his love affairs. He had never touched anyone with anything but lust burning in his mind and passion sizzling on his fingertips but *this* ... this was different. *Cherry* was different – and not in the way people often say they're different. This wasn't the eating-dessert-before-dinner different, nor was it the I-sleep-with-my-head-at-the-foot-of-the-bed kind of different. Those people were normal people who did different things out of habit. Habits they'd picked up from other inherently normal people. Cherry herself, her soul and her spirit, were different. It wasn't just that she didn't do or see normal things. Cherry also took the bad things she saw and tried to flip them to do good. She had a genuine desire to help people, *all* people, people she'd never met, and that was what made her different to anyone Chase had ever met. Chase had seen people joyously hating one another, feeding off their love of others' misfortune. He'd seen happiness where there shouldn't ever be happiness, but in Cherry it fit like a perfect glove.

His hand moved to the back of her neck and he brought her in closer to him. She gently lifted herself onto tiptoe and their lips, finally, touched. Both Chase and Cherry had had kisses before but this may as well have been their first – it was like no kiss either of them had experienced before. As soon as their lips parted, they could taste the Belonging and Honesty on each other's tongues and they laughed into each other's mouths.

Chase slipped an arm around Cherry's pyjamaed waist and pulled her closer to him and held her there.

'I'm sorry,' she whispered.

'For what?'

'For leaving.'

He pushed her away gently so he could look her in the eyes. 'So you've decided, then?'

'I can't think of another way around it,' Cherry said, tears coming to her eyes.

'There must be something else we can do!' Chase said urgently.

'Live normally?' she said and shrugged. 'Try to ignore what we can see and just live with it. Stop helping people.'

'Would you be content with that?' he asked and she shrugged again. 'Then that's not an option. I'm not having you unhappy.'

'If I go to the Guild I'll be ... nothing. Unhappy is better than nothing. And then we can stay together.'

'True, but there has to be a better way. One that won't make you miserable. We'll figure this out, I promise.' And then he pulled her in to taste that concoction of Belonging and Honesty once more.

Cherry's phone buzzed in her pocket.

'Mood killer,' Chase said against her lips.

'Sorry.' She pulled the phone out of her pyjama pocket. It was a Facebook notification from the Psychic Sisters page, letting everyone know about their event tomorrow.

'They don't hang about, do they?' Chase laughed. 'That

reminds me ... money! You actually asked for money!'
Cherry had almost forgotten about the wad of cash sitting
in her other pocket.

'I was planning to split it between all their clients.
The ones most affected, at least. Seems only fair they get
something back.'

Chase curled out his bottom lip and nodded approvingly.
'Nice touch. You definitely should have pushed for more,
though. I can't even begin to fathom how much of this
town's cash has paid for Dani's acrylic nails. Too much.'

'Well, at least—'

BANGBANGBANG!

Cherry and Chase both jumped apart at the sound of
Sally slapping her open palm against the door. Cherry
unlocked the door and beckoned her in.

'Sally?' Cherry said, 'What's wrong?'

'Have you seen it?!' Sally shrieked.

'Seen what?' Cherry asked.

'HAVE YOU SEEN IT?!' Sally shrieked again.

'Have I seen what, Sally?' Cherry said patiently, holding out her arms to calm Sally.

'The event. Velina. Danior,' she said between breaths.
'The event. At their shop. Tomorrow.'

Chase and Cherry shared a look. 'Yes, I did see, actually.' Cherry reached behind her for her mug of tea and
sipped it, trying to hide her smile.

'No one can go,' Sally said, holding Cherry's gaze. 'I
won't allow it.'

'Am I missing something?' Chase asked.

'No one can go!' Sally said louder. 'I won't let them!'

'Why, Sally? Why shouldn't anyone go?' Cherry was trying to keep track of what Sally was saying, but it wasn't making much sense.

'Because it's *me*.' Sally dropped to her knees and started sobbing. These weren't the practised crocodile tears they'd seen earlier. Her shoulders heaved up and down and the tears ran in long streams through the gaps between her fingers. 'It's me. It's me, it's me, it's me.'

'Oh, Sally! What's going on? What's you?' Cherry sank to Sally's side and put her arms around her but Sally pulled away, holding out her trembling hands, fending Cherry off.

'No, please don't give me sympathy. I can't stand it. I don't deserve it. Least of all from you.'

'Sally. Please. Talk to us,' Cherry pleaded. 'Tell us what this is all about.'

'Sally ... you don't just go to my mother for readings. Do you?' Chase said quietly. He had remained standing and Cherry looked up at him in confusion. What was going on? Sally shook her head, more tears pouring onto the slate floor.

'What do you mean? What do you go there for?' Cherry asked.

Sally steadied herself with a few deep breaths and once her lip had stopped quivering she said, 'I go there ... to snitch.'

16

The Snitch

Sally sat on the floor clasping a cup of tea with both hands but the shock had made her bones cold and there was no warming her up. She was now sitting cross-legged and refused to move anywhere more comfortable.

'So you became a sort of ... spy? For Velina?' Cherry asked, rubbing Sally's shoulder.

'Not sort of. That's exactly what I am.'

'But ... why? Why would you do that?' Cherry was trying so hard not to judge but the news had come so out of the blue she couldn't help but feel betrayed.

'It wasn't out of choice.' Her lip started to tremble but she shook her head and blinked several times, pushing the tears back down. 'I was married, did you know that?' She smiled. 'We were childhood sweethearts. Met when we were just fifteen. He asked me on a date and took me to the ice cream parlour. We shared a banana split and that was it.' She looked wistful for a moment, lost in her memories. 'Just like that our fates were intertwined so when he died, he ... he took a part of me with him. It's inevitable, I guess. We were married for over twenty years so of course that was going to happen. I went to Velina and Danior hoping they could help me. I was desperate – there were so many things I never got to say to him, so many things I wanted to apologise for, and Danior said she would help me.'

A muscle in Chase's jaw jutted out from his cheek.

'I went back to them, time and time again. I was fed lie after lie and so much false hope at each meeting but I couldn't see through it, until one day Velina said something that didn't match up. Ron and I had this ridiculous way of saying we loved each other. I'd kiss the air twice and he'd shoot the kisses down with his hands as if they were guns. Just a bit of fun, y'know. Something no one else understood apart from us.' Sally became a younger Sally as she talked of times gone by. Cherry caught Chase wiggling his fingers subtly towards the window but only he could see Nostalgia, waltzing outside the window.

'There was one particular session when Velina told me Ron was in the room,' Sally continued. 'I asked her what Ron did when I kissed the air twice and she said he simply blew kisses back at me. It was like flipping a switch. In an instant I realised it had all been lies and deception. I couldn't take it, I couldn't believe that all that time when I thought I had this connection with Ron ... Well, angry doesn't cut it. I shouted, screamed, I even ripped down half of that bloody beaded curtain.' Sally laughed bitterly. 'I stormed out of their shop, determined to out them as frauds when Danior caught up with me and told me she knew.'

'Knew what?' Cherry asked, drawn in.

'She knew about ... ' Sally swallowed hard and spoke into her lap, '... my ... other man.'

'Other man?' Cherry's hand faltered at Sally's shoulder.

'You cheated on Ron?!' Chase gasped.

'Please don't judge me,' Sally said. 'I loved Ron, I did, but I fell for someone else too. I never wanted to hurt anyone. It just happened.'

'But, Sally,' Cherry said, glancing out the window. 'That doesn't justify—'

'I know! It's been over thirty years. I know what I did and just how wrong it was and I've had to live with that guilt every. Single. Day.' Sally sniffed. 'And then Danior ... she saw me with ... the other man after Ron's funeral. I was breaking it off,' she added quickly before Cherry's expression could contort into one of disapproval. Sally kept her composure but the tears kept pouring down her cheeks. 'I loved Ron with all my heart, I really did. I still do. He really did take a part of me with him when he died and I just wanted to move on and honour his memory. It was my small way of trying to make it up to him but when Danior found out, that was the end of that, and the end my life as I knew it.'

'How?' Chase asked.

'I wasn't the only person to love or miss Ron. Everyone knew him, everyone loved him and the whole town mourned him. Everyone would have burnt me at the stake had they known what I'd done.'

'Why did anyone have to know? What you did was wrong, but it was still your business. No one else's. And you were trying to move on,' Cherry said.

'It became Danior's business as soon as she realised she could use it to her advantage.' Sally's lip trembled.

'My aunt,' Chase said, 'has a way of using people's personal and private information against them and to her advantage. I've watched her do it over and over again. Had I known, Sally, I—'

Sally held up her hand and shook her head. 'This was my bed and I had to lie in it.' She took a sip of tea. 'Danior said that she'd tell everyone, that she'd announce it at a town hall meeting or at church or she'd tell each of her clients when they came in to the shop. She threatened to turn me into the most hated woman in town and I couldn't face losing anything else after losing Ron. I was scared.'

'Anyone would be,' Chase said. 'My aunt can be ... quite intimidating when she wants to be.'

'So I begged her not to say anything,' Sally said in a small voice. 'I told her I'd do anything as long as she kept my secret.'

'And what did Danior do?' Cherry asked, but she already knew the answer.

'She took advantage of the situation,' Sally said.

'Of course she did,' Chase almost spat the words out.

'And now she's taking advantage of everyone else too. Because of me and what I've told her and Velina.' Chase and Cherry shared a look.

'What do you mean?' Chase asked, leaning his elbows on his knees.

'This town may not be huge, but its secrets? It has so many, and I've uncovered many of them over the years. Especially recently.' Sally's eyes flickered towards Cherry but she quickly took another sip from her mug. 'I've told them everything I found out and they used that information when customers would come in for genuine readings. But they've been up to something else the last couple of times I've been in there, scheming secretly, and it got me worried. I told them yesterday that I wouldn't do it any more. I said enough is enough and it had all gone too far and now this! Now they're holding this stupid event and I know they're going to tell everyone my secret. They're going to use what I've told them against everyone too and it's all my fault!'

'No, they won't,' Cherry said determinedly. 'It's going to be okay.'

'Cherry ...' Chase warned, thinking of Happy and the Guild. 'You need to be careful.'

'It'll be fine,' Cherry said. 'We'll figure it out.'

Chase shook his head. 'There's no stopping those two. They're villains, cold-hearted villains.'

'Villains are always defeated,' Cherry countered.

Chase stretched out his hand, taking Cherry's hand, her palms slippery against his, cold and dry. 'But this isn't a story and in the real world, the wicked usually win.' He squeezed her fingers to try to make her understand, but she pulled away.

'I refuse to accept that,' she said.

'Chase is right,' Sally sniffed.

'No, he's not.' Cherry said and then after a moment added, 'He's only right if we do nothing. If we give up, Velina and Danior win by default. We don't have to make it easy for them and we won't ever win if we don't even try.'

Chase couldn't help but smile at Cherry's conviction. 'Okay,' Chase said. 'What do you propose exactly?'

'The event is tomorrow,' Sally said. 'We won't be able to stop it in time.'

'I'm not saying we stop it,' Cherry said quickly, sharing a look with Chase. They still needed the townspeople to take the Normality pills, after all. 'It will look too suspicious if it's called off so quickly. We'll need to think of something else to make sure Velina and Danior don't hurt anyone.'

'We have less than twenty-four hours,' Chase pointed out.

'Jack Bauer only had twenty-four hours. The crew

of the Protector only had thirteen seconds when the Omega 13 was activated.'

'That's *Galaxy Quest*!' Chase said.

'So?'

'It's *fiction*. This isn't.'

'It's stranger than,' Cherry said.

'That doesn't matter! This is real! These are real people with real lives and ... ' Chase caught Sally's head bowing further towards the ground and he realised she was accepting her fate. A fate he was condemning her to with absolute certainty by refusing his help. 'And ... and ... we'd be fools not to try,' he sighed. Sally sobbed softly and Cherry clapped her hands together.

'GREAT!' She grinned.

'But how?' Chase asked. 'What are we going to *do*?'

Cherry started to pace. 'Tell me about your mum and aunt. Be specific. I need details.'

Chase groaned and swept his hands through his hair. 'They're awful, *awful* people.'

'Tell us something we don't already know,' Sally said, trying to push herself up onto the nearest bench.

Chase moved behind her to take hold of her under her arms and hoist her up. 'Dani is more blatant about her wrongdoing ... ' He struggled with Sally's weight, 'but Velina is quiet yet calculating.' He exhaled. 'It makes her more dangerous somehow.'

'It's always the quiet ones. Thank you, dear,' Sally said now that she was settled and patting Chase's hands resting on her shoulders. 'They lie and lie and lie and lie. It's all they've ever done and all they'll ever do. They don't need *humble* pie. They need *honest* pie.' Sally chuckled to herself. 'Then again, I reckon they could do with a lot of humble pie too, y'know. I've never met anyone else with so little human decency in my entire life and do y'know what else? I think they've never in a million ...' Sally's voice drifted up and away, almost colliding with the lightbulbs above, making them flicker. Cherry was lost in her own thoughts and Chase looked at her, hard. He had a horrible feeling he knew exactly what she was thinking.

'You can't,' Chase said, making Cherry jump.

'Can't what?' Sally asked, confused.

'I *can*!' Cherry said, marching through to the kitchen. Chase followed her, leaving Sally looking after them in bewilderment.

'No, I mean ... you literally can't,' Chase said once they were out of Sally's earshot. 'Happy. The Guild. They've got tabs on you. Big Brother is watching you. If you dish out anything to anyone they're going to know. They'll take you away and put you in one of their prisons.'

Cherry paused and drummed her hands on the kitchen counter. 'Is that really worse than working for the Guild?' she asked. 'Worse than doing nothing to help Sally, and stop Velina and Danior?'

'I don't know! Maybe!' Chase grabbed Cherry's hands. 'I don't want to lose you. I've only just found you.'

Cherry was caught off-guard. She'd only ever had to think about herself for the last few years. But now Chase was here ... and everything was different. 'Chase, I ... don't want to lose you either but we need to do something. Your mum and aunt are hurting too many people.'

Chase sighed. 'I know. You're right. But there must be another way.'

Cherry shook her head sadly. 'This is the only way. Will you help me?'

Chase kissed Cherry's forehead and pulled her into a hug. 'I'll help you,' he whispered. 'I don't know how to say no to you.'

'What are you to up to in there?' Sally called.

Cherry smiled up at Chase. 'Planning!' she called back.

'Plotting,' Chase muttered.

Sally appeared in the doorway, wiping her nose on her sleeve and brushing her silver dreads back into place. 'Look at you two. You're thick as thieves! What changed?'

'We just realised ...' Cherry shrugged at Chase so he finished the thought for her.

'We've got a lot more in common than we first thought.'

Cherry had never broken the law before. She'd never even thought about it. However, now that she was putting the finishing touches to a plot that would break the laws of a world she had only just discovered even existed, she was finding any way possible to justify it.

'I mean ... it's not really breaking the law if you're helping people, right? Surely that's a flaw in the law, not with me.' She worked her rolling pin at double speed, squashing the pastry beneath so it was as thin as paper.

'I mean ... how valid is this Guild of Feelers anyway? How can they enforce actual laws?' She overloaded the pie crust so that the cherries spilled out onto the chopping board beneath.

'I mean ...'

'Cherry.' Chase reached out and steadied the pie tin that was shaking precariously in her hands. 'It's going to be okay.' He took the tin and placed it back onto the counter. 'One last touch.' He gathered all the spit he could muster at the front of his mouth and while thinking of every truth he'd ever told and all the truths he wanted the world to know, he swilled it around between his teeth and sloshed it back and forth over his tongue. He spat it into a bowl, took up a basting brush and glazed the top of the pie. 'There we are! All done!' he said, pleased with himself.

'Grim.' Cherry grimaced and Chase grinned as he opened the oven and slid in the pie.

'Sally seemed a bit shaken. Maybe we should have walked her home?' Cherry said.

'I'm sure she'll be fine. She seemed to want to be alone

anyway,' Chase said, dusting off his hands on his grey jeans, leaving floury handprints on his thighs.

'So how should we do this?' Cherry said. 'Do we leave the pie for them anonymously?'

'No. They'd be suspicious. They've got too many enemies so they'd probably throw it straight in the bin if they didn't know who it was from,' Chase said. 'I'll say it's from me. They think I'm loyal now, remember?'

Cherry bit her lip but nodded her agreement. 'But we have to make sure they eat it,' she said.

'Easy. I'll eat some too. I could do with being a little more honest,' Chase said with a smile.

'The only other problem with making them more honest is that we need to get to them first, before the pie kicks in. Otherwise they're more likely to expose Sally too. No doubt they'll make a speech.'

'Maximum humiliation,' Chase said.

'Exactly. So we just need to make sure we interrupt them before they get to that.'

'Make a fool of them before they can make a fool of anyone else. I like it! How long does that honesty last for?'

'It depends on how much they eat,' Cherry explained. 'The average slice? Probably about three to four hours. Just long enough for them to get their comeuppance.'

'Perfect.' Chase leaned against the counter and put his hands in his pockets. 'You've got flour in your hair,' he said, his voice dropping to a whisper.

'I always have flour in my hair,' Cherry said, smiling at him.

'I know. You wouldn't look like you without it.'

They stood there, their gazes locked for a few moments, before Cherry reluctantly looked away. She bent down to check the pie through the oven window. 'Well, let's hope they have a decent-sized kitchen in those prisons.'

'You seem very calm about the whole jail thing.'

'Weirdly, I am. It just doesn't feel that real to me. It feels like Monopoly jail. Do you know what I mean?'

Chase nodded. 'Yeah, I understand. Doesn't it creep you out, though? This idea that we're part of this whole community that we didn't even know existed? How many other ... *Feelers* have we met and not known that's what they were?' Chase sat down on the kitchen floor next to Cherry.

'I've not even thought about there being others like me since I met you,' Cherry said shyly. 'Have you?'

'Yes, but I didn't really think about it properly,' Chase said. 'I mean, I'm twenty-six! What are the chances of going that long without meeting anyone else like us?'

'We must be rare,' Cherry said.

'Not *that* rare if there's a whole Guild of Feelers who are after us,' Chase pointed out, laughing.

'True. They must be very good at hiding in plain sight, then,' Cherry said. 'It's mad, really, when you think about it. A Guild of Feelers ...'

'Any part of you feel like running?' Chase asked.

Cherry frowned. 'What do you mean, running?'

'From the Guild. Keep doing what you do but run to stay out of prison. Why don't you fight them?'

Cherry blinked slowly, thinking about it. 'Maybe I could run for a while but I just ... don't think I could run all my life.'

17

Cherry Pie

The pie wobbled fiercely on Cherry's lap on the boat ride to The Barbican. Not because of the waves that gently rolled underneath them but because Cherry couldn't stop bouncing her knees up and down. Cherry's eyes were fixed on a pale yellow flyer that a girl not much younger than Cherry was holding. She must have been twenty at most, her cheeks rosy in the sea wind, her dangling dreamcatcher earrings becoming tangled in her blonde hair. Cherry could just about make out the words PSYCHIC SISTERS across the top of the flyer. Chase put a steady hand over the pie to slow her jittery legs.

'All is going to go according to plan,' he whispered. Cherry watched the blonde girl take her purse out of her bag and count through the notes and hoped that Chase was right.

When they disembarked the boat they saw hundreds of yellow flyers fluttering in the hands of nearly everyone in sight, all of them heading in the direction of Psychic Sisters.

'At least they'll have a crowd to embarrass themselves in front of. Come on.' Chase went to grab Cherry's hand but she pulled away. 'Cherry? What is it?'

'I don't know if I can do this,' she said in a small voice.

'What? But last night you were so sure.'

'I know, I know. But who are we to decide who deserves to be punished?'

'Who else would decide that?' Chase said. 'The Guild? You want to leave everything up to them?'

'I don't know.' Cherry gestured the pie up to the sky. 'The universe?' She shrugged. 'Surely not us.'

'They're my family and I know they're bad people but it still hurts me to say that we need to stop them. They're going too far.' Chase stopped pulling Cherry's arm and reached to take the pie from her but she nimbly moved it behind her back. 'Cherry ... we're not doing this out of spite to hurt them. We're doing this to help Sally and to stop more people being hurt and blackmailed.' Chase placed his hands on either side of Cherry's face. 'We're the heroes in this story, okay?' Chase turned her around and took the pie out of her hands.

210

'Then why do I feel like a villain?' Cherry groaned and started to trudge in step with everyone else.

'Because you don't ever want to do anything mean to anyone. Whether they deserve it or not.'

'And you *do*?' Cherry asked, wrapping her chunky knit cardigan around her.

'Maybe at one time, yes, I did mean things willingly.' Chase looked sideways at Cherry. 'But things are changing for me now.'

'How so?'

'Because I know it's not just about me any more. There's a bigger picture to think about. Tricking my family into eating the pie might feel wrong, but we're doing something only *kind of* bad for the greater good. We're balancing each other out, Cherry. If anything, the scales are tipping further in *your* favour.'

'Are you calling me fat?' Cherry mocked.

'What? No, of course not! Where did you get that ... oh, I see. Very good. Well done,' he said when he caught her smirking. 'At least you're smiling now.'

But that smile was short-lived. When they reached the shop they saw that Velina and Danior had erected a small podium directly outside. On it stood a small table dressed with a red velvet blanket and with a crystal ball placed in the centre. Two black chairs had been placed either side of the table. Even though the Facebook invitation had said to be there at midday and it was only half eleven, the crowd was already at least six people deep and everyone looked worse for wear. Most were sporting obvious bed-heads, some were yawning, some still had fake, plastic smiles plastered on their faces. And every single person had a Meddlum. All of the Meddlums, most of them being different sizes of Guilt and Confusion, lined the other side of the street opposite the shop. They wrestled and jostled, filling the air with their inhuman grunts and howling. It was a mess.

Chase scanned the crowd of Meddlums. 'No one looks happy and there aren't a lot of good feelings out there.'

'*No one?*' Cherry asked. 'Some of them are smiling . . . sort of.'

'I think that's just a leftover from what they had at your bakery. Very few have any good feeling and even then they're mild.'

'Tea?' A woman wearing large sunglasses and black lipstick approached them, carrying a wobbling stack of polystyrene cups and a big silver thermos.

'Er . . . yes please . . . ' Chase said. He took the cup from her and oddly, she curtseyed and skittered off to pour more unsuspecting townsfolk tea. Chase slurped the smallest sip. 'Normality,' he confirmed. 'They're giving it out before they appear. No doubt they think it's going to make everyone more susceptible and more willing to give bigger donations.'

'They've certainly thought it through. Will they be inside the shop now, do you think?' Cherry asked.

'They do like to make an entrance so they're probably

waiting for the crowd to get bigger and for the tea to kick in. They'll be inside dolling themselves up, making themselves pretty for any press. Come on.' Chase started to push through the crowd, the pie cradled protectively into his chest. Chase didn't bother to knock on the closed door of the shop but regretted that decision when he walked in on Danior wearing nothing except a pair of knickers and her silk robe, which was swinging open.

'Oh *Jesus*, Dani.' Chase averted his gaze and wished he wasn't holding the pie so he could cover his eyes with his hands. 'You know that window isn't frosted? People can actual see in and see ... *you*.'

'In all my glory?' Dani held her robe open and out to the sides like a butterfly and bit her lip.

Cherry leaned over his shoulder and saw Dani's untamed, sagging breasts, gasped and threw her hands over Chase's eyes. 'He's ... he's your *nephew*!' Cherry hissed.

'Nothing he hasn't seen before.' Dani shrugged and tied the robe closed.

'Sadly, that's true,' Chase said, gently shaking Cherry off. 'Why are you even undressed anyway?'

'I'm getting changed for all the photographs. I've got to look my best,' she said, holding her new orange acrylic nails up to the light to check they weren't already cracked.

'I see,' Cherry said, nudging Chase. 'Well, we thought we'd come along today.'

'Yeah and ... I brought you a pie to say ... to say ...'

'Good luck!' Cherry said, splaying her fingers to make jazz hands.

'Yeah. Good luck!' Chase said, with a big smile and held the pie out to Dani.

'Did someone say pie? Oh marvellous! I'm absolutely starving.' Velina appeared from behind the beaded curtain, its rattle ricocheting through Cherry's head. Only now did she realise that the beads on one half of the curtain were looking sparser than the other. *Sally*, she thought and tried hard not to smile.

'Apple?' Danior asked, piercing the foil over the pie with a nail. Chase pulled it away and placed the pie on the front desk next to the till.

'Cherry,' he said, uncovering the pie and revealing the red fruit poking out from the lattice.

Danior gave one short snort of a laugh and rolled her eyes at Cherry. 'How quaint.'

'We just wanted to celebrate all your upcoming success. Let me get some plates.' Chase disappeared up the stairs behind the desk. Cherry stood wringing her hands, waiting for Chase to return. She looked around at the pictures on the wall, avoiding Velina and Danior's gaze but feeling their eyes on her wherever she moved, like old creepy paintings in an abandoned house. Chase finally clinked back down the stairs with plates and a knife.

'Who wants a slice?' he asked, presumptuously cutting into the pie.

'Oh, not me, darling. I'll never get into my dress,' Dani said.

'It's not the Oscars, Dan. One tiny slice of pie isn't going to make a difference,' Chase said.

'Even so, better not risk it!'

'Oh, that is a good point,' Velina said. She disappeared back through the curtain and returned a few moments later holding out a gold sequinned dress that looked like it belonged in a production of *Chicago*.

'TA-DA!' Velina shook the dress so that the sequins caught the light and glimmered.

'That's very ...' Chase didn't know whether to be nasty or nice.

'Very ... um ...' Even Cherry was fighting an urge to say something less than lovely.

'... short,' Chase said.

'... sequin-y,' Cherry said.

'How insightful,' Velina said, dropping the dress a little.

'It's lovely, really!' Cherry said quickly, trying to back-track.

'Wait until you see mine!' Dani said, scuttling through the beaded curtain and returning with exactly the same dress, only this time in silver.

'It's the same dress!' Chase laughed.

'Yes, but I'll wear it better.' Dani nudged Velina playfully but Velina didn't look all that amused.

Chase shook his head, trying not to laugh. 'Well, I'm

telling you now, a mouthful of pie isn't going to hurt,' he said trying to get back to the matter in hand.

'And I'm telling you, I don't want to risk it.' Danior slid her hand under the pie dish and moved to take it upstairs to where Cherry assumed the kitchen was. Chase stood in Danior's way, blocking her path. She narrowed her eyes at him and growled, 'I'm not playing games, boy. Move.'

Chase's mind flashed back to all the times she'd called him *boy* and he had to take a deep breath in order to keep calm.

'It's just a little slice of celebratory pie.' He chuckled and tried to keep his voice light but Cherry could hear his nerves. Surely the sisters would too?

'Oh, for goodness sake, Chase! If you want pie so badly why don't you just HAVE SOME!'

SPLAT.

Danior pushed the pie onto Chase's face. The sauce dribbled out of the sides and the pastry cracked and crumbled down Chase's front. Danior threw her head back and cackled. Cherry gasped as she watched Danior give the pie tin a little twist on Chase's face with added venom. Chase pulled the tin away with a great sucking noise only to find that most of the pie was still stuck to his skin.

'What. The actual. Fuck.' His words bubbled through the sauce.

'Oh, stop whining. It's not *your* big day.' Danior dismissed him with a wave of her hand, before pushing past him and heading upstairs with her dress. Cherry heard the curtain rustle and turned to see Velina leave the room without so much as a backward glance. Cherry turned back just in time to see Chase licking his lips.

'Chase. Stop eating it!' she whispered.

'I can't help it! It's everywhere! And I was going to have some anyway so it makes no difference. Fuck,' he said looking down at himself.

'Yeah. Fuck,' Cherry said.

'Right. So ... erm ...' Chase looked at her, holding out his red-stained hands in defeat.

'That wasn't exactly part of the plan,' Cherry said helplessly.

'What do we do now?' Chase asked quietly.

'I don't know!' Cherry hissed, clenching her fists.

'It's okay. Just ... listen, take a breath. We'll figure this out.' Chase tried to rub the sauce from his face but Cherry could see he was only rubbing it in, his skin getting pinker and pinker underneath.

'Calm down?!' Cherry slid her phone out from her pocket. 'We have fifteen minutes. FIFTEEN!' she cried, raising her voice. Chase rushed to her and pushed her towards the door.

'Shhh!' he hushed. 'Just go outside.'

'What?!'

'Go outside! I have an idea but you can't be here. They don't trust you. You saw how Danior looked at you. As much as I hate to say it, I'm family, and even though they don't think much of me, they still trust me. Just let me try one last thing. What other options do we have?'

'Okay,' she said. He was right – there were no other options.

'Okay?'

'OK. I'm out of ideas. But just please ... be careful and ... and ...'

'I'm not going to screw this up.' Chase kissed her on the forehead, leaving behind some sticky, cherry-flavoured debris. He ran across the shop and up the stairs. 'Mum! Dani!' he called.

Cherry left the shop and instantly found herself pushing through the restless, humming crowd. She took deep breath after deep breath, her chest rising and falling underneath her wool cardigan. Someone accidentally stood on her foot and the pain triggered the prickle in the back of her eyes and the sound in her ears started to wane in and out. 'Oh, God.' She let out a sob and there, in the middle of the crowd, she sat down on the pavement, pulled her knees up to her chest and rested her forehead against them. She couldn't separate out any of the noises until she latched onto the only sound she was waiting for: the bell above the door of Psychic Sisters.

The crowd fell silent.

18

As Rare As A Unicorn

'I'm not really one for speeches ...' Velina began. She stood on her tiptoes so she could reach the mic that was duct-taped to the front of the lectern. Danior pushed her aside and rested her hands on the edge of the lectern, with her elbows sticking out so Velina couldn't get any closer. Cherry could only hear their voices and when she opened her eyes the sight of all the yellow flyers made her stomach flip.

'I, on the other hand, *am* one for speeches!' Danior cackled and snorted and the speaker that was teetering on the front of the small podium squealed in response. 'Welcome one and all, young and old, to our humble shop. For almost four decades we've been here, in our little hovel, helping you all realise your greatest dreams and making all your lives brighter with the knowledge you crave but are unable to reach. We *can* reach that knowledge, however, and so have worked hard for most of our lives giving you, our loyal friends and customers, just what you need.' Danior licked her lips, transferring more of her lipstick to her teeth, which she then bared to the crowd in a grin. 'Ladies and gentlemen, boys and girls, today we want to thank you for all the ... love you've given us by letting those you care about who have passed communicate through us. All we require is a ... small donation. Baskets *and tea* are being passed around. Make sure you find both!' Danior wiggled her fingers dismissively to her side and Velina produced two wicker baskets from underneath the podium and handed them to the front row of the crowd. 'Good, good. Keep them moving!'

'You all right down there, Miss Redgrave?'

'Oh, George. Hello. Yes. Fine.' Cherry took the hand he was offering to her and he hoisted her off the floor. Her cheeks burned. She needed to pull it together. She couldn't fall apart every time something bad happened.

'You looked comfy down there.' George gestured with his other hand that was holding a cup of tea. 'I wouldn't. Disgusting stuff,' he said when he caught Cherry eyeing the cup. 'Not even really sure what I'm doing here but everyone loves something free.' He took a breath and then said very quickly, 'Listen ... I'm so sorry about the other day. I should never have got into that state and I should've listened to you about Chase. It's not like you to get angry and I should have been a more supportive friend to you and stayed away from—'

'Actually, it's all okay,' Cherry said, her breathing back to normal now. 'Chase and I have . . . worked things out. We've been talking a lot recently. I think we both misjudged each other.'

'I see,' George said, an uncertain smile slowly spreading across his face. 'Well, good for you . . . I think. Chase is a . . . handful.'

'I know.'

'Then again,' he said playfully, 'you punched him, so I guess . . . so are you.' George nudged her with his elbow and Cherry's cheeks rounded up into a smile.

'Did you get your job back at the library?' she asked.

'Nah. I think that chapter of my life is well and truly over.'

'Oh, George. I'm so sorry. I thought Sally would be able to get it back for you. She was furious when she left.'

'It's not that,' George shook his head. 'She *did* get me my job back but . . . I said I didn't want it. I kept thinking about what you said, actually.'

'Oh, no. What did I say?' Cherry's stomach somersaulted again.

'You said "It's never too late". It probably wasn't an original quote but it stayed with me all the same.'

'It's never too late for . . . ? What now? Do you have a plan?'

'I'm putting my degree to use! Applying for jobs. There's one in Truro that looks promising.'

'Cornwall?'

George nodded. 'I've never been, but as they say there's a first time for everything.'

Cherry couldn't help but feel impressed. Who would've thought George would take a risk like this? She smiled at him. 'That's terrific. I'm really proud of you, George.'

He blushed. 'Well, it's all down to—'

He was interrupted by the bell above the Psychic Sisters' door ringing out again, but Cherry was too short to see what was going on.

'Who was that? Leaving the shop? Was that Chase?'

'Er ...' George was taller than Cherry but still had to tiptoe to see. 'Yeah, I think so. Someone's behind the podium anyway. Passing Velina ... two glasses, I think. Champagne, it looks like.'

'Ah, *yes*!' Danior's voice boomed through the mic. She swiped up her glass. 'While you all have our,' she smirked, 'traditional tea, we thought we'd have something a bit stronger. We are celebrating, after all!' She knocked back the glass and swallowed its contents in one. Velina sniffed hers first, as it seemed to have an odd froth floating on top, but after seeing her sister's enthusiasm, she swallowed her drink down quickly too.

'Cherry!'

Cherry turned to see Chase hurrying towards her. He swerved and ducked through handfuls of coins and the tea-filled cups. He'd cleaned most of the pie from his face but there were a handful of tell-tale stains on his clothes.

'Chase! What did you do? I mean how did it go?' She added quickly, turning her face away from George.

'My aunt and mother never could resist a drink or two,' Chase whispered, his lips brushing her earlobe. His hand found hers and he squeezed it. Cherry glanced at George, who was staring straight ahead – but she was certain he'd seen the intimacy between her and Chase.

'Right! You all came here for a show, so let's get started, shall we?' Danior swirled the glittery hem of her dress, showing off her liver-spotted thighs, and sat in one of the black chairs.

'It's so cold out here,' Cherry said, pulling her cardigan around her. 'I don't know how they both aren't freezing in just those dresses.'

'It's the evil in their veins. It's made of the fires from hell. Keeps them toasty warm while they carry out their sordid deeds.'

Cherry looked at him in surprise. 'Will you keep your voice down?' she hushed.

'No, do you know what? I don't think I will. Excuse me! Velina!' Chase shouted over the crowd but he tried to mask his face with his hands at the same time. 'Is it true you can't actually speak to the dead?'

'Yes,' Velina said instantly, nodding enthusiastically. Danior looked appalled. She leaned across the table and slapped Velina hard across the cheek and the crowd gasped.

'And is it true you've been taking everyone's hard-earned money when they ask you for help, even though you know you don't have any supernatural abilities?'

'Yes!' Danior said, the word sliding off her tongue before she could catch it. Velina leaned over and returned the slap, twice as hard. The crowd was beginning to unsettle, with a few people starting to shout out.

'Disgraceful!'

'You're fakes!'

'I want my money back!'

'And, Danior, is it true you used to steal my pocket money to buy yourself cigarettes?'

'YES!' Danior shrieked and Velina slapped her so hard, she knocked the crystal ball off its small gold stand and it rolled off the podium and into the crowd.

'Sorry, I couldn't help myself,' Chase said, a small laugh escaping his lips.

People moved and created a path for the ball as it rolled to a stop at Cherry's feet. She was suddenly in the direct eyeline of the sisters.

'YOU!' Danior pointed a claw and Cherry was sure she was envisioning sinking it deep into her eye sockets. Dani walked back over to the lectern on shaking legs. She didn't understand what was going on but she had this overwhelming urge to be very, very honest all of a sudden. 'You think you're *so* clever with your little bakery and your ridiculous pyjamas but a SILLY LITTLE CUPCAKE CAN'T STOP ME!' Danior's eyes were painfully wide and her eyeliner and eyeshadow were merging to create thick lines above both of her eyelids. 'Let's start with Bruce, shall we? Bruce Bunting, are you here?' No answer. 'Hmm? Can't hear you, Bruce? But then again I doubt anyone would be able to hear you over the deafening sound of your wife's betrayal!' There was no gasp from the crowd, only concerned murmurs – but whether they were for Bruce or Danior's mental wellbeing, Cherry couldn't decipher.

'We have to stop this,' Cherry whispered urgently to Chase, who had paled now things had taken a turn for the worse. 'This is exactly what we didn't want to happen.'

'We're too far away,' Chase said. He and Cherry tried to push their way towards the front but the crowd, so engrossed in what was going on on stage, weren't budging. Cherry and Chase looked at one another, defeated. How could they stop this? They'd promised Sally they were going to *help* her, not ruin her.

'What about, Margie? Is she here?' Danior was on a roll. 'Because Bruce, did you know that if you ever wanted to leave your cheating wife, there's a lonely widow waiting over in the dress shop who would happily have her sloppy seconds!'

Cherry looked around until her gaze fell on Margie's glistening eyes, just a few people away. Cherry squeezed Chase's hand, then wriggled her fingers out from his and tried again to elbow her way through everyone to get to her but Margie started to push forwards, moving away from her. She was having better luck than Cherry and was moving at a faster pace than Cherry was.

'Wait! Margie!'

'AND I've not even got to the good bit. SALLY LIGHTBODY! Are you here?!'

'Stop it!' Margie raised her voice louder than Cherry had ever heard her speak before but it still wasn't loud enough to cut through Danior's wailing.

'Because I think everyone should probably know that SALLY LIGHTBODY ...' she paused, savouring every word, 'HAD AN AFFAIR! She CHEATED on Ron. Remember Ron? Dearly beloved by all! A wonderful man who loved Sally more than anything and yet she had ANOTHER MAN!' Danior screamed.

'STOP!' Margie shouted. She'd made it to the edge of the podium and was staring up at Danior. The crowd hushed so Margie dropped her voice, feeling exposed. 'You are embarrassing yourself.'

'*I'm* embarrassing myself? Haven't you heard all the things I've said?! This whole *town* has embarrassed itself!'

'Yes, I did hear what you said. Every word. But not a thing you said has shocked me.'

Danior's face fell. 'What do you mean? You can't possibly—'

'I already knew it all,' Margie said.

'So did I,' Bruce said, appearing beside Margie but not quite able to meet her eye. Suddenly, voice after voice rose from the crowd.

'And me.'

'Me too!'

'We've known for ages!'

'No ... this isn't possible. *How* could you have known?!' Dani shook her head furiously, unblinking.

'Think about it, Dani.' Margie's voice was clear and confident. 'We'd all be blind fools if we didn't see all the things that were happening under our noses. These things aren't secrets because nobody knows; they're secrets because ... we don't talk about these things out of *respect* for one another. It's not for us to judge what Sally did, nor should we interfere *en masse* in what's going on between Bruce and his wife, and it's no one's business how I feel about—' she coughed, '—how I feel. If I want to talk to someone about it, I will, and so will anyone else, but we're not gossips. We don't talk about people behind their backs, filling other people's heads with half-truths when we don't have all the facts. We live and let live. We don't interfere. We're not entitled to each other's private lives and just because we accidentally heard something or someone let something slip, it doesn't give us the right to stick our oars in.'

Danior took a step back from the crowd, clutching at her heart.

'Margie's right,' Bruce said. 'People will ask for help when they need it and we'll offer it when things get bad. But most of all, we don't hold our mistakes against each other or bring them up to win a cheap point in a nasty argument.'

Danior took another step back, her breathing shallow.

'Saying that, and forgive me, Sally, but I need to clear your name just a little.' Margie scanned the crowd until she found Sally. In a moment Sally understood that Margie knew what she'd kept hidden all these years. She nodded her consent that yes, Margie could tell everyone the truth.

'Ron had a secret too. Something he didn't want anyone to know and his reasons for that were his own, but the truth was that Ron was gay. And I know you loved him, Sally, but no one is judging you for seeking physical comfort elsewhere, because yours and Ron's wasn't that kind of love. I just wish he felt he could've opened up to us, his friends, and that you didn't have to spend all these years thinking we would think any less of you.'

'But it's so wrong,' Danior whimpered. 'They were married. She shouldn't have—'

'Like you're such a saint!' Margie whipped around to face the podium again. 'These things are never black and white. Feelings and friendships and relationships – they're complicated. Even when things are going well, it can still be so messy.'

'Those who live in glass houses shouldn't throw stones,' Bruce offered, 'And by the sounds of it, you two have been chucking bricks.' Bruce shook his head and laughed at his own joke.

Danior took one last step back and her heels slipped

off the back of the podium. Flying backwards, her arm caught the Psychic Sisters shop window and it shattered, shards of glass raining down around her. The crowd gasped and pushed forwards but Velina screamed, 'LEAVE HER!' No one had noticed the tears pouring down her face. She clambered down off the podium as best she could in her ill-fitting dress and helped her sister to her feet, Danior's arm streaked with blood.

'Leave us. All of you,' Velina said, opening the door to the shop.

'You're all terrible people!' Danior wailed, wrapping the ends of her headscarf around her hand and arm. 'You keep dreadful secrets and act like saints but I know the truth! I know the truth! I know the—'

Velina slammed shut the door, cutting off Danior's voice. The crowd remained stagnant, lost without someone or something to look at and listen to. A flock of sheep without a shepherd.

'Is that really who we are?' whispered the girl with black lips. 'Are we terrible?'

'Of course it isn't!' Bruce exclaimed.

'Well . . . it is . . . and it isn't,' Margie said, facing Bruce and the rest of crowd. 'We've all done stupid things. Bad things, even. Things we aren't proud of but . . . ' Margie tried to push herself up onto the podium but her arms slipped.

'Here . . . ' Bruce interlinked his fingers and opened out the palms of his hand. Gratefully, Margie put a hand on his shoulder, placed her foot into his hands and he hoisted her onto the podium to stand before the crowd.

'Where was I?'

'We're terrible people!' Chase called out, some residual Honesty still left in his system.

'Thank you, Mr Masters. No. We've done stupid, ill-advised things but that doesn't make us bad people. The fact that all of the things disgracefully announced on this stage today were secrets we hid from each other doesn't mean that we're bad. We just weren't ready to share them with one another.' She turned her kind eyes to Sally. 'And even when you think you've done a bad thing and it isn't a bad thing at all, it can still make you feel remorseful.'

'What does that prove?' Sally said, her cheeks wet and burning.

'Do you think bad people feel remorse for the things they do? No. We feel bad even when we haven't done any-thing wrong! We feel shame and we feel lonely. And we try to be better because we don't want the world to think we're terrible people because deep down, we know we're not. We just ... we just ...'

'Fuck up?' Chase offered again. Honestly.

'Exactly. We just *fuck up*.'

'Nice one, Margie,' Cherry whispered in Chase's ear, linking her arm through his.

'Everyone's getting their mojo back,' Chase said. He watched tiny spots of light begin to appear above people's heads.

'You can see that?' Cherry said in a low voice. 'Their happiness is coming back?'

'Happiness. Hope. Even Horniness! You name it. They're just not depressed any more.'

'Hey, no one was depressed. Just a bit . . . ' Chase raised an eyebrow. 'OK, perhaps,' Cherry sighed.

Chase watched the lights transform as Margie kept talking. At first they were just little blobs of gold, blue and pink but then they took shape and became Hope, Acceptance and Pride.

'We're *people*. As much as we try to be perfect something is always going to go a little bit awry somewhere along the way. While we should accept whatever consequences come our way as a result, none of us should be defined by our mistakes, nor should we be subjected to ridicule by some silly little ninny in a dress that, I promise, did not come from *my* shop.' Margie laughed. 'We're human. That's all there is to it!' Margie shrugged, suddenly embarrassed and very aware that everyone was staring at her. The crowd whooped, cheered and clapped as Margie accepted Bruce's hand and delicately climbed down from the stage.

'I've never seen her like that!' Chase said, admiration in his voice.

'Looks like a bit of Normality did her some good!' Cherry laughed.

'Or a bit of you, Cherry,' Sally said, joining them.

'What do you mean?' Cherry asked.

'She looks up to you!' Chase said. 'It's obvious.'

'Is it? No offence meant to Margie, but ... she's almost double my age!'

'So?' Sally said. 'Whenever she's in your shop I can see her mimicking you. When you stand up tall, so does she. When you talk a little louder, she raises her voice too. You told her you were once an anxious person and now look at you! You're a confident young woman with a business of her own who makes friends on a daily basis. You're an inspiration.'

'Plenty of people who were once anxious manage to get themselves out of the house and talking to people.'

'True, but they're as rare as unicorns and out of all of them, Margie met you. You're *her* unicorn and now she wants to be a unicorn too.'

'I'm not sure about that, but she did pretty well up there. I'm proud of her,' Cherry said, watching Margie shake hand after hand after hand.

'Look at you two,' Sally said, pointing at Cherry and Chase's linked arms. 'Thick as thieves. Well, they say opposites attract!' Sally squeezed their shoulders then wrapped her arms around herself.

'Are you all right, Sally? You're shaking,' Chase asked, concerned.

'Just a bit too much excitement for me today. I need a glass of brandy and a lie-down after all that!'

'I think we all do. Home?' Chase asked.

'Home.' Cherry smiled – but then everything went black.

No one else had noticed. Or rather, no one else could *see* that there was something blocking the sun. There was a large shadow ahead of them, bigger than Chase and Cherry combined. The edges of the shadow were fuzzy and gently undulating but very clearly on the top of its head were two jagged horns. They twisted in on themselves and then snaked back up to the sky and tapered off into long, perfect points.

'Chase. Just stop for a moment.' Cherry tried to stay calm as she turned towards the gin distillery to see the Meddlum the shadow belonged to. She gasped. Now she saw the edges of its shadow had been writhing because it was burning like an ember. There were no flames but smoke poured off it in thick plumes that covered the street around it. Cherry's heart started hammering in fright and Chase could feel its thrum in her fingertips as she dug them deep into his forearm. Most of the crowd has dispersed and Cherry was grateful she and Chase were alone. There was no way she'd be able to cover for what she was seeing now.

'What can you see?' Chase whispered. 'Cherry, talk to me.'

'I've seen big Meddlums before but nothing so ... *hellish*.' Cherry's eyes tingled and she wondered if the smoke from Hate was affecting them. Chase peered closer.

'Wait ... Cherry, I can see it! In your eyes! I can see the reflection of it in your eyes! Holy *shit*.' Chase covered his mouth, watching the creature burn in her irises.

Cherry stood, transfixed, the two burning coals that were the monster's eyes boring into hers.

'*Oh my god*. You see these things on a daily basis?!'

'I tried to tell you.'

'I know but ... how are you not more emotionally mangled by it?'

'I *am*. I'm just really good at hiding it.'

'Oh, Cherry. I'm so sorry. I had no idea,' Chase wrapped his arms around her but she was still frozen in place. He pulled away and looked into her eyes again. 'Who does it belong to?'

'I don't know. I can't see through all the smoke.' Cherry squinted and Chase looked around, trying to match the Meddlum to anyone nearby.

'Wait ... there ...' Cherry noticed the smoke at the foot of the Meddlum had started to spin into tiny tornadoes. 'Can you see anyone? I can only see smoke ...'

Chase nodded. 'Yeah, there's someone there but ... he just looks like a regular guy.'

'He's coming into focus now. I still can't make out his face, though.'

'He's in his twenties, well groomed, doesn't look particularly happy or ... wait ... Cherry ... I can't see anything ...'

'What? Is the smoke getting in the way?'

'No, I can't see the smoke, remember? It's just that ... Cherry, he has no good feeling. Like ... nothing. I can't see anything good.' Chase instinctively put an arm in front of her.

'But his Meddlum is so big . . . '

'What kind of Meddlum is it?' Chase asked, still not used to the name Cherry had given the demons she saw.

'*Hate*,' she said, blinking hard. 'I've never seen it so big before.'

'Hate for what?' Chase looked at her as a tear ran down her cheek.

'. . . himself,' she whispered. And then a face broke through the smoke – a face Cherry would recognise anywhere.

Cherry would have run if she hadn't been sick. Bent double, she threw up until there was nothing left in her stomach. It was all on the cobbles in front of her, the black smoke covering the mess.

'What's going on?' Chase rubbed her back.

Cherry waved him away, swallowed hard, coughed, gagged again, anything to avoid having to answer but her head snapped up when she felt the sun on her shoulders.

'Where did he go?' The Meddlum had disappeared, leaving only thin grey wisps rising into the air. Its owner had vanished too.

'As soon as you . . . y'know . . . ' Chase mimicked her gagging, 'he turned and ran in the other—'

'Miss Redgrave. Mr Masters. I've been looking for you.'

Cherry and Chase both whipped around to see a familiar and yet unfriendly face.

'Happy,' Chase said.

Her expression, as usual, did not change. She wore the same shade of yellow as she had worn before but this time she was wearing a suit. Her briefcase dangled by her side.

'Correct. You made a decision, Miss Redgrave. Did you not?'

'Well, I . . . ' Cherry said.

'You meddled again, did you not?'

'No, she—' Chase said.

'We have evidence. And you knew you were strictly forbidden to meddle if you weren't in the Guild's employ.'

'It's not—'

'—what it looks like? No, I'm sure it's not but even so, looks like we'll have to be taking you in.'

Cherry hadn't noticed the van parked on the side of the road behind Happy. Three men in blue suits were climbing out of the double doors at its rear, unfolding a wheelchair. The image of the van rattled in Cherry's mind and she shrank into Chase's side.

'This isn't right. Get behind me, Cherry,' Chase, yet again, put his arm in front of her and pushed her behind him. 'She's not going with you.'

'No, I know she isn't . . . ' Happy said. She lowered the briefcase to the ground, clicked open its clasps and the foam on the inside glowed against her pale skin. Happy fiddled for a moment behind the lid. She stood and tapped the air bubbles out of the syringe she held in her hand, poised and ready. '... but you are, Mr Masters.' Happy's hand darted out towards Chase's neck before he'd even uttered a word in protest. All that escaped his lips was a guttural groan as he slumped forwards into the wheelchair the men in blue had strategically placed. Chase's body fell the wrong way, his stomach on the seat, his head hooked over the back and his knees digging into the foot rests.

'STOP! PLEASE STOP!' Cherry cried. 'What are you doing to him?! It's me you want! Let him GO!' She stepped forwards to help him but Happy held out the syringe in her direction and she halted.

'A little bit of Compliance makes someone do whatever you say but a concentrated dose means you can do whatever you want *with* them. I wouldn't step any closer if I were you. Unless you'd like to join him?' Cherry hesitated and then moved towards Chase. Happy stepped to the side, blocking her path. 'Oh, I see,' Happy said, her face unmoving. 'The Hermit has found love? Interesting. Still, I don't think where he's going is quite the place for you. I *would* be careful though, Cherry.' Happy lifted the collar on Chase's jacket and wiped off a little of the sauce left over from the cherry pie. She sucked her finger. 'A little Honesty goes a long way so let me be quite frank. You're one step away from the back of that van.' Happy clicked her fingers and the men in blue started to pull Chase away. His arms hit the wheels and his feet dragged across the cobbles. One of his shoes caught and slipped off as they bundled him through the double doors but none of the men stopped to pick it up.

'No!' Cherry started forward, without thinking, and before she knew it Happy had inserted the very tip of the needle into her arm. She injected a tiny amount of what was left in the syringe and said, 'Stay where you are please, Cherry.'

Cherry couldn't move. Her mind wanted her to move but her body wouldn't . . . comply.

'Just be grateful there wasn't enough left to . . . ' Happy gestured towards the van.

'Happy . . . ' Cherry wheezed.

Happy turned slowly and clasped her hands in front of her. 'Yes, Miss Redgrave?'

'I hope the woman you are underneath everything the Guild has done to you is no different to who you are now.'

'How sweet. And why is that?'

'Because, now, you've taken the one person I've truly felt like I've belonged with since my father died. Now you've taken Chase from me, this is personal.' Cherry's body may have betrayed her but her voice held firm and steady. 'So I hope you've always been a monster. Because that way, when I take you down, I won't feel too guilty about it. And I will come for Chase, you can count on that.'

Happy looked at Cherry blankly before climbing into the van and driving away. But to where? Cherry didn't even know where to begin. She knew the likelihood of the Guild being someplace conspicuous or marked on a map somewhere was non-existent. Eventually Cherry's body became her own again and she walked over to where Chase's shoe lay on the cobbles and picked it up. She thought of him, how little time they'd had together, and the big gaping hole he'd left. She cursed whoever was listening for making her part of this torturously twisted fairy tale.

Cherry needed help. Before she'd learned of the Guild, Cherry had only known two people who were like her. One of them was Chase and the other was the man she had recognised in the smoke: Peter. She was sure it had been him. He was a man now and not the child she'd known him as, but it was undeniably his face she'd seen. She'd seen that hateful seed on their final day together at school and ever since it had been growing into a giant ball of living fire. *Poor Peter*, Cherry thought. Had Peter come to find her? Had he come to help? Had he been to the Guild? Is that where he'd been taken all those years ago? Cherry had to know because if he did know where the Guild was, he could help her get Chase back.

Grey clouds were hanging overhead and a thick drop tumbled from the sky here and there as Cherry ran to the water's edge. She was rarely fond of her abilities but at that moment, she knew they would be the key to finding Chase. She turned back towards the town and, against the grey sky, she saw a stream of black smoke pouring upwards into the clouds. Without hesitation, Cherry ran towards it.

The Lovers

'If no one loved, the sun would go out.'

Victor Hugo

19

Shura

When you've come to call four white walls home, anything different, anything beyond, holds a beauty all of its own. Green floors become lush grass and blue-tinged fluorescent lights become clear skies but Peter wasn't a fool. Peter couldn't be tricked into feeling grateful to be let out of his white cell for a change of scenery when he'd seen real grass and he'd seen the sky in his lifetime. He knew what real beauty was and would accept no substitutes, which is why when he saw Shura within the confines of the Guild for the first time, he thought she must be a hallucination brought on from too much time alone.

'Fourteen?'

The blue suits came for him every time he acted out. This time he had bitten a white coat during a dental examination. He'd wanted to see if he could make the white coat feel something, *anything*, but all Peter had done was make him bleed and the white coat's expression had remained vacant. The blue suits escorted him to an examination room. He'd lost count of the number of times he'd been inside one of these rooms. Once upon a time he used to keep track but when he realised the visits would never stop he gave up keeping count. He hadn't seen the point in carrying on. Now, the two blue suits forced him into the familiar green leather chair and they tightened the straps around his ankles and wrists. They pulled them tighter than necessary and they pinched and caught at the hairs on his skin.

'That'll do,' the nurse said and she shooed the blue suits away. Once they were gone, she turned to Peter and he saw her face for the first time. She looked at him from under the dark tendrils that had come loose from the bun on the back of her head and all of Peter's anger melted away in a moment. The door slid closed and once the nurse had heard the thud of its automatic lock clicking into place she started unfastening the straps.

'Peter Fenwick, I assume?' she said. Her voice sounded like velvet.

'Um ... experiment fourteen,' he corrected. She wandered around him and he felt suddenly hot and exposed in his green gown.

'I think Peter will do just nicely. As long as you don't mind?' Her brown eyes shone when she spoke. 'I'm Shura.'

'You don't seem qualified to be a doctor,' Peter said. The thought had fallen out of his brain, through his mouth and onto the floor before he'd had a moment to process it.

'I'm a nurse,' she said. 'And I'm perfectly qualified to carry out what we're here for today.'

'What I mean is, you don't seem qualified to work . . . at the Guild. You're not . . . brain dead,' Peter said in a rush, keen to explain his clumsy comment.

'No, I'm not brain dead.' And then she smiled, as if to prove it.

It was the first real smile Peter had seen since arriving at the Guild all those years ago, when he was just a child, and he couldn't look directly at her for too long for fear of crying. The way her thin but perfectly rounded lips curved, the right side a little more than the left . . . how the sides of her eyes creased . . . the slight breathy laugh that escaped when she flashed her crooked front teeth at him. There was so much beauty in that smile that Peter couldn't help but grin himself.

'And neither are you, it seems!' She laughed but then quickly put a finger to her lips. She pulled the last buckle loose on Peter's right ankle, ran to the door with a skip and pressed her ear up against it. 'I don't think they'll hear us if we talk quietly.'

'Why are you doing this?' Peter whispered.

'What? Being a decent human being?' She raised her eyebrows. When Peter nodded, she simply said, 'It costs nothing to be kind.'

'You'd be surprised,' Peter said. 'In this place, it seems to cost the earth. Why are you even working for the Guild?'

'Family tradition. My mum worked here before me. Although things were different when she was here. It wasn't as cruel back then and I didn't want to follow in her footsteps but you know what the Guild are like. They can be . . . persuasive.'

'I know that only too well,' he said waving the hem of his hideous gown. 'I don't wear this as a fashion statement. But why aren't you all . . . zombified like the rest of them?'

'You'd be surprised at how many of the white coats here aren't. Some of us here just want to help people. It's just the Feelers who need to be . . . well, zombified, I guess. And it doesn't hurt if you have acting skills when it's called for.' Shura straightened out her face and blinked mechanically.

'That's even more depressing. How many white coats who still have their feelings still carried out the tests on me? Because this is definitely the first time anyone has spoken to me like a human being.'

'Shhh!' She hushed as he started to raise his voice. 'If we get caught we might both be on the receiving end of a couple of hundred volts.'

'They're not going to hear us if you turn that thing on. It'll drown us out.' Peter pointed to the grey machine that had come to haunt his nightmares.

'Good thinking!' Shura flipped a couple of blue switches and turned a dial. She took up the two black discs that were attached to the machine by coiled wires and placed their metal surfaces face down on the leather chair. 'You're going to have to scream, though,' she said, her finger on the final switch. 'They'll be expecting to hear you.'

Peter smiled, happy at the thought of getting one over on the Guild. 'It's better when it's fake.'

And so Peter screamed and groaned, while Shura laughed. They had a snatched, whispered conversation in between the fake cries and when Peter went back to his four whitewashed walls, he didn't feel angry any more. How could he when he could close his eyes and see *Shura*?

20

Peter

The smoke had led Cherry to a rundown house. The windows were boarded up, an old three-piece suite and a broken TV had been dumped in the overgrown front garden and the gate was completely rusted over and sealed shut. The place looked abandoned and yet the black tornado of smoke that was swirling out of the chimney was a sure sign that this was where Cherry would find Peter.

Cherry was unsure of what she was going to say when she saw Peter. She just knew she needed to get to him as soon as possible. She pulled herself up and over the gate, struggling in the process because Loneliness had hooked its arms around her waist to try to stop her. She dropped to the other side and looked up at the house, watching the smoke rise and fade away.

What do I say? What. Do. I. Say? 'Hi, remember me? Your one and only friend from when we were children? We bonded over the weird shit we could see that no one else could and then I watched you get dragged away by men in blue coats which coincidentally has just happened to a friend of mine so it turns out, you've shown up just as I need your help! Oh, and how have you been?' Cherry rubbed her face with her hands and muttered, 'Just knock on the door,' and walked up to the front door.

There was no door handle or knocker so she pulled her cardigan sleeve over her fist and hammered on the wood. She was certain she could hear footsteps approaching the door but nobody opened it. Smoke started to pour out of the rectangular hole where a letterbox flap used to be.

'Peter? That ... that *is* you ... isn't it?'

'Who is it?' replied a low, gravelly voice.

'Erm ... Cherry. Cherry Redgrave. Do you remember me?'

'*Cherry?*' A sooty hand appeared through the letterbox hole and it pulled the door open just enough so that an eye could peer through the crack.

'Yeah, I'm Cherry. We went to school together. When we were like ... seven, I think.'

'Cherry ... *Redgrave?* I did know someone with that name once.'

'Well, that was me. I'm Cherry Redgrave.'

'Prove it.'

'Prove it? How?'

There was a pause and then he said, 'I told Cherry something when we were kids that I haven't told anyone since. I shared a name with her. A name for *something*. What was that name?'

Cherry nodded. 'It's a name I still use today. Meddlum. You and I can see Meddlums. I saw yours earlier – that's what led me here – and it's terrifying.'

Peter flung the door wide open and pawed at Cherry's shoulders until she was in his embrace, smoke engulfing them both.

'I,' he sobbed, 'thought,' another sob, 'I'd never,' more sobbing, 'see you again.' Sob. His chest heaved against Cherry's and his fingers dug deep into her neck. She hugged him back, hard.

'I didn't think I'd ever see you again, either.'

The moment Peter had been dragged from school and bundled into the back of a van flashed through Cherry's mind. She remembered the rush of fear that had coursed through her veins that her fate may be the same, but most of all she remembered the icy touch of Loneliness as it plunged its hands into her stomach and tied it into knots. It had kept a firm grip on her heart for months and had given it a firm squeeze each time she had turned to where Peter used to sit and seen his empty seat. Cherry had been certain her friend had been lost to her for ever but now he was here, a man so unknown to her but there was a familiarity there too that made

251

her eyes sting with tears she didn't know she'd needed to cry. Loneliness tried to reach out for her but its fingers fell short.

'Why are you wearing pyjamas?' he said, sniffing.

Cherry rolled her eyes over his shoulder and ignored the question. 'What happened to you? Where did you go?' she asked instead.

'The Guild. It's a long story. Come inside, quickly.'

Peter let go of Cherry and pulled her inside. He leaned out of the door, looked left, then right, before slamming the door closed. Cherry found herself standing at the foot of the smoking Meddlum. It looked down at her with less fire in its eyes than it had done earlier. The ceiling to the bottom floor of the house had caved in, Cherry guessed, due to water damage, as half the roof was also gone. This meant Peter's Meddlum could stand upright in the house. It was quite the sight to behold.

'This way.' Peter walked past Cherry, through his Meddlum's legs and disappeared into the smoke.

'Didn't anyone ever tell you smoking is bad for you?'

'You're hilarious! I've been trying to quit for years.' His voice was getting further away.

'Where have you gone? It's kind of hard to see around here, Peter, and this house is a bit of a deathtrap.'

'Safest place for an escapee!' he said, his hand appearing through the black cloud. Cherry took hold of it and he gently guided her through the house and into a back room where his Meddlum was too big to follow and he closed the door behind them, tendrils of misty smoke sucking at its edges like tentacles.

'She's a little monstrous but ... she's actually quite friendly,' Peter said.

'She?'

'I think she's a she, don't you? And she was a feisty lady, from what I can remember.'

'From what you can remember?' Cherry asked, frowning. She didn't understand.

'I can't see her any more.' Peter pointed to his eyes. 'I wear these lenses that—'

'What? Why do you have a pair of those?' Cherry cried.

'You know what the lenses do?' When Cherry nodded yes, Peter said, 'Please, sit down. We've got a lot to talk about.'

Cherry looked around her and saw that the room they were in was mostly bare. A few dustsheets lay in the corner along with a large rucksack and there were small puddles of melted wax from where Peter had been lighting candles just as he was doing now. He struck a match, lit five candles of varying size and then carried them over to Cherry on two halves of a broken plate.

'I try not to let the wax get on the floor.' He shrugged, letting wax drip onto the floor. 'Please. Sit,' he said again. Cherry was about to ask where when Peter crouched and sat cross-legged on the floor, placing the candles in front of him, so Cherry did the same.

'You said you were in the Guild?' Cherry asked.

'That's right,' Peter said. 'You've heard of it?'

'Yes, but only recently.'

'Lucky you,' Peter said. 'My brain still buzzes from time to time.'

'What do you mean?'

Peter regarded Cherry for a second. 'How much do you know about the Guild?' he asked. 'Do you know what they do?'

'Only a little bit. I don't know much, to be honest. Just that it's a kind of headquarters for people like us to keep an eye on people like us.'

Peter shook his head sadly. 'That's not strictly true. The Guild isn't so much a HQ for our kind. It's more like a laboratory. The Guild want to know why we are the way we are, so they conduct tests on us. It's genetic, they know that much. We inherit it.'

'We *inherit* it? Genetically? From a parent?' Cherry asked.

'Mm-hmm. Always from the mother,' Peter said.

Cherry didn't have a mother. Biologically she did, of course, but the woman who had given birth to Cherry had decided to give up her baby from the moment she found out she was pregnant. Cherry had never known her and had never had any need to, but with those four words, Peter had changed that.

'Do you think that's why your mum left, because she didn't want to see you go through it?'

Peter shrugged. 'Maybe. That could be why your mum put you up for adoption too.'

'You remember that about me?'

Peter nodded. 'And I remember your dad's *amazing* cherry pie!'

'That's sweet of you, to remember.' Cherry smiled at the thought of her father.

'Your dad and his baking are hard to forget.' Peter's eyes glinted with the memory.

'Can you tell me more about the Guild?' Cherry asked. She wanted to talk about her father some more but she needed to find out as much as she could about the Guild if she was going to help Chase.

'Why are you so curious?' Peter cocked his head to one side. 'What's got you so interested?'

Cherry thought of Chase, unconscious, being dragged away from her. Did she tell Peter straightaway? As much as their reunion seemed amicable, Cherry couldn't be sure if Peter could be trusted immediately. Not when his hate-filled Meddlum was quite literally as big as a house. She needed to tread carefully until she could be sure about Peter.

'I'm new to this,' she said. 'I only found out there were more people like you and me about forty-eight hours ago. And I had no idea the Guild existed before then either. I figure the more information I have, the better.' She shrugged, trying her best to look unconcerned and nonchalant.

'Well, the Guild isn't for people like us. Not really. That's how it started, I think, but that's not how it carried on. The Guild was founded by people like us centuries ago and its aim was to help people learn how to use their ability, so they started conducting research to understand us better. They thought finding out why we are the way we are would be the first step. Took them years to figure out it was genetic, and then over the years they stopped trying to help us. It just became about finding out as much as they could about us, and then it became about stopping us. They thought what we could do was dangerous so they decided to track down everyone who had this ability and began building a database. Then their children were tracked and their children were tracked and you can see how it evolved. You and I were never *off* their radar, Cherry. They've always known about us.'

'But Happy told me—'

'You've met Happy?' Peter growled. 'She's one of the worst!' Smoke seeped in under the door and Peter coughed.

'Happy told me they only find people when they start acting up. When they start making a scene and drawing too much attention to themselves. That's how they find us.'

'"How do you know whether someone is a serial killer until they've murdered six people?" I must have heard her say that a million times. Utter bollocks. They've known about us from the day we were born. I caused trouble from an early age which was why they took me away when we were in school. If you've only just found out about the Guild then you must have only just started causing trouble for them.' Peter raised his eyebrows in question.

'All I did was bake a few bloody cakes,' Cherry huffed defensively.

'Doesn't matter. You started using what you can do in a way that attracted too much attention. The Guild are all about containing it. They bring people in who have been messing around with normal people's feelings and they tell everyone they're being taken to prison but that's not true. They experiment on them, to try to make them normal.'

'Normal? As in ... *not* able to see anything?'

'Nothing at all.'

'I don't understand – why would they do that? Happy told us about those lenses that can prevent us from seeing the Meddlums. Isn't that enough?'

'They're only temporary. They don't last for ever and they don't take away our abilities for ever. Not only that, but they're linked to the Guild. Anything you can see, they can see. It's a surefire way to get yourself caught if you're doing anything ... unsavoury. A few little twerps sit at their screens and just watch us all day long. Which is pretty gross when you think about it. They want to get as many of us wearing them while they find a better solution, something more permanent. Which is why anyone who gets dragged into the Guild wakes up with a pair already "installed".'

'Happy said there was a two-year waiting list . . . '

'*Sure* there is. They just say that to make us want them more. It makes them sound more exclusive which means if you get a pair, you feel *lucky* to have them. It's a mind game, and the Guild loves mind games.'

'Can't you just . . . take them out?'

'Once they're in, they're in until either the Guild removes them or the system they're linked to goes down. The Guild's endgame is to find a cure and they've become more ruthless as time as gone on. They've tried splicing, dicing, cognitive behavioural therapy, electric therapy . . . you name it, they've already tried it. They hit dead ends and then kept hitting them as hard as they could just to make sure they haven't missed something.' Peter stared into the flames of the candles, his eyes bright in the glow. His voice dropped to a whisper. 'For so long they thought it was something in the eye itself. So they kept taking them out. People would wake up and their eyes would just be . . . gone. They cut them open, trying to find anything that pointed to an answer. It took jars full of discarded and mutilated eyeballs before the researchers decided to try something new.' Peter blinked furiously a few times. 'It made me really appreciate my sight – normal and abnormal.'

'Oh, Peter.' Cherry wanted to reach over and take his hand but he crossed his arms, signalling that that part of the conversation was over. She thought it best to move the conversation on so she said, 'So let me recap. You were taken away in a van as a child.'

'Correct.' Peter nodded.

'And you were taken to the Guild.'

'Correct.'

'Where people like us are experimented on to try to find a way to fix our sight.'

'Correct.'

'So we can live normally.'

'Yup.'

'At least that's what they tell themselves.'

Peter nodded.

'But really they don't understand us and think we're dangerous.'

'That's right.'

'And most of us end up blind, or worse, dead?'

Peter nodded again.

Cherry's stomach dropped at the thought of Chase being held by these people. What were they doing to him? 'How long were you there?'

'Until yesterday.' Peter dipped his fingers in the wax of the candle nearest him.

'What?' The word snagged in her throat.

'Yesterday,' Peter repeated.

'So you've been in the Guild ever since you were taken away as a child? And they just ... let you go?'

Peter raised an eyebrow and said, 'Would I be sat in an abandoned house lighting crappy candles if they'd just let me go?'

Cherry leaned forward eagerly. 'You *escaped*?'

'Yes. Like I said, this is the safest place for an escapee.'

'I thought that was a weird joke that I just didn't get!' Something occurred to Cherry. 'How did you survive in there for so long if so many people died in there?'

'Well, it helps to have a mother who works there.'

'Your *mother*?'

'Turns out she left me to work for the Guild.'

'Ooookay.' Cherry stood up quickly, causing her head to spin. 'Oookay. This is a lot to take in. I just need a second.'

She tried to organise her thoughts into some kind of order but there were too many of them clamouring for attention. She paced around the room and Peter simply watched her, his head swaying one way and then the other as Cherry moved from wall to wall. Eventually she stopped and turned to look at Peter. 'Okay. All right. Start from the top.'

'My mother left to work at the Guild. She's one of the few who can see both good and bad Meddlums so she's got more reason to want to switch off that kind of sight than anyone. When I was taken in, I guess her maternal side hadn't been entirely eliminated by all of the Guild's experimentation so she convinced the people in charge to leave me alone. I was put into a special unit instead. Solitary confinement, basically. It was a lonely existence but at least I was mostly untouched.'

'Mostly?' Cherry started to pace again, breathing in for three steps and out for the next three.

'The solitude got to me every few months, I hated it, so I acted up now and then and they would take me in for electrocution therapy. It would . . . keep me calm, more docile, for a while. I was less trouble for them that way.'

'Why didn't they just remove your feelings permanently?'

Peter gestured towards the smoke that was still filtering in underneath the door. 'Have you seen her? They couldn't get her off me. They tried hacking her down like a tree at one point but she just wouldn't budge. Our *attachment* is a little too strong. She loves me too much. That's why they never let me go. She was too big. All they could do was return her to her original, less real form, lock us up and keep up the electrocution whenever they thought it was necessary. They didn't care about the effect it had on me,' Peter added bitterly.

Cherry looked at him with sympathy. 'I can't imagine it . . . what you went through. All those years, locked up. I'm so sorry that happened to you.'

'It's not your fault,' Peter said quietly.

'But still, I *am* so, so sorry,' Cherry said. 'So how did you get out?'

'After all those years locked up there, I eventually found a weak link. The Guild employees have to undergo electric therapy every three months to keep them numb and that takes its toll on their memories.'

'Every three months?!' Cherry gasped.

Peter nodded sadly. 'They think feelings get in the way

of their so-called law enforcement. Fewer real feelings equals better judgement, is how they justify it, but it's another excuse to cover up the fact their "better judgement" means they're bringing people in for the smallest "crimes" simply so they have more guinea pigs to experiment on. So many kids were brought in after accidentally making someone feel something they weren't supposed to.'

'They bring in kids?' Cherry shouldn't have been surprised, especially as she knew Peter had been taken away as a child, but she'd so been wishing that had been the exception rather than the rule.

'Mainly teenagers. Kissing is a minefield.'

Cherry touched her lips and her mouth filled with Belonging. *Chase.*

'Teenagers being free and easy with their kisses is a problem for the Guild, especially if the teenager hates the world. One misjudged kiss and all hell could break loose.'

'I didn't really do much kissing when I was younger. The little bit that I did do probably caused Confusion more than anything.' Cherry shook her herself. She was getting off topic. 'Tell me about what the therapy does to memories.'

'The human body can only handle so much of it and continuous treatment meant that Feelers like Happy became more and more forgetful. One of the guards would bring me food three times a day and yesterday the guard who brought me my lunch forgot to lock the door to my cell. It was the first time it's ever happened so I knew it was my one and only chance to get out of there. I found a spare uniform in one of the supply cupboards and then I just had to put on a gormless expression and leave. Once I was in the uniform, I looked like all the other workers and no one noticed me. I just needed to get out of there. They were starting to get desperate.'

'What do you mean?'

'Bad Meddlums are becoming bigger. The suicide rate of people like us is at an all-time high. There have even been some cases of PTSD where Meddlums have been so monstrous, they've frightened people to their wits' end. The Guild doesn't know how to help people with these kind of mental health issues so they just up their dosages, ramp up their therapies and experiment more aggressively.'

Cherry was at a loss for words. The more she heard about the Guild, the more desperate she became. How was she going to get Chase out of there?

'They will have noticed I'm gone by now, though,' Peter continued. 'This is where it gets dangerous. Getting caught after I've escaped will be game over for me. They won't just put me back in a cell. They'll make an example of me to send a message.'

'Why haven't you been caught already? You've got lenses, right?' Peter nodded and blinked hard. Cherry went on, 'Surely they can just hack into your sight and find out where you are, can't they?'

'They should be able to,' he said, a look of confusion on his face. 'So either they're happy to be rid of me or there's a serious glitch in their system.'

'So you can't get caught?'

'Doesn't seem that way, no.'

'And you can't go back?'

'No way.'

'Not even for a friend?' Cherry pushed. She knew she asking a lot from him but she didn't see that she had any other choice.

Peter held her gaze and then said, 'Your turn to tell me everything. What's going on?'

'They took a friend of mine. Chase Masters.'

'He's like us?'

'He is. He sees good feelings.'

'Lucky bastard.'

'Not really,' Cherry said. 'It made him pretty bitter about life – he couldn't understand why he couldn't have the happiness other people had. He was ... a difficult man at times.'

'He sounds lovely.'

'He *is*,' Cherry insisted. 'He just thought he was alone. Didn't we think the same at one point? But he's a good man underneath it all – only now he's gone. They've taken him.'

'Why?' Peter asked. 'Why did they come for him?'

'We sort of ... started a fight. A turf war, you could call it.'

'What the hell does that mean?'

Cherry sighed. She didn't have time to go into all the details. 'I've been baking cakes for years to help people but he started making drinks to cause trouble. People were starting to become reckless. We kept trying to outdo each other and the whole town got caught in the crossfire and everyone, well, everyone went a bit ... mad.'

'That sounds like enough to make the Guild intervene.'

'Happy paid us a visit and gave us some Normality to fix things. But she said I had to stop using my gift to help people otherwise I'd be taken away. Either that or I had to become a Feeler.'

'So why did they take this Chase instead?'

'I don't know!' Cherry cried. 'I thought they were coming after me but they took him. And now he's probably going to have his brain fried or have his eyes gauged out of their sockets or end up ...' Cherry couldn't bring herself to say the word. *Dead.*

'So what are you going to do?' Peter asked. Cherry stopped in front of him and looked at him, her eyes full of hope. 'Not a chance in hell,' he said, standing up and backing away. 'No. Way.'

'Peter, please.'

'I'm not going back in there!'

'They might kill him!'

'If I go back, they'll kill *me*! I don't know who this guy is. I don't owe him anything. *And* he sounds like a bit of a prick!' Peter put his hands on his head and pulled at his hair, hard, for a few seconds. He spun around with his fingernails digging into his scalp. He looked utterly mad. Cherry took a step back and wondered exactly how much electrocution he'd experienced over the years. 'This isn't a game, Cherry! If I get caught, I won't be coming out again. If you want to risk your life for him, then fine but ... I can't.'

Cherry took in the panic in his eyes, the desperation on his face, and her heart sank. She couldn't ask him to go back there for her. It was too much. There had to be another way. 'Okay, I'm sorry. I shouldn't have asked. I get it – it was too much.' Cherry dropped her tone, trying to soothe him. 'But do you think you could maybe help me from the outside instead? You could tell me where it is, draw me a map and tell me anything I need to watch out for. And *who* I need to watch out for?'

'Cherry ... ' Peter warned.

'*Please*. I can't do this without you.'

'You shouldn't be doing this at all.'

'I can't leave him there.'

'Like you left me, you mean?' Peter spat.

Cherry was stunned. 'Peter – I was seven. What could I have done?'

'I don't *know*. Something. *Anything*.'

'I had no idea the Guild even existed. I thought you'd been taken away to ... to an asylum or something! I was a child. No one would have believed me if I'd told them you weren't crazy and I could see the monsters too. I would have ended up right there with you.'

Peter dropped his head, deflated, the fight gone from him as quickly as it had reared up. 'I know. I'm sorry. There's nothing you could've done.'

'You don't have to come with me, Peter. I understand. I *completely* understand. Just ... please help me. You know what it's like in there. Don't let someone else suffer if they don't have to. I can't leave him in there but I need your help. Help me save Chase.'

Images flashed through Peter's mind. Blue suits, bottles of pills, gloved hands holding his nose, bleeding eye sockets, jars full of eyeballs staring back at him, grey skin and finally, a lifeless, limp hand with a yellow rag tied around the ring finger dangling from under a crisp white sheet. Peter squeezed his eyes shut and shook his head, hoping the memories would fall from his head and burn in the flames of the candle. He opened his eyes and saw Loneliness pulling at the boards nailed to the window, trying to reach out for Cherry. Peter sighed.

'What kind of a name is "Chase" anyway?'

Peter had been kept in solitary confinement for most of his time in the Guild so it turned out that he didn't know what the rest of it looked like outside the section he'd been kept in. He didn't even know how big the Guild was. What he did know was that it was in Cornwall, somewhere called Warleggan, and that it was all underground.

'I was planning on finding part-time jobs here and there, and working my way up the country and then flying abroad. I didn't bargain on finding you on my first stop,' he said while he mapped out what he knew of the Guild with charcoal on the floorboards.

'You mean, you had no idea I was here?' Cherry asked, kneeling next to him to look at his work.

'Nope. There's no way I could've known, is there?'

'Wow. If anything's going to make you believe in fate it's something like that, eh?'

'I guess. Now, Happy is the worst,' Peter said, getting back to the matter at hand. He drew a smiley face on the floor.

'What about Grumpy?' Cherry smirked.

'Who's that?' Peter asked. 'I've not met them.' He scratched his head.

'No it's . . . come on! *Snow White*?'

'Who's she?' Peter asked.

'Forget it. Remind me later to make you watch that movie. OK, so Happy is the worst. Who else?'

'For the most part, no one else will be too concerned with you but you'll definitely be on Lonely's radar because that Meddlum has been buzzing around you like a fly since we were kids.' Peter pointed towards the thumping sound coming from the patio doors. Loneliness was sat with his back against them and was banging his head over and over.

'Happy and Lonely. Got it.'

'Conveniently, everyone who works for the Guild wears specific colours, depending on their roles. The white lab coats are, obviously, the doctors. They carry out all the experiments. Most are completely brainwashed but a few of them only pretend to have had treatments. If you can find one of the normal ones, you might be able to get them on your side.'

'How do you know that?'

'There was a nurse,' Peter said softly. 'She was kind to me. She never carried out the treatments on me when she was supposed to. She'd turn the machine on without me connected to it and I'd scream for a while so no one got suspicious, and then we'd just talk. She helped me. She stayed at the Guild so she could help people like me.'

'Oh, yes?' Cherry nudged Peter's arm and his face flickered for a moment, like his heart was remembering something, something that made him look like he'd missed the bottom step in a flight of stairs and fallen further than he thought. And as quickly as it was there, it was gone again.

'The blue suits are the guards and the henchmen,' Peter went on and Cherry didn't probe him any further. 'They do all the heavy lifting and all the dirty work but it's everyone in yellow you really need to watch out for.

They're the Feelers. It's their job to watch everyone. You sneeze, you wipe your arse, you dump your feelings in someone else's cake, they'll know about it.'

'Yes,' Cherry said, 'I'm starting to realise exactly how much Feelers can see.'

'If you don't get caught, you probably won't see any of the Gelders,' Peter said.

'Gelders?'

'The Guild Elders. They're the ones in charge.'

Cherry blew out her cheeks in frustration.

'What's wrong?' Peter asked.

'It's just all a bit ... mad, isn't it? White coats. Blue suits. Feelers in yellow. And now bloody Gelders. It's a lot to get my head around.'

'Things do go mad when you've got a bunch of people who want to control something as uncontrollable as feelings. They're never going to get that control because it's impossible. The more they try, the madder it gets, and they fail all over again. What started out as a quest for knowledge about something potentially incredible and life-changing and *good* has turned into a lust for power fed by the fear of something they can't understand. For people like my mother, that cycle will never end and so it just keeps going on and on and on.'

Cherry let Peter's words sink in. This was so much bigger than she'd anticipated. 'Something potentially incredible?' she asked. 'Do you *like* seeing Meddlums?'

'I did, before they put these lenses on me. You can

pinpoint exactly how someone's feeling without even talking to them, without knowing a single thing about them. Then imagine the possibilities once you do get to know them. You could unravel their most complex issues and thoughts within minutes.'

'You sound like you'd make an excellent therapist,' Cherry said.

'That's the plan. These lenses might mean I don't see Meddlums anymore but I still want to help people. Like you do.'

'Just be careful it doesn't backfire on you like it did for me.'

'You could always ... come with me?' Peter neatened the outline of the smiley face with his finger, avoiding her gaze.

'What do you mean?' Cherry asked, also avoiding his gaze.

'It's easier to hide from the Guild when you know they're watching. We could change our names, dye our hair, keep moving around so they can't find us ...'

'I don't want to live like that,' Cherry said.

'You don't really have a choice now. Especially if you rescue your friend. You'll always be running from them.'

'That's different,' Cherry said.

'Why?'

'Because I'll be—' She caught herself before the words slipped out onto the floor and ruined Peter's drawings.

'With him?' he finished for her anyway.

Cherry fiddled with a splinter jutting out from one of the floorboards and didn't say anything.

'I get that,' Peter whispered. 'I do, really. Don't feel embarrassed by it. If I had the chance to run away with Shura, I would have taken it.'

Cherry hadn't shied away from saying the words because she'd been embarrassed. She'd shied away because she'd surprised herself. Something that she hadn't thought through properly had almost fallen out of her mouth and that rarely happened. Cherry was an over-thinker. Her anxiety had conditioned her to be that way. Yet somehow, when it came to Chase, she defied that trait in herself. When it came to Chase, Cherry was involuntarily impulsive and while it made her hands tremble and her knees go weak, it also made her heart swell.

'Is Shura the nurse?'

'Yes ... she is.' Peter rubbed out the smiley face he'd drawn and wiped his hands on his jeans. 'I don't really have any more to tell you. I've told you everything I know.'

'That's okay,' Cherry said, once again choosing not to push Peter when it was clear he didn't want to talk. 'You've told me plenty. What I need to figure out now is how to get in.'

'The place is underground and security is round the clock. They have cameras everywhere and they'll see you coming from miles off.'

'So it's impossible?'

'Pretty much.' Peter raised his shoulders in apology.

'There's got to be something.' Cherry wasn't going to be put off. 'An air vent? A rubbish chute? Anything?'

'It's just not going to be that easy! And you're stealing back a *man*. He won't exactly be inconspicuous when you try to smuggle him back out.'

'There's got to be a way!' Cherry threw her hands up in frustration.

'Well ... ' Peter began. 'There might be a way but it's suicide.'

Cherry frowned. 'I'll try anything. What is it?'

'Getting caught.'

'Oh.'

'Yeah. *Oh*.' Peter shook his head and laughed at his own stupidity. 'I told you it was suicide. It's a mad idea. Don't—'

'If I were to get caught,' Cherry interrupted, 'hypothetically, of course ... where would they take me?'

'Cherry ... ' Peter warned.

'Just hypothetically!'

Peter narrowed his eyes. He didn't believe this was hypothetical and yet he still found himself saying, 'They'd probably take you to a holding cell in the first instance while the higher-ups were alerted. You're probably of interest to them so certain people will want to be told you're in the Guild.'

'Okay. Will Chase be in a holding cell?'

'If he was only taken today then yeah, most likely he'd

be in a cell. They won't start experimenting on him until they've run all the preliminary tests on him. That gives you at least twenty-four hours.'

'Peter ... ,' Cherry said slowly. 'I think I've got a plan but ... I'm going to need your help.'

'I can't go back in there! Please!' Peter began digging his nails into his scalp again.

'It's okay! I'm not asking you to!' Cherry looped her fingers around his wrists and stroked them with her thumbs until he loosened his grip on his skull. 'Just answer me something. Your Meddlum ... she creates smoke when you feel hate, right?'

'Right,' he mumbled.

'And the more hate you feel, the more smoke she gives off?'

'That's about it, yeah.' He looked up at her and Cherry smiled at him.

'Well, then. Let's fire her up.'

21

Captured

Cherry thwacked her spoon against the side of the mixing bowl. The batter sprayed across every surface of her kitchen and slopped onto the floor, while she skipped around the central island.

'I'm baaaaking agaaaain!' she sang. 'And there's nothing you can do about it!' Cherry picked up a bag of Cheery chocolate chips and twirled it around her head so that most of them ended up on the floor rather than in the bowl.

'Baaaking is really great, filling Plymouth with lots of HATE!' Cherry yelled.

She mustered up as much Hate as she could in her mouth and spat it into the bowl. She stirred the mixture furiously.

'Cakes and cookies are a must, when sharing out your Love and Lust!'

She scooped up a handful of pistachios, put them in her mouth and chewed them into tiny pieces, concentrating all of her sexual desire into them. She opened her lips and let the masticated mess fall into the batter.

'All my treats must be filled, with feelings to piss off the Guild!'

Cherry had started to sweat. She put the bowl down and listened, hoping to hear the sound of a van pulling up outside, but all she could hear was Loneliness tapping its foot.

'Are you serious? Where are they?' Cherry hit the handle of the wooden spoon that was sticking out of the bowl. The end in the batter flicked up and a large dollop of the batter hit Cherry on the forehead and slowly slid down her face. 'Brilliant,' she said wiping it out of her eye. 'The Guild have been sniffing around here for the last week and now that I need them, they're nowhere to be seen,' she huffed. 'They're probably too busy prodding at Chase's eyeballs with hot pokers or shoving bolts of electricity through his hippocampus. Oh God, this is impossible.' She put her head against the kitchen counter, a chocolate chip sticking itself to her cheek. Cherry was getting ready to throw in the towel when there was a knock at the door.

'*Finally.* COMING!' She yelled, grabbing her coat as she skipped through the shop, but her feet slowed and shuffled the last few feet to the door when she saw George standing at the window. 'Urrggghhh,' she groaned, unlocking the latch.

'Lovely to see you too!' George said, an amused look on his face.

'Sorry,' she said, taking her coat off again. 'Sorry, George – I'm just ... expecting someone.'

'Oh, yeah? It's not Chase by any chance, is it?'

'Erm ... no. He's ... not here but ... he's not who I'm expecting.' Cherry sighed. 'It's complicated.'

'Sounds it. Well, anyway, I won't keep you. I just wanted to say thanks for everything.'

'Thanks?' Cherry asked in surprise. 'What for?'

'For everything,' George said. 'I mean it. I'm so much happier now and it's mostly down to you so ... thank you. People just don't say it much so I wanted to say it to you: thank you.'

Even with everything going on, Cherry knew how much this meant to her friend, to be able to say those words to her. She smiled, trying to cover her feelings about what was going on, but George wasn't fooled.

'Cherry ... is everything all right? You seem ... very on edge.'

'I'm fine. Just a lot going on. Up here.' She tapped her temple and the chocolate chip fell off her cheek. 'Oh God, I must look like such a mess.'

'I hate to think what your kitchen must look like,' George said, laughing. 'Look, is there anything I can help with? Anything at all?' George stepped closer to her.

'No, I'm fine.' Cherry shook her head, her mind full of thoughts of the Guild and Chase and Peter.

'Clearly you're not fine, Cherry. You're a mess. And I don't just mean from the baking.' He stepped closer again.

'I know but ... '

'Please let me help?' He placed his hands on her shoulders.

'I ... '

'Please.'

He squeezed her shoulders lightly and an idea ignited in Cherry's brain. It took hold like a fire spreading through a forest and before her morals had a chance to snuff it out she threw her arms around George and kissed him with everything she had. George dropped his hands in shock, several thoughts racing through his mind. *What about Chase? Is she confused? You did offer to help, after all. This isn't okay though, is it? She's climbing me like a squirrel on a tree! WHAT IS SHE DOING?!*

George very firmly pulled Cherry's hands away from his neck and pushed her gently away.

'Cherry ... I know you're ... upset ... about something ... but ... '

'I. Am. So. Sorry.' Cherry stepped away and turned around, too embarrassed to look him in the eye. 'I don't know what came over me.'

Cherry knew what she'd done was wrong but she was desperate. She needed to get to Chase and the simple act of baking had not brought forth the wrath of the Guild. It had suddenly hit her that she needed to somehow impact the life of someone else before they would intervene and George had been in the wrong place at the wrong time.

'It's okay. I mean, it's not okay but I forgive you. You're going through something ...' George's vision started to swim. He shook his head, trying to straighten it out but his eyes kept drifting to the left. '... you're ... Chase's ... squirrel ...'

George fell forwards and Cherry managed to catch him but they both hit the floor with a small thud. Cherry tried to turn him over as best she could but he was heavy and she could only get him onto his side. Quickly, Cherry ran behind the counter, found a Post-it note and a pen and scrawled out an apology. She stuck it on George's head, grabbed her coat and ran into the street.

'YOU CAN'T IGNORE THAT!' Cherry shouted. 'I HAVE INTERVENED AND YOU NEED TO COME AND GET ME OR SO HELP ME I WILL TURN THIS ENTIRE TOWN UPSIDE DO—'

THUNK.

Cherry felt a twinge in her right buttock, like something had bitten her. She twisted her leg and saw a small dart with yellow feathers sticking out. '*Ouch*,' she said as she pulled it and the needle twisted out of her flesh. A strange warm sensation started to spread down her leg, up her side, and into her arm. Her fingers could no longer grip the dart and it fell to the floor. Cherry stumbled a few steps backwards towards the bakery and slumped against the door. She slid down onto the pavement, her head lolled to the side and just before her heavy eyelids closed, she saw the blur of three blue dots moving towards her, followed by a bright yellow glow.

22

Professionals

Cherry awoke, her skin prickling with cold and her eyes streaming. She blinked a few times. Everything was a blur and when she reached a hand up to wipe the tears away, her other hand followed. *Handcuffs,* she registered. They were cold, tight and, in her opinion, unnecessary. Cherry blinked again and again but still couldn't figure out why her eyes were stinging.

'It'll wear off in a few minutes. Your eyes just need to get used to the lenses.'

The lenses. They'd fitted her with lenses. Cherry felt an immediate sense of loss. She couldn't imagine a world where she couldn't see Loneliness or anyone else's feelings. Strangely, without Loneliness in her sight, she felt its presence all the more.

'Chase?' Cherry croaked. 'Chase, is that you?!' She could only see a blurry outline of someone across what she thought was a corridor. The more she rubbed at her eyes the clearer the image became.

'Yeah, it's me. I wish it wasn't, though. I wish I wasn't here and I'd really rather you didn't see me like this.' Chase sighed.

'Oh God. Oh God, oh God, what have they done to you? Are you hurt?' Cherry gasped. 'Did they electrocute you?'

'No! No, no, I'm fine, nothing like that. They haven't hurt me yet. I'm just ...'

Cherry's vision was starting to clear and Chase came into focus. He was wearing what looked like a pale green hospital gown that came halfway down his thighs. He was sat with his back against the wall, and his hands were handcuffed too.

'It's worse when I stand up,' he admitted. 'It's not really long enough but it helps that you came dressed for the occasion too.' Chase tried to laugh but it sounded hollow. Cherry looked down at herself and saw the reason why she was so cold.

'Oh, how lovely. Matching outfits. I've always wanted to be in one of those couples.'

'That makes one of us.'

'At least I've still got my underwear on,' she said, groaning as she pulled herself up to sitting. The feeling was starting to come back in her legs.

'Lucky you. My bare balls are touching the floor over here! They're the coldest they've ever been.'

'Then please, I beg you, don't stand up.'

Their attempts at humour were falling short of the mark but Cherry did find a little comfort in hearing his voice again. He was alive and he seemed to be OK. That was a start.

'How did you land yourself in here?' Chase asked and instantly Cherry's face flushed with embarrassment.

'I ... er ... I kissed George,' she said fiddling with the end of her gown.

'Oh ...' Chase's face fell. 'I see.'

'Not because I wanted to! I was trying to bake cakes again so that Happy or whoever would turn up but no one showed. They just weren't having it unless I truly interfered with someone's feelings. George just happened to turn up at the right time.'

'Right.'

'Don't be like that. I did it so they would bring me here, so I could save you.'

'Really?' Chase said. 'You did that for me?'

Cherry nodded. 'I couldn't leave you here.'

Chase sighed. 'I just wish it could have happened a different way.'

'I was running out of time. All I could think about was getting to you.' She smiled feebly and she could see him smile too. Cherry could now make out that she and Chase were in separate cells that were divided by a corridor, like dogs in a pound waiting for someone to come and take them home. Except the first person to approach their kennels wasn't a happy, homely family looking for a new member. It was a man in a white coat with a clipboard whose skin reflected the colour of the mint green floors.

'How are you feeling, 601?' the man said, avoiding eye contact.

'601?' Cherry asked Chase.

'I'm 598,' Chase explained wearily. 'Two other people were brought in before you, which means you're 601.'

'They've *numbered* us?' Cherry was incredulous. 'Right. Well, I'm wonderful, thanks. Aside from being naked, handcuffed and not being able to see properly, that is.'

The man didn't react – he simply scribbled on his clipboard. He jabbed a full stop on the page and said, 'Your examination will begin shortly,' before walking away.

'They're a cheerful bunch, aren't they?' Chase tried to move his legs underneath him without exposing himself.

Cherry crawled to the bars to watch the doctor walk away. 'He hardly seemed human,' she said.

'The examination is pretty standard,' Chase said. 'They prod you a bit. Weigh you, take some measurements. There's nothing too scary involved so don't worry too much.'

'It's what comes after that, that I'm terrified about,' Cherry said. 'Is there anyone around here that can hear us?'

'No guards or anything that I've seen,' Chase replied. 'There are other cells around here but I reckon everyone in them will be on our side.'

'You got that right!' an Australian accent called from somewhere along the corridor.

Even if that was the case, Cherry still didn't want to risk exposing themselves so she dropped her voice. 'I've got a plan.'

'To get us out of here?' Chase whispered.

Cherry threw up her hands. 'No, a plan to turn these cells into a nice permanent two-bedroom home. You don't mind spending the rest of our lives here, do you?' Before Chase could answer she growled, her voice rising, 'Of course it's a plan to get us out! I found an old friend who was being held here. It's a long story and I don't have time to explain everything now but he's like us, and he sees the bad stuff like me. I trust him and he told me things about this place and he said that all the lenses are linked to a central system. If we can find the control panel for the system and destroy it, then all of the lenses will go down and everyone will get their sight, their *real* sight, back again.'

'We'll see everyone's Meddlums again?' Chase crawled to the edge of his cell and knelt up against the bars.

'Since when did you call them Meddlums?'

'Since you,' he said, smiling.

'That's lovely, darling heart, but can I hear the rest of this plan?' the Australian voice called out.

'Shh!' Chase hushed.

'If we can destroy that control panel, Peter will take it from there.' Cherry knelt up against the bars of her cell too, mirroring Chase's pose.

'Peter?'

'My friend, the one who used to be in here.'

'What kind of friend?' Chase said.

'What does that matter?'

'Just seems weird, that's all.'

Was he seriously sulking? 'Really, Chase?' Cherry said gently but firmly. 'With everything that's going on, you're worried about another man? Look I trust him and so should you.' When Chase didn't respond, Cherry said more softly, 'Trust me.'

Chase's eyes softened. 'I do trust you.'

'Good, because you need to trust me now. We have to find that panel and switch it off.'

'That's it?' Chase said.

'That's it!'

'Sounds too simple, love,' said the Australian. 'Something always gets in the way.'

'We'll be fine,' Cherry said, although the chain connecting her wrists rattled against the bars of the cell as her hands shook.

'Of course we will,' Chase said. He smiled at her and she instantly felt better, knowing that they were in this together.

'601!'

Cherry jumped, the sudden shout startling her. The bars to her cell began to vibrate as they started to lift from the floor. Cherry skittered back, the floor cold against her skin, and she could feel a sore spot where the dart had hit her.

'Come forward, 601.'

Cherry pushed herself off the floor, careful to keep her hospital gown flat against her legs. She winced as the pressure from her hands caused sparks of pain to shoot up her legs. She looked down and saw that her legs were covered in scratches. She wondered if the three men in blue suits had dragged her the same way she'd seen them drag Chase: with no compassion or consideration. She walked out of her cell and into the corridor. Chase reached his hand through the bars as far as he could before the cuffs stopped him and Cherry held onto his fingers.

'We have to find that panel,' she whispered. 'And when it happens, run.'

'When what happens?' he asked.

'601. You are due for an examination. Please move forward.'

'*Just run*,' Cherry repeated urgently, before letting go of Chase's hand.

A woman stood at the end of the corridor near a small green door that had a keypad next to it, mounted on the wall. She had straw-like hair that stuck out on her shoulders, making her head look triangular, and she wore a lab coat and held a clipboard like the man that had visited a few minutes earlier. 'Follow me,' she said curtly. She slotted the card that hung by a lanyard around her neck into the reader and entered a seven-digit number. The door juddered open to reveal a long silver corridor, reminiscent of an air vent, and the smell of disinfectant stung Cherry's nostrils. She tried to pull her robe closed behind her but in doing so the front lifted higher, exposing more of her uppermost thigh. She took a deep breath. *You are in your pyjamas*, she told herself. *Really baggy, breezy pyjamas.*

Cherry followed the woman as she walked quickly down the corridor. They turned left into another corridor, this one lined with windows on one side. Cherry seized the chance to look outside – if her plan didn't work, she might never escape the Guild and she wanted to see the sky one last time – but instead all she saw was the inside of a huge grey hall. Men and women dressed in blue suits sat behind desks that lined the floor of the hall. On each desk there was a large screen displaying what looked like some kind of first-person shooter video game.

'The lenses,' Cherry said under her breath.

'What did you say?' the straw-haired woman said, turning back to see Cherry had stopped halfway down the corridor.

'Er ... the lenses you put in my eyes. They're great. Thank you,' she said through gritted teeth.

'Lenses?' the woman said, her own eyes glazing over.

Then as if a light had been switched on, 'Oh! Yes. The lenses. Marvellous, aren't they? Clearer vision means a clearer mind!' she recited. 'Follow me.'

Cherry's gaze darted over the hall, desperately trying to spot anything that looked remotely like a control panel. She was hoping for something huge and obvious. Maybe even a large sign that said *Control Panel*, but she knew it would never be that easy. Most likely it was small and discreet, hidden away and impossible to find. All of a sudden she had an overwhelming certainty that she wasn't going to be able to pull this off.

'In here.' The woman opened a white door and the light that spilled out was blindingly bright. Cherry squinted and cautiously stepped over the threshold but refused to move any further until her eyes adjusted. The straw-haired woman closed the door behind her, leaving Cherry on her own.

Or so she thought.

'Nothing in here but me for now. Come in. Take a seat,' a voice said.

'The light. It's too bright.' Cherry rubbed her eyes but stopped when feeling the edges of the lenses under her eyelids made her cringe.

'Your lenses have made your eyes sensitive, that's all. Once you're in here I'm sure they'll adjust and settle.'

Cherry took one step in and blinked.

'Now, 601—'

'Cherry.'

'—you seem to have been quite the troublemaker and we usually find that those who cause trouble have lots of trouble of their own.' Cherry could now make out a white table with a large divider running down its centre and a white chair on either side. 'Come and sit opposite me. This mirror here is a special device our team have developed.'

Cherry moved slowly towards the chair and lowered herself into it. The 'mirror' in front of her was as clear as glass and she could see a woman on the other side in a yellow suit. Her hair was the blackest black Cherry had ever seen, her skin was paper thin, and her sunken eyes had deep purple bags hanging underneath them.

'You're Lonely,' Cherry whispered.

'How ever did you guess,' Lonely said without the inflection of a question. She swivelled her chair to a touchscreen behind her, pressing it a few times. 'I've sent a message down to the control board to shut your lenses off while we conduct this examination so when I do this,' she tapped a series of buttons on the screen behind her and the glass frosted for a moment and then a silvery sheen glazed over its surface, 'you'll be able to see your own reflection and that of your own emotional baggage too.'

'I can only see me,' Cherry said. She leaned in closer to the glass and noticed a scratch on her forehead that hadn't been there before.

'Give it a moment. They're probably still just fixing your lenses.'

Cherry linked and unlinked her fingers under the table.

She cracked her knuckles and traced the palm over her hands over and over, killing time, until finally she noticed a small black blob in the mirror, just above her right shoulder. It stretched upwards and expanded until she could see Loneliness in the mirror.

'I see Loneliness. You're looking taller,' Cherry said sadly and held out her fist over her shoulder which Loneliness fist-bumped and then promptly drooled on. 'I can see it without the mirror, though. Why do you need to look at it through the mirror?'

Lonely tapped another corner of the screen and the image of Loneliness froze in the mirror. Cherry looked at the real Loneliness as it looked at the image of itself, twisting its head from left to right like a confused puppy.

'We capture images of feelings so we can compare them and see how they differ from person to person, and how they adapt to their owners over time. By the size of this Loneliness, I'd say it's been around for almost two decades, is that correct?'

Cherry tried to remember the first time she'd seen Loneliness. 'I was seven when we first met, so ... seventeen years.'

'Yes. Almost two decades, then,' Lonely repeated.

'Oh ... ' Cherry said. Had it really been that long? She glanced up at Loneliness, who grinned at her, almost affectionately.

'And it seems like you're very cooperative towards it. That usually happens the longer a feeling has lingered.

You have a routine. You don't fight against it and it doesn't fight against you.'

'No ... we ... erm ... we get along just fine.'

'Interesting.' Lonely typed some notes onto the screen. 'It'll be quite the monster to remove.'

'Remove?' Instinctively, Cherry reached out behind her and simultaneously Loneliness clutched Cherry's shoulders. She didn't want to feel lonely any more but Cherry didn't like the way Lonely had said 'remove'.

'Mmm, yes.' Lonely nodded. 'Remove. We're going to get rid of it.'

'Why do you need to get rid of it? Can't I just have lenses and then I won't even know it's there?'

'You already *have* lenses. This is something more permanent.'

'Why can't you just shrink the feelings gradually? Give everyone a dose of the counteracting feeling? Like—'

'Like you did? Yes, we've all heard about your kind-hearted approach.'

'And what's wrong with that? It worked.'

'It takes too much time.' Lonely threw up her hands. 'It's as simple as that. No one wants to be told their heartbreak will go away *eventually*. They want it gone immediately. We can offer that to people.'

'Wait ... do you mean ... normal people? People who can't see what we see?'

'Come here,' Lonely said, beckoning Cherry over to the screen.

She pressed the pad of her thumb onto a small green square on the bottom right hand corner. The screen went dark and then flashed, capturing an unflattering image of Cherry's face that remained on the screen for a brief moment before disappearing and leaving a four-way split screen showing security footage in its place.

'These are the live feeds from our main examination rooms. They took 555 down about half an hour before you arrived so they should start her removal process ... ah, yes. There we are.'

Lonely touched the top left quarter and it filled the screen. It took a moment for Cherry to figure out what was going on but when she did, she watched in horror. A large, grey Meddlum was on its haunches, cowering, its long claws covering its ears and clutching its head. There was a woman on the other side of the room writhing around. Her mouth was wide open, her teeth bared like some kind of animal. Her hair was slick with sweat and plastered across her forehead and she was scratching at her shoulders, her chest, her stomach, as though her whole body was on fire. If the three doctors in the room hadn't been moving at a normal pace, Cherry would have thought this footage had been sped up. Cherry peered closer, noticing something between the woman and her Meddlum.

'What are all those red ... strings?'

'When we bring a Meddlum into our world, when we make it real, we also bring form to the attachments it has created between itself and its owner. To detach a Meddlum, one simply has to ...' Lonely gestured to the screen as one of the doctors took a scalpel and reached out to slice through one of the strings. Each half fell limp and the woman in the corner dropped to her knees, writhing in even more agony than before.

'... cut the ties! Marvellous, isn't it?' Lonely said, without a trace of remorse.

'No.' Cherry shook her head. 'It's barbaric! She's in pain! They both are! How can you think putting someone through that much agony is OK?'

'We've tried all kinds of anaesthetics. We've tried every painkiller under the sun, but we're dealing with emotions. It's not the same as physical pain. Nothing will dull it. Besides, she asked for it.'

'No one deserves this,' Cherry said, clenching her fists.

'No, 601, I mean she actually asked for it. That woman came here voluntarily. It's rare but it happens. She signed a contract – I assure you she's here of her own free will. Look a little closer at what she's trying to get rid of.'

Cherry squinted at the screen. 'Is that Grief?'

'Precisely. This is a far briefer torture than if we'd let her be. When it's over, she won't feel a thing and Grief will be gone for good.' Lonely laid her hand flat against the screen, turning it to black.

'Surely not ... for good? It's like cutting down a tree, isn't it? It'll just grow back ... won't it?' Cherry asked, walking back around the table to stand in front of Loneliness.

'Not if you pull it out from the roots. You're better off leaving it to the professionals, 601,' Lonely said, taking up a clipboard and sitting down on her side of the table.

'It's Cherry and it doesn't seem right when the "professionals" don't really know what they're doing. You don't know what kind of lasting damage you're doing to her. She needs to learn how to live with her grief otherwise she'll never get over it. Not really. That's why I opened my bakeries—'

'Baking cakes doesn't mean anything here, 601.'

'*My name is Cherry.*'

'Not here it's not.' Lonely looked up at Cherry, her eyes and words vacant, and yet Cherry could hear them in her head, full of vitriol.

'Is that the plan? Give everyone a number, take away their feelings and turn them into ... into robots?'

'The world would be far more efficient that way, don't you think? Feelings get in the way of rational judgement. Anger and resentment break up families. Heartbreak and grief linger and become distractions. It's all unnecessary. Taking away those feelings means people can continue with their lives '

'That's madness! Feelings are part of life! Feelings *are* life! If you take away what people feel you take away anything meaningful. People's hearts break because they once cared. They cared so much for something that the loss of it actually makes them feel like they have a hole in their chests.'

'And we can fix that.'

'No, you're missing the point. You're essentially taking away consequence. If you take away Heartbreak, people will care less about losing what they love so that won't be real love at all. If you take away Guilt, people will drink, eat and gamble their lives away without thinking about how that might affect people they care about. If you take away Loneliness ... ' Cherry's voice broke, 'you're taking away what it means to be loved. What it means to be surrounded by people who cherish you. What it means to be so scared of being alone that you treasure every single day that the people you care about are by your side. Wanting to diminish the evil in this world is a good cause, one I have fought for the majority of my life ... but not like this. I won't let you do this.'

Cherry ran for the door. She smacked her fist against it until she could feel the bruises forming. All the while Lonely simply watched her. Had her emotions not already been deadened and numb, she would have watched with amusement. Cherry kicked the keypad. Cherry thought of Chase in his cell and kicked it again. She thought of Peter running and hiding for the rest of his life and she kicked it again. This time she heard a sharp crack and the keypad broke clean off of the wall. The door, finally, slid open and Cherry ran.

'SUITS!' Lonely shouted without a trace of feeling. In

her mind, she was only shouting to raise awareness, not because emotions were running high. 'SUITS! WE HAVE A BREAK OUT!'

Cherry ran out of the room and along the window-lined corridor but four blue suits were already charging at her. She came to a halt, her bare feet slipping on the shiny green floor, and turned around only to see three more blues coming for her. Cherry backed up against the windows, Loneliness next to her, scratching the glass. Cherry looked at it but its fingers started to fade. They've turned the lenses back on, Cherry thought. Loneliness kept clawing and whimpering and fading, and Cherry kept blinking and rubbing her eyes, trying to stop the lenses from turning on again, not wanting to feel like she was losing her feelings. Not yet.

But it was no good. Loneliness had completely vanished. Cherry knew it was still there, but she hated not being able to see it. 'Don't do this,' she said to Lonely, who had caught up to her, a syringe in her hand.

'Like I said, 601.' Cherry didn't bother struggling as the needle was plunged into her arm. 'Leave it to the professionals.'

23

Inside The Guild

Cherry sat bolt upright on the green floor. She looked around but with just one light working in the centre of the room, it was hard to see clearly. She knew she wasn't in her cell, though.

'Why do I keep waking up in different rooms?' Cherry mumbled, her arm tingling.

'I keep asking myself the same question,' came Chase's voice. He was sat a few feet away from her, still in his gown, looking at her in concern. 'Are you all right?' he asked.

'Fine. I think.' Cherry rubbed her arm, her skin cold. 'You?'

'My eyes are still stinging but I'm as good as I'll ever be while I'm here.' Chase then looked over his shoulder and mouthed, 'They're watching.'

Cherry glanced at the wall behind Chase and saw that there was a large rectangular mirror. She guessed that a whole host of white-clad, sadistic scientists were on the other side of it, watching them. A speaker in the corner of the room crackled.

'598 and 601, please stand on the black Xs on the floor.' It sounded like a woman's voice but without inflection or tone, it was hard to tell. Everyone sounded too similar.

'Best just do it,' Chase said, standing up awkwardly and pulling his gown down, not minding if it slipped off his shoulders as long as it covered everything below the waist. Cherry held her gown closed behind her back and found one of the two exes just left of the centre of the room. Chase stood on his X and faced her.

'Commencing Realisation in five . . . '

Their exes lit up beneath their feet. Cherry tried to move but she was rooted to the spot.

'Realisation?' she said, her heart thumping. Her legs felt like lead so she grabbed her knees to try and get them to move but something had her trapped.

'Four . . . '

'What's going on?!' Chase shouted.

'Three . . . '

'STOP!' Cherry screamed, putting her hands over her ears, her vision starting to fade.

'Two . . . '

'Breathe, Cherry.' Chase's voice soothed her and she clung onto that feeling.

'ONE!'

There was a moment of silence before the room filled with bright, white light and a gentle hum filled the air. Cherry felt a sensation in the base of her neck, like a beetle was burrowing itself into her brain. She scratched desperately and when the sensation became a sharp pinch she started to pull at her hair, tears streaming down her cheeks. The hum elevated to a crescendo and Cherry's body filled with heat. As the sound intensified, so did the heat. It was a slow build-up at first and then all of a sudden Cherry felt she might burst into flames. She screamed. She squinted through her streaming eyes and brought her hands to her face – they were white hot and smoking. Chase had tried to hold in his pain for as long as possible but finally his voice barrelled out of him in a roar. Both of them tried to move their feet, tried to run but it was as though they were melted to the floor. They were trapped. The light disappeared and the two of them dropped to the ground immediately. Smoke continued to rise from their bodies but the fire in their veins was subsiding. Cherry moved in and out of consciousness, her vision fading until she finally gave in and let the darkness consume her.

Cherry stirred. Her skin was sore and tender but when she brushed a hand over it, it felt smooth and unharmed.

However, when she reached up to delicately stroke her aching head, some of her hair came away in her hand, crispy and charred. She opened her eyes slowly but caught in her eyelashes was a thick piece of red string. She lifted her arm to find several strings were attached to her, trailing all the way up to her shoulders. Cherry sat up and looked down at her legs which were also tangled in red strands that all disappeared off into the darkness on the other side of the room.

'So these three are what you can see when you look at me?' Chase said. He was sat in the opposite corner to Cherry but he didn't look at her. Instead he was watching the darkness intently where three pairs of glowing eyes were staring back. Frustration, Mischief and Cynicism were standing in a row, holding hands.

'You can see them?' Cherry said.

Chase nodded once. 'Thanks to our friends here at the Guild, I'm not entirely in control of what I do or don't see any more.' Chase gestured to the mirrors.

'*Realisation*,' Cherry murmured. 'Chase, I think ... I think they're real. They've made your Meddlums ... *real*. They've given them form so they're visible to everyone.' Cherry remembered what she'd seen on the screen in the examination room and she was filled with trepidation. She knew what was coming next.

'How can you see past them? They're ... *monsters*. I'm a monster,' Chase whispered.

'What do you mean? They're ... they're Meddlums.

302

They're the worst parts of ourselves. Every bad thing we ever feel manifests itself in them but they aren't us. They don't have to define us.'

'No, Cherry. Monsters like these could only belong to a monster,' Chase spat out, taking a step towards his three vices. They shuffled backwards.

'Do you really believe that?' Cherry stood shakily.

'You don't?' Chase said, finally looking at her.

'I think it's time you met someone.' Cherry walked towards Chase but she looked past him, past Frustration, Mischief and Cynicism and into a pair of eyes that were barely visible in the dim light of the room. Its fur was so dark that it had been hidden well until Cherry beckoned to it. The red strings attached to her arms tightened as Loneliness stood. Most of the time it was hunched so it could look Cherry in the eyes but now as it straightened up properly, Cherry could see it was at least seven feet tall. Since Chase had been around, Loneliness hadn't been in the best shape so clumps of fur were missing, its claws were chipped and its eyes were bloodshot and yellow.

'What is that thing?' Chase backed away from Cherry and her Meddlum and pressed his back into the wall.

'This is Loneliness. My lifelong companion.'

'It's ... oh God, Cherry, it's hideous.' He looked horrified.

'I know, Chase.' Cherry turned back to Loneliness who reached out and held her hand. Its scaly hands were cold and clammy and twice the size of hers but even so, it wrapped both of them around her palm and squeezed. 'But it's mine.'

'How have you lived your whole life, knowing it's there, lurking behind you? How have you never tried to get rid of it?' Chase slid down the wall until he was sitting on the floor.

'I *have*. You know I have. It's not as easy as it looks. You can't switch your emotions on and off like a light and when you've grown up with ... *this* ... ' She pointed at her eyes, 'with what we can do, you don't end up with many friends. My dad left when I was a kid and then my other dad died and ... I didn't have a lot of people to love and care for, okay? But Loneliness has followed me everywhere I go. There have been times when it's shrunk and there have been times it's been ten feet tall and it's blocked out the sun, but don't you see? If Loneliness hadn't always been there, reminding me of everything I didn't have, I wouldn't appreciate having you in my life half as much as I do.' Several tears spilled over and Loneliness caught them on its finger and wiped them on its fur. Cherry moved over to Chase and crouched next to him, bundling up her attachments to Loneliness and putting them in her lap, careful not to entangle them with Chase's. 'As much as you hate it, they are yours.' Cherry looked over at Frustration yanking Mischief and Cynicism into itself to create a creepy family portrait. 'You have to take the bad with the good, and the bad make you grateful for the good you have in your life. They don't make you a monster. You're a good man, Chase. You can work to make them smaller or you can wallow in this self-pity, but either way,' she lowered her voice and turned her head away from the mirror, *we have to get out of here.*' She took Chase's hand, stood and gave him a tug but he didn't move. 'Chase ... come on.'

'I don't think I want to leave just yet,' he said, looking at the floor.

'*What*? Chase, what are you talking about?'

'It might help, what they do here might help me ... get rid of them.'

'Chase, no!' Cherry grabbed his hands urgently. 'This place is ... *evil*. There's no good here. They don't care about you, about me. They literally sever you from your feelings. I watched a woman almost claw her body to shreds because of the pain of it all. This won't help. It will make you less ... *you*.'

'But how do you really know that? It might not be that bad.'

'Chase ... you're scaring me now.' Cherry crouched back by his side, desperation settling over her.

'If someone wants to stop feeling frustrated or cynical, why shouldn't there be a place they can go? What if someone's constantly feeling bitter and defeated and they can't help taking it out on the world? Why shouldn't they have the choice to be free of that?'

'Because it's a cop-out, Chase! It might get rid of the

feelings but it'll deaden the rest of your emotions too, and you'll be less of a person. You can't help how you feel, but you *can* choose how you treat other people as a result. You are in control of that. If you want to stop being an arsehole, you work on not being an arsehole! But if you want to stop feeling frustrated with the world and cynical towards every kind-hearted person you meet, then *talk* your problems away! Find a friend, a professional, someone you can confide in. You don't let some experimental scientists, who don't know what they're doing, come at the fabric of your soul with a fucking knife and turn you into a robot! NOW GET UP AND HELP ME!' Cherry yanked his arm and he slid towards her a fraction, his resistance still putting up a fight.

'*Chase* . . .'

'I'm staying, Cherry. I don't want to be the owner of *them* any more.'

'Can't you see all the good there is, too?'

'Everything good has gone,' Chase said miserably.

Cherry looked at his Meddlums and at her Loneliness, then over at the mirror. 'No, it hasn't. They're controlling what we see! Don't you understand? It's the lenses! They're filtering out everything good you've got going for you so they can trick you into thinking you only have bad feelings. They need you. If they get rid of every bad thing you feel it'll be easier to manipulate you. I don't know what for. I can't figure out why any of this is happening but I just know you'll be playing into their hands!'

'I just . . . want to be better. I want to be good enough.'

'Oh, Chase,' she whispered. 'This doesn't make you better. It makes you . . . a coward.' Her voice faltered on the final word. She didn't want to say it but she had to make him see sense.

'A coward? How the hell does wanting those monsters gone make me a coward?'

'Because this is easier! You can't even accept your own flaws. You can't just work on them and make yourself a better person by learning how to live with them. You just want them gone, never to be seen again – but that's not a solution, Chase.' Chase's eyes darted briefly to his Meddlums but his face contorted and he lowered his eyes to the floor, not able to stand the sight of them. Cherry tried again, 'Imagine never getting frustrated again? Imagine having someone treat you like shit and you have no choice but to stand there and accept it because Frustration doesn't know how to latch itself onto you any more. And . . . and if you're never cynical of anything ever again you're just going to trust everyone, including all the people you *shouldn't* trust. That protective instinct will be gone. And Chase . . . it would *kill* me to never hear that mischief in your voice again. To know I'd never see that playful, cheeky smile again . . . it breaks my heart.' Cherry laughed through her tears. She hadn't even realised she'd started crying. 'And I wouldn't wish that heartbreak away, either! Because it means I care about you and even if I have to leave here with heartbreak instead of you, I'll just be glad to that we met and that you changed me.' Tears caught in the corners of her lips. They tasted of Sorrow.

'Are you coming?' Cherry stood over him and Loneliness joined her side. Chase shook his head but didn't look up at her. 'Then I'm sorry.'

'Sorry? For what?'

'For not letting you get what you want.' Cherry looked up at Loneliness and nodded. Loneliness ran to the wall opposite the mirror and began rubbing its back against it. It cracked its neck. 'You see,' Cherry said, 'they've made a slight mistake in all of this. It's quite dangerous to make a Meddlum real so it's not limited to its owner.' Loneliness started panting. 'Especially one that's as big as Loneliness. Especially one with incredibly sharp claws and three rows of teeth, I believe?' She looked at Loneliness and it grinned, showing every pointed tooth it could. 'And it's especially dangerous to make one real who belongs to someone so desperate never to be lonely again that she will do whatever it takes to save you, Chase.'

Loneliness howled and pushed off from the wall, launching itself into the mirror. It shattered into hundreds of tiny pieces and revealed four men in white coats on the other side. Loneliness was sprawled over three of them, and the fourth was reaching for the phone when Loneliness bit his leg, pulled him to the ground and headbutted him so hard he passed out.

'Chase. I swear to you we will get rid of your Meddlums together but right now it's time to GO!'

Chase looked at Cherry then and like a bolt, he knew he couldn't leave her. What was the point of anything if she wasn't with him? He took the hand she held out for him and squeezed it. 'I'm sorry,' he said. 'I just wanted to be free.'

'You will be free,' Cherry said. 'I promise. But we have to go. Come on!'

They jumped through the hole where the mirror used to be into the next room, Mischief, Cynicism and Frustration tumbling after them. Chase grabbed a key card from the pocket of one of the unconscious men and used it to open the main door.

'LONELINESS!' Cherry called as the door was closing behind them, the red strings tightening and pulling at her arms. Loneliness's hand stopped the door from shutting fully. It pushed it open and ran after Cherry, Chase and the rest of the Meddlums.

'It won't be long before they realise we're missing,' Cherry said. She pulled Chase into a small alcove between examination rooms. 'And it's harder to hide because of them. There's six of us now.'

'And we can't split up because there won't be any guarantee that we'll both get out.'

'Exactly. So we have to act fast.'

'HEY!' A distant voice yelled. 'YOU SHOULDN'T BE THERE!'

Cherry poked her head out into the corridor and saw Loneliness biting at one of the windows, one of his crooked teeth cracking the pane.

'Looks like we've got to be *really* fast,' Chase said.

Loneliness pushed his shoulder through the broken glass and plummeted into the hall below. Cherry's stomach flipped as she waited for the strings to tighten and take her with him but they seemed to stretch. *Or maybe it's like silk from a spider?* she thought, *Maybe the strings are never-ending*. There wasn't the time to think about that now. Cherry turned back to Chase.

'We need to find the main panel that controls the lenses and shut it down.'

'And then what?' Chase asked, breathless.

'Peter will take care of it.'

'How will he even know?'

'He has lenses installed too – he'll know when they stop working. He'll take care of it.'

More shouts erupted from below and yet there was nothing panicked or worried about them. The shouts were merely to alert security that something in their serene and robotic routine had been disturbed.

Chase and Cherry ran out from their hiding place and to the shattered window, Frustration, Cynicism and Mischief following closely behind. Loneliness was in the hall filled with desks, ripping computers from tables with one hand and he was gripping a blue suit's neck in the other.

310

'Loneliness!' Cherry screamed. 'Stop hurting people!'

Loneliness put the blue suit down just as another blue suit broke a chair over its head.

'Unless it's necessary!' Chase called.

Loneliness grinned up at him and then swiped the woman's legs out from underneath her, her head cracking against a desk on her way down. Cherry hit Chase lightly in the stomach.

'What?' he said. 'Am I wrong?'

'STOP THEM!' It was Lonely's blank, emotionless voice.

'I've never hated anyone's face more,' she whispered to Chase and then yelled, 'HELP!' through the missing window. Loneliness dropped the man it was holding at its feet. 'JUMP!' Cherry yelled. She took Chase's hand and before he was able to react, she toppled over the edge and pulled him with her. Loneliness got there just in time to catch them both. Cherry landed on its back and it caught Chase in a fireman's lift. Chase's three Meddlums landed in a heap on the floor but they had no chance to orientate themselves before Loneliness took off carrying Cherry and Chase, and dragged them behind it.

'We have to find the control panel,' Cherry said into Loneliness's ear. It nodded enthusiastically, its long purple tongue hanging out of his mouth. Chase's Meddlums crashed into desks, chairs, computers and people as they ran past, too fast and strong to be caught.

'LEFT!' Cherry screamed, seeing a door that was

marked PRIVATE and taking a chance. 'Anything that's marked private in a locked underground bunker in the middle of nowhere is worth looking at,' she said, feeling herself slipping further down Loneliness's back. Loneliness barged, shoulder first, into the door, catching Cherry's hand. She yelped and slipped and Loneliness slowed down, looking around at her. She climbed back up as best she could. 'Keep going!' she gasped.

Beyond the now-broken door was a short corridor. A man was standing at the other end, in front of another open doorway, pushing a cart covered in empty plates.

'No!' Cherry shrieked but she was too late.

Loneliness ran at full speed and kicked the cart into the man. He fell backwards down the stairs and landed with a gruesome crack.

'No, stop it! How many more people are we going to hurt before we leave?' She buried her head in Loneliness's shoulder, hoping the man wasn't dead.

'Cherry,' Chase said, panting. 'I don't think Loneliness thinks that way. It just wants to get out.'

'So do I,' Cherry sobbed, 'but we have to stop hurting people.'

'It's going to take force to get out of here. They're not going to just let us leave.'

'We don't have to push people down the stairs!'

Loneliness turned to look at Cherry and she was certain it understood what she was saying.

'We're already underground,' Chase said. 'How much

312

further down can we go?' He craned his neck over Loneliness's arm but all he could see were stone stairs spiralling down in the dark.

'Must be something they *really* don't want us to find.' Cherry squeezed her heels into Loneliness's sides and it continued on down the stairs. Frustration, Mischief and Cynicism stumbled down each step, each falling over the other two. A stench filled their nostrils the further down they went and Cherry gagged.

'What does this panel look like?' Chase asked.

'I don't know. Peter didn't say exactly. He kept calling it a control panel so I'm guessing something with lots of buttons?'

'Surely he would know what it looks like,' Chase reasoned. 'Why didn't he just tell you what to look out for?'

'I don't know. I don't think he had seen it himself, otherwise he would have said . . . ' Cherry said, not doing a very good job of convincing herself, let alone Chase.

'Peter isn't exactly a fount of knowledge, is he?'

Cherry opened her mouth to defend Peter but was distracted by something at what she assumed was the end of the staircase. Several streams of white light danced about the floor, crossing over one another and flickering.

'Can you see that? It's beautiful.'

Loneliness stopped on a step a few from the bottom and put Chase down. Cherry climbed off its back and walked into what appeared to be a large, empty cave. She checked to make sure their strings weren't in too much of a tangle.

'Cherry . . .'

'One sec,' she said, fiddling with a string that had become twisted.

'Cherry . . . Look!'

'What is it?'

She looked up at Chase to see that the tiny rivers of light were dancing over his gown, weaving in and out and under and over.

'Oh God, Chase!'

'It's OK, Cherry. It doesn't hurt, but *look*.'

Chase touched her shoulders and she turned to look at where he was pointing. She gasped. Ten pairs of brightly lit eyes were glowing in the dark.

24

The Control Panel

'Why have you come?' said a voice. It was soft and sang like a wind chime and reverberated off the walls. Cherry stepped forwards. 'Stay back!' warned the voice. 'We are not to be seen.'

Chase reached for Cherry's hand and pulled her closer to him.

'Who are you?' the voice said.

'We don't work for the Guild. We were brought in. For experiments,' Chase said, his hand sweating against Cherry's.

'As were we,' the voices said.

'Experiments?' Cherry asked. 'Are you all right?'

'We are what we are. Nothing can change that now.'

'So ... you *don't* work for the Guild?' Chase said.

'We are kept here against our will, caged up like animals. We do what we must to survive but no one in this room is loyal to the Guild.'

'We're trying to find the control panel. We want to shut off everyone's lenses so we can get out of here,' Cherry blurted out, relieved at the glimmer of hope that these people, whomever they were, might offer them some help.

The eyes grew brighter and a chorus of voices rang out as they all said, 'You have found us.'

'What do you mean?' Cherry said, frowning.

'You have found us,' they repeated.

'We're looking for the control panel. For the lenses,' Cherry tried again. She had to make them understand.

'You have found us.'

'My friend Peter . . .'

'Peter?' one of the voices said.

'Yes . . .' said Cherry. 'Do you know him?'

One pair of lights blinked and when they opened again, instead of light pouring out, they projected an image of Peter's face onto the floor. In it, he had a black eye, his hair was charred and sticking up and Cherry could see that he was wearing one of those hideous green gowns but despite all of that, he was smiling.

'Peter,' the voice said and the picture came alive. Peter was laughing and speaking in the video but there was no sound. 'He was kind.'

'He's safe,' said Cherry. 'And when I get out of here I

will make sure he stays that way but I need your help. I need to find the control panel.'

'You have found us,' they said again.

'Cherry ... I think ... I think *they* are the control panel.'

'You have found us,' one of them said.

'Come closer,' said another. Cherry stepped forward and pulled Chase with her. 'Just the girl.' Cherry tried to let go but Chase tightened his grip.

'It's okay.' Cherry raised his hand to her lips, planted a kiss on his knuckles and let go. As Cherry stepped forwards, all the eyes turned to her and illuminated her face.

'My name's Cherry.'

'We know,' they said.

'How?'

'We see everything,' said the wind chime. 'We are the Guild's greatest experiment and the Guild's greatest secret. I am Experiment 341 and we, in this room, were the first to be installed with the sight. Our eyes are linked to the others. We watch over our kind.'

'You're kept down here?' Cherry asked.

'We see everything. All the time. The darkness helps us to focus. We are alone here, free from distraction.'

'Don't you want to leave?'

'No one leaves the Guild.'

'They do! You can!' Cherry took a step forwards but all of the eyes flickered so she stayed where she was. 'Sorry. I'm sorry. I didn't mean to scare you. But I can get us out.'

'No one is allowed to leave.'

Cherry blew out her cheeks, frustrated. 'You can see anything one of our kind has seen, right?'

'We see all through the lenses,' Experiment 341 said.

'Can you rewind?'

'We can see into the past but not the future.'

'Then look back to what Peter saw yesterday.' *Was it yesterday?* Cherry thought. *How long have we been here?* 'Maybe not yesterday. Check the last twenty-four hours and look for Peter and a bad feeling the size of a house.'

'That is not possible,' Experiment 341 said.

'Let us try,' a different voice said.

'We cannot,' Experiment 341 began again but was interrupted by another voice repeating, 'Let us try.'

All of the eyes closed, apart from one pair. Experiment 341 hesitated and then she closed her eyes, too.

'We see it,' they said. 'It's monstrous.'

'And can you see Peter?' Cherry asked eagerly.

'We can.'

'Then you see that you *can* leave,' Cherry said. 'Please help us and we'll take you all with us. You can leave the darkness behind.'

The eyes bobbed up and down, nodding their heads in agreement. 'There is only one way to turn off our sight.'

'Tell us how,' Cherry said. 'We'll turn it off and then we can leave.'

'I'm afraid it's not your decision,' one of them said. 'It's up to us.'

318

'What does that mean?' Chase said, moving to stand next to Cherry. 'Surely it's simple to switch your lenses off?'

'We do not have lenses,' they chorused.

'Come closer,' Experiment 341 said, closing her eyes. Cherry took one step forwards and the other lights guided her across the dark floor until she was standing in front of Experiment 341, close enough to touch her. 'Do not be alarmed.' Cherry felt 341 put her face next to hers and she opened her eyes, careful not to blind Cherry with their light. And then Cherry saw that they were not eyes at all. They were glass orbs, millions of images dancing across them all at once so that they blurred into one glowing light. The pictures flickered so fast that Cherry couldn't focus on one at a time. Loneliness whined.

'Our eyes were taken and replaced with orbs. They are like your lenses but on a much stronger level. We see everything. You see what we want you to see. We are the filters to your sight.'

'How can you take all of that in? There are too many and they move so fast,' Cherry said in awe.

'We've been down here a long time. Practice makes perfect.'

Loneliness groaned again, scratching his back up against one of the walls.

'But Peter said there were people who watched screens all day. To watch over what everyone like us is doing. He never said it was like ... *this*.'

'Not everyone here knows about us. Secrets and theories become urban legend and everyone thinks they're the truth. Peter didn't know about us.'

'How do you know that? Did you know Peter?'

'I used to,' 341 whispered.

Cherry looked into the orbs again, overwhelmed by the sheer volume of what she was seeing. How did they live with this, day after day? 'Is there any way to make it stop?' she asked.

341 took Cherry's hand and squeezed it. Cherry looked down at her black skin contrasting against 341's caramel tones. 341 pulled her hand away and Cherry thought she saw a glimpse of yellow around her wrist but couldn't be sure.

'The only way to stop the sight is by shattering our orbs,' said 341, her voice steady as the other experiments nodded.

'But . . . you'd be blind,' said Chase.

'We're already blind,' said the experiments.

'I can't do that,' said Cherry, the hairs on her arms rising. 'You wouldn't be able to see anything.'

'You can see things now,' said Chase. 'You see more than anyone else sees.'

'Perhaps,' one of the other experiments said. 'But it is a burden. This is not a life any of us chose and now that we can see it is possible to leave it behind, we would be grateful if you kept your promise and helped us. You need to shatter our orbs.'

'Couldn't you have done it yourself? Shattered the orbs, I mean?' Chase asked. He pulled Cherry closer to him.

'We've tried. They're tough to break. We're not strong enough,' they said. Loneliness let out a long howl.

'What makes you think we'd be strong enough?' Cherry asked. Loneliness's howl grew louder.

'That creature is driving me mad,' Chase muttered.

Cherry could only make out Loneliness's outline as it ambled towards them. It veered to the right towards an experiment whose lights started to blink rapidly.

'It's all right, 347. I believe Loneliness is just trying to help.' 341's voice was low and soft.

Loneliness whined and lifted its hands up to 347's face, its large palms covering 347's ears. It closed 347's eyelids with its thumbs, extinguishing the light, but keeping the pad of its thumbs there. The crunch of glass reverberated around the cell and Cherry's stomach turned as 347 screamed.

'Stop!' she yelled.

'No,' said 341, reaching out for the hand Chase wasn't holding.

Loneliness pulled its hands away and covered its head, whimpering, drool spilling from its lips and pooling around his feet. 347 clutched his bleeding face but through his sobs of pain he whispered, 'Thank you, thank you, thank you,' and Loneliness kissed his forehead.

Cherry sobbed and Chase brought her in closer. 341

nodded at Loneliness who shuffled its feet to Experiment 308 whose eyes were already closed, ready and waiting.

Peter pulled grass from the ground in clumps and watched it float away into the breeze. 'Come on, Cherry,' he groaned. She'd already been in there longer than she should have. Peter had refused to go back into the Guild but he'd been prepared to help Cherry in another way. Even so, he thought he'd seen the last of Warleggan. There was nothing for miles, and the light was fading fast but he was determined to wait. He had faith in Cherry, but it had been hours and he couldn't keep from fidgeting impatiently. The cold was settling in for the night and the only thing to warm him was the thick heat coming up from the vent he had strategically placed himself in front of. He closed his eyes and threw himself backwards, flinging his arms above his head and let out a sigh. He opened his eyes but all he could see was black. Had he fallen asleep and day had turned to night? Peter rubbed his eyes hard but still the black smoke clouded his vision.

Smoke.

'Ohmygod!' he yelled, scrambling up and looking up into the burning face of Hatred. 'OH MY GOD, SHE DID IT! She did it! She did it! She did it!' he chanted and Hatred threw her head back and laughed. 'Right. We've got work to do. Stand there.' Peter pointed to the edge of the vent and Hatred waddled as fast as she could so that her large toes curled over the edge of the metal slats. Peter closed his eyes and thought of his mother and how she'd kept him locked up in that place for almost his entire life. More and more black smoke started to pour off Hatred's body but before it rose and disappeared into the darkening sky, Hatred sucked it up into her mouth and blew it down the vent with as much force as she could.

'This is for you, Shura. This is all for you.'

'How do we know it's worked?' Chase asked.

He was creeping back up the stairs with Cherry, Loneliness, his Meddlums and the ten prized experiments in tow. They held each other's shoulders as they ascended the staircase. Cherry tried not to look behind her but Curiosity took her chin in its hand and turned it over her shoulder. The blood from their hollow eye sockets was glittered with glass dust, their hair was singed and charred and their gowns were filthy and reeking. They had been treated like animals for so long they had started to resemble them.

'It will have worked. We are the control panel but we no longer see,' said 341 in Cherry's ear.

'Then let's hope Peter has held up his end of the deal,' Chase said.

They slipped and stumbled up the spiral staircase, the

experiments' legs stiff from lack of use, but their hearts lifted them and they moved forward slowly but with purpose.

'We may have a lot of company when we get upstairs,' Chase said.

'I know. I know.' Cherry rested her forehead against Chase's back, trusting him to guide her up the final steps. Her feet reached flat ground but she didn't dare look up at what was inevitably going to be a corridor full of blue suits, white coats and Happy with a syringe.

'Cherry.' Chase wiggled her wrist. 'Looks like Peter came through.'

Cherry snapped her head up, saw nothing but black smoke and smiled.

25

Loneliness

Cherry put a finger to her lips and turned to the experiments, but then realised they couldn't see her. 'We've got to be quiet,' she whispered to 341 who whispered to 347 and the message was carried quietly down the line. They crept to the end of the corridor although any noise they were making was drowned out by the sirens and the screaming. People were running through the smoke, some were screaming at the fire, some were screaming at the monsters that had reappeared after years of not being seen. Fear filled the air.

'I don't know which way is out,' Cherry said.

'We'll figure it out. We just need to move,' Chase said, ready to run out into the busy hall.

'Take my hand,' said 341 and without question Cherry

interlinked her fingers with 341's. 'I worked here for years before I was turned into a guinea pig. I know my way around this place whether I can see it or not. You just need to give me a starting point. Describe exactly what you can see.'

'A lot of smoke.'

'You don't know where we are?' 341's voice faltered.

'Erm ... ' Cherry tried mentally retracing their steps. She remembered jumping through the window and how Loneliness had carried them diagonally across the hall.

'We're on the right side of the hall. Top right. To get to you we came down a corridor and then through a door marked Private. That's where we are now. Where that door used to be.'

Blood was seeping out from under 341's closed eyelids. It had started to collect and clot and soon she wouldn't be able to open them. Fresh tears sprang to Cherry's eyes.

'Got it. Let's go.' 341 pulled at Cherry's hand and for someone who was blind she moved incredibly fast.

They stayed close to the walls and white coats flashed by in the smoke but no one noticed the silent, soon-to-be escapees. 341 turned left and started to pick up speed down a corridor where red flashing lights on the ceiling were penetrating through the smoke. They were losing cover.

'Chase, have you got Loneliness?'

'It won't let go of my gown,' Chase growled.

'Good.'

'The other three are riding the experiments.' She could almost hear him roll his eyes.

'How much further?' Cherry whispered to 341.

'There's a lift at the end of this corridor that will take us up and out but we need a key card.' Loneliness tugged at Chase's gown and waved the key card Chase had swiped earlier in front of his face.

'Oh ... nice one.' Chase pressed the card into Cherry's hand.

'Got one!'

'Perfect. Once the doors close, they won't open again until we're upstairs. Once we're upstairs, and the doors open, we have to run. Fast.'

Cherry nodded. 'Towards the smoke. We need to run towards where the smoke is the thickest. Make sure everyone knows that.'

The smoke was starting to fade. More and more faces were becoming visible and Cherry caught sight of Loneliness's monstrous face. How was she going to hide it in the real world, now that it was a form everyone could see? She shook the thought from her head. She'd figure it out. Right now she had to think of the task at hand. 341 bumped up against the glass lift doors and fumbled trying to find the keypad.

'Let me.' Cherry took the card in her own shaking hands and swiped it. The doors opened and Cherry, Chase and 341 piled in.

'QUICK!' she screamed as Frustration, Mischief and

Cynicism skittered in around Chase's feet and held onto his legs. The other experiments, with no one to guide them, bumped into each other in the confusion. Cherry saw Loneliness's claws reach out but two men in blue suits suddenly appeared.

'STOP THEM!' Happy was barrelling down the corridor as the doors began to close, leaving Loneliness on the other side, clawing at the glass.

'NO! LONELINESS!' Cherry's hands searched the walls for any buttons to open the doors once more but there was nothing. She beat her fists against the glass, screaming as Loneliness wrestled with the blue suits. It thrashed ferociously against them, breaking a window with its large foot.

'The lift's leaving!' said 341, holding Cherry's heaving shoulders. 'You can't stop it!'

'The strings! They're going to drag the lift down!' said Chase, trying to prise the doors open with his fingers.

'NO! We have to go back for the others. Loneliness!' As the lift started to rise, Loneliness ripped one of its arms free, closed its claw around a piece of broken glass and before Happy could sink her syringe into its fur, Loneliness grabbed every red string that attached it to Cherry ... and cut.

26

Smoking

The doors opened and Cherry fell face first onto the floor of a dank cave.

'We've got to move.' 341 stumbled forwards and Frustration took her hand. 'Will you guide me?' she asked and the Meddlum yapped its acceptance. Mischief moved behind her and Cynicism stood to her left so they formed a semicircle around her and together they started to run. The lift doors closed and the lift immediately sank down into the floor, no doubt having been called by Happy. Before Chase's strings became too taut, he scooped Cherry into his arms and followed after 341.

They came out into a forest but the trees thinned out quickly as they ran and Chase could see a road up ahead.

He didn't dare look down at Cherry's face. He could feel that her body was limp in his arms and there was something trickling down his arm which he thought might be her blood. Her severed red strings hung underneath her and fluttered against his bare legs. Twigs and rocks dug into his feet but he kept running until 341 called back to him, 'Can you see smoke?!' 341 had reached a road up ahead but there was no smoke.

'No! Just keep running!'

'Smoke . . .' Cherry murmured. 'Smoke . . .'

'Hold on, Cherry. They're not going to catch up to us. I won't let them.'

'Smoke . . .' She whispered again and this time, she raised her arm and stretched out her hand, pointing to the van that was barrelling towards them, smoke trailing behind it.

'This way!' Peter appeared out of the sunroof, flailing his arms above his head. 'Over here!'

Frustration picked 341 up and carried her towards the van, Mischief and Cynicism not far behind. Chase hesitated, the strings between him and his Meddlums straining. He couldn't see Hatred, just the smoke coming out of the exhaust. The van screeched to a halt halfway down the road, kicking up a cloud of dust and the driver's door opened.

'Chase!' shouted Sally, 'YOU GET THAT GIRL IN THIS VAN THIS INSTANT!'

Chase didn't need to be told twice. He started to run

but a sharp pinch in his neck caught him unawares and as he stumbled, Cherry fell from his arms. He whipped around, his limbs already numbing, and Happy stood over him, a syringe held neatly between her dainty fingers.

'Clever, 598.'

'Chase,' he corrected, slurring.

'No, 598. I don't know how you pulled off this little stunt but it's time to get yourselves back inside.'

Chase's knees buckled and they slammed into the ground. A blue suit ran at him and tried to pull one of his arms behind his back. Chase struggled and caught the man across the jaw but he threw himself off balance and landed face-first in the grass on the roadside. Sally ran from the van and screamed their names but Peter couldn't risk it. He ducked back inside the car and started to rock back and forth.

'*Can't go back. Can't go back. Can't go back*,' he mumbled.

'I suppose it's quite endearing,' Happy said to Chase, 'that you thought you could escape.'

'Happy ...' said a blue suit.

'But I don't feel endearment, so it was all for nothing, really.'

'Happy!'

'So it's lucky for you I'm just—'

'HAPPY!' The blue suited man screamed as experiment 347 climbed onto his back and clawed at his face.

Happy spun around and stared into the eyeless faces

331

of nine experiments she'd had a hand in caging up for almost a decade.

'No ... no, you shouldn't be here. What happened to your faces? YOU.' She kicked Chase in the neck. 'That's how you did this. That's how you broke the lenses. *Shura*. WHERE IS SHURA!'

'Shura?' Peter's head snapped up.

'I told you I'd find a way back to you,' Experiment 341 said from the front passenger seat. She didn't look around for fear of what Peter would say when he saw her face but it was undeniably her voice.

'*Shura*!' Peter clambered between the seats and into the driver's side next to her. Tears poured down his cheeks when he saw that underneath the burnt hair, the blood and grime it really was her and he knew for certain when he saw the yellow rag, now bloodied and full of holes, wrapped around her ring finger that he had tied there years before as a promise. A promise that he would always be hers. A promise he'd been willing to keep even when he saw her lifeless body wheeled away in the Guild, sure she was dead. Yet here she was. His Shura. 'Oh God!' he cried.

'Where are you? Let me hold you.' Her hands tentatively reached out and searched for him and at first, Peter just watched her hands colliding with nothing but air but then, he circled his fingers around her wrists and gently guided her hands to his face. She traced the outline of his nose, his eyebrows, his cheeks, his chin.

'Peter,' she sighed, smiling through her tears.

'CHERRY!' screamed Sally, crouching down by the back tyre and clutching the mud guard, not knowing what to do. Cherry's body lay still on the ground and Chase was barely moving.

'Wait here,' Peter said to Shura, planting a firm kiss on the top of her head before getting out of the car and walking towards Happy with a determination so strong that the ground shook.

'What did you do to her?' Peter said, crouching down next to Cherry. Five of the experiments had blue suits pinned to the ground, fighting them with all the hurt and anger they'd been saving up while they'd been locked away.

'Ahh, Peter, dear son. Couldn't stay away from Mummy for too long, could you?'

Peter narrowed his eyes at Happy. 'You may have given birth to me, but you're *not* my mother.'

Happy tutted. 'Come now, why would you say such a thing? I do my best.'

'*This* is not your best.' Peter stepped over Cherry and Chase and stood between their barely conscious bodies and squared up to his mother. 'Your best would've been staying. Not leaving me and then locking me away.'

'I didn't want you to turn out like me,' Happy said matter-of-factly.

'I was always going to be like you. It's because of you that I'm like this.'

'I didn't know that when I left, Peter. And you ended

up here anyway, so you got what you wanted. We were together at last.' She looked at him blankly.

'Got what I wanted? As soon as I arrived you put me in a cell! You didn't treat me like your son, you treated me like any other experiment. You even gave me a number! I was seven years old and I was experiment fourteen.'

'I couldn't have shown any favouritism, now could I? Nepotism is—'

'Nepotism? Is that what you think it would've been?! Stopping them from locking me in a cage wouldn't have been favouritism. It would've been *human*!' Peter spat. Out of the corner of his eye, he noticed the four other experiments silently making their way towards Happy. The blue suits now lay unconscious in the trees so Peter knew all the experiments were getting ready to pounce. He inhaled deeply. 'Occasionally, *Mother*, I still jerk and jolt like the electricity is still passing through my body while you were trying to pull all of my feelings out of me. Hatred stuck by me through it all and now she's bigger and far more dangerous than you could ever have imagined.' Hatred heard her name and waved a hand that was covered in embers. The wind fanned it and it burst into flames, making Happy jump.

'You can hardly blame me for that,' she said. 'That's just what happens to people who don't know how to behave.' Happy clasped her hands together and shrugged.

'You're a lost cause.' He shook his head, a tear running down his nose.

'Look how sad you are, Peter. We can fix that.' Happy took a step towards him.

'*We can fix that. Clearer vision means a clear mind.* I've heard it all, *Mum.* Sooner or later everything you've done is going to catch up to you. Or ... maybe they already have.'

Peter's gaze shifted from his mother to the experiments who had moved so stealthily they were standing behind her, close enough to touch her. 347 led the charge. He jumped on her, knocking her to the ground. 349 straddled her and slapped her hard across the face over and over and over and she stayed straddling her while 345 and 348 took Happy's legs and dragged her into the forest where the trees were thickest.

My oldest friend,

I'm sorry I won't be there when you wake up. We couldn't risk getting dragged back to the Guild so we've gone into hiding. Eloped, actually. My Shura and me. But I wanted you to know that we'll always come back should you need us. You found her for me and that is something I will spend the rest of my life repaying you for. I also discovered why the Guild couldn't find me when I escaped. Shura. Shura was blocking any trace of me from their systems. Everywhere I went, she made sure no one followed, and now we're together again because of you.

I've left all my details with Sally (who said Shura and I are destined for a strange but happy life together . . .) so you'll know how to get in touch initially. It may just take us a little bit of time to get back to you. I'll find a way to let you know where we move on to when the time comes. Who knows where we'll end up. Then again, who knows where you'll end up. I assume the Guild will take some time to regroup. We caused a lot of damage when we destroyed their control panel. It was at the heart of all they did and without it, they're stuck. But we must remain careful – they will find a way to return and I worry it will be more dangerous and painful than before. We're safe for a while, though. We've got a head start so we need to make the most of it.

There's nothing you can't do though, Cherry. When life tries to cut you down you seem to get taller and stronger.

You're my hero.

Peter

P.S. I'm sorry about Loneliness but if it's any consolation, it wouldn't have lasted much longer, not now that Chase is around. He's a really good guy.

P.P.S. I'm trying to quit "smoking", I promise.

27

Loneliness Escapes

Cherry awoke with a start. It took her a moment to realise where she was: in her own bed in the flat above the bakery. Chase was lying next to her, his hand in hers. She tried to sit up and her whole body throbbed. She groaned in pain.

'Who's up? Oh, Cherry, you're awake. What can I get? Are you hot? Cold? Thirsty? Hungry? I can get you anything you need?' Margie stood up from her chair in the corner and ran downstairs before anyone could answer.

Bruce laughed. He was curled up on the rug on the floor. 'She's become a whole new woman in the last few days, Cherry!'

'I think that's your doing though, Bruce,' Sally said, from her position at the foot of the bed.

'What's going on?' Cherry croaked. Her lips were parched and her tongue stuck to the roof of her mouth. 'Why are you all here?'

'You don't remember?' Sally said. 'I was your getaway driver.'

'Getaway driver?' Cherry rubbed her head and tried to sit up again. Bits and pieces started coming back to her. The Guild. Chase. Peter. Shura. Happy. Loneliness. 'I do remember but, Sally, how did you know where to find us?'

'Your friend Peter. What an oddball he is! Such a fidget, he wouldn't sit still the whole way there. Then again that lovely little thing that came back with him kept him quiet on the way home. He couldn't stop looking at her and I don't think it was because of all the blood. That reminds me,' Sally dug into her bag and pulled out a piece of folded paper, 'Peter asked me to give you this. I tried to make him stay until you were up and about but he seemed pretty adamant that they leave as soon as possible.'

Cherry felt an urgency start to boil in her own stomach. 'We have to leave, too,' she said, reaching for Chase's hand. 'Chase!' She shook him lightly and then more vigorously as panic set in.

He woke abruptly, startled. 'What's going on?! Cherry, you're awake!' He sat up as quickly as he could, trying to blink the sleep out of his eyes. A rattling came from the stairs and Margie appeared in the doorway with a tray full of mugs and plates.

'I didn't know if you'd prefer tea or coffee so I made both and I've also brought up some biscuits but I thought then again maybe you might not have an—'

'I'm sorry. We have to go. They'll be looking for us.' Cherry threw back the covers and despite the pounding in her head and the metallic taste of blood at the back of her throat she forced herself to stand. 'We have to *go*.'

Margie quickly set the tray down on the floor and tried to steady Cherry. 'Now, I don't know what happened, but no one's looking for you!'

Chase kicked the blanket off his legs and got out of bed quickly. He held Cherry's gaze, knowing they were thinking the same thing, and then bolted out of the room and down into the bakery. Cherry strained her ears to listen and the panic bubbled harder when Chase's footsteps were heavy and fast as he ran back upstairs.

'We have to leave. Now,' Chase said.

'Are they here?'

'The van's outside but I can't see anyone out there.'

'Oh, God.' Cherry sank onto the bed and put her head in her hands, the red strings swinging back and forth. Chase opened Cherry's wardrobe, found her case and started to throw anything he could find into it. Cherry watched him as he frantically tried to close the zip when it was full but it whined at his efforts.

'Chase, is this what it's going to be like?' she whispered. 'Running all the time?'

'I don't know, Cherry. We'll talk about it later.'

'We can't keep running,' she said.

'We have to! Right now, that's our only choice.' He hit the top of the suitcase.

'I'm not sure what's going on here,' Margie said, 'but it really can't be so bad that you have to leave.'

'No, you don't understand – if we stay, we could be killed,' Chase said.

'Killed?!' Margie gasped.

'What *was* that place, Cherry?' Sally sat next to Cherry and put her arms around her. 'Tell me what's going on.'

Cherry hesitated. She'd kept her secrets for so long, she didn't know where to begin. 'Chase and I aren't like most people. We see the world differently. And that was a place that ... tries to put a stop to that.' Cherry chose her words carefully.

'We know you and Chase aren't like the rest of us. You never have been.' Sally shot a sideways glance at Chase. 'If running away right now means not getting hurt then you need to run but Cherry's right, Chase. You can't run for ever.'

'I know we can't. We'll figure it out, but right now ...' Chase pulled the case off the bed and wheeled it to the door.

Margie took Cherry by the hands and helped her to stand. 'This is all a little over my head, love, but you need to be safe. Whatever it is that's making you think you're not safe, then get away from it until you are safe.' Margie pulled Cherry in tight to her chest and hugged her hard. Cherry sank into the hug, grateful for the unbidden kindness.

'How do we get out of here without being seen?' Chase asked.

'Is there a back door?' Bruce suggested.

'There is, but it leads out into an alley that loops back around to the front of the shops. We'll be seen no matter what,' Cherry explained.

'Take my car. It's parked outside.' Sally pulled her keys out of her pocket and pressed them into Chase's hand. 'You can thank me later.' She winked and Chase kissed the top of her head.

'Listen, Sally, I'm so sorry. About my mum and my aunt. And for me. Had I known, I would have stepped in and—'

'We can't help who we're related to and I don't hold their wrongdoings against you. It wasn't your fault. Now GO! This isn't goodbye, so stop trying to make me emotional. We'll see you again.'

'Don't be a stranger, you hear?' Bruce said, reaching up to squeeze Cherry's hand. He looked taken aback, unsure of what was happening, but he knew his friends were leaving and that made him sad.

'We're so grateful you moved here,' Margie said, taking Bruce's other hand. 'You changed my life.'

Cherry looked between Margie and Bruce and saw the mutual affection there and she smiled. 'Take care of each other,' she whispered, a lump forming in her throat.

'Cherry,' Chase called.

'I know. Come on.'

They walked downstairs as though they were part of a funeral procession. Margie and Bruce led the way, Chase took Cherry's case as she gingerly walked behind him and Sally took up the solemn rear.

'Are we going to have to make a run for it?' Cherry ducked halfway down the flight of stairs and peered round the corner. All she could see was the blue van parked outside. No sign of blue suits, white coats or Feelers in yellow.

'I think so,' Chase said. 'Best to be as quick as possible.'

'I say go now rather than wait for something to happen,' said Bruce, rolling up his sleeves. Chase went to open the door.

'Wait!' Cherry ran to him and held the bell still. 'Okay, now.'

Chase opened the door and they ran to Sally's old car. Chase slung the case in the back seat and ran to the driver's side while Cherry hopped in the passenger side. Chase put the key in the ignition and started the car.

Then the bell above the door rang out as Sally slammed the door closed and shouted 'CHERRY!' and Cherry looked up and saw them. Blocking the end of the road was a human wall of blue suits and two more vans.

'Shit,' Chase said.

Cherry reached for Chase's hand but he shifted the gear stick into first and took off the hand brake.

'Chase! You can't run them over!' She yelled as the car started moving.

'Why not?'

'Chase!'

BANG!

At first Cherry thought they were shooting at them but when she looked up, the blue suits were unarmed and starting to back away. The bang had come from above them and when she looked up, two large footprints were imprinted on the roof.

'What the—'

BANG!

Something jumped down onto the bonnet, tipping them forwards, the back tyres coming off the cobbles and then thumping back down as Loneliness leaped off the car. It turned to look over its shoulder and grinned at Cherry.

'But how . . .'

'I don't understand . . .'

Chase and Cherry looked at each other in disbelief.

Loneliness let out a roar and the windows of all the shopfronts rattled. It roared again and they shattered, shards of glass raining onto the street. It scratched at the cobbles with its claws and beat the ground with its fists and then it ran straight for the blue suits. Some of them ran away but others stayed, foolishly thinking they could take on the monster – but they had no idea how strong it was. Without a moment's thought, Loneliness tossed them aside like they were nothing.

'No!' Cherry screamed, her eyes widening in horror. Chase's face paled.

This wasn't the Loneliness Cherry had spent most of her life with. This ... beast was violent, dangerous, murderous. One by one, it picked up the blue suits and tore them apart, limb from limb. Cherry tried to block out the screaming but it was no good – she'd remember that sound for the rest of her life.

'We have to help them,' she sobbed.

'It's too late, Cherry,' Chase said through his own tears. 'They're all gone.'

Cherry couldn't bring herself to have one last look at the town she'd come to love or her old friend Loneliness. She didn't want her last memory to be stained in blood, so she closed her eyes as she and Chase sped past the chaos and away, for good.

Dear Peter,

We're safe. I think. As safe as we can be while the Guild is still in business, but I don't think I'll ever be happy with a life on the run. I've always tackled everyone's issues head on but now that it's me I have to save, I have to run away? I know I don't really have another option. It could be life or death but it just feels so . . . wrong.

There is one thing that helps me sleep at night though, Peter, and I hope it may give you some comfort too. Something that the Guild overlooked. Something that I didn't realise until now, either. On the day we left Plymouth, Loneliness came back to save us. It had escaped, Peter! It found us and saved us but . . . it wasn't the Loneliness I knew. It was violent and brutal and more terrifying than I had ever seen. It had become an actual . . . monster. Loneliness had been mine since I was a child. It had been with me for seventeen years and not once had it been violent. Not once had it raised even the smallest finger to me. I was the only one it could touch and it never hurt me, not physically. Meddlums are still able to influence us. They can still stop us from being who we want to be and make us be someone completely unlike ourselves and yet Loneliness had never once made me violent or been violent itself. If it had violent tendencies, why did it never make me do violent things? I think it's because I had as much influence over Loneliness as it had over me! I can see that now. No one can help how they feel so I was stuck with Loneliness. But I had a

347

choice. I could let Loneliness consume me for the rest of my life, give in to it and let it control me like a puppet . . . or I could fight back. When it would whisper in my ear and tell me to lash out at those I loved, to push them away, I'd say no. When it tried to keep me lonely I would hold it at arm's length and . . . it would listen. I pushed it away so much that I accidentally drew a line across the door of my bakeries so it couldn't come in. I created a safe space for myself that Loneliness had no choice but to respect because, while I couldn't control its existence, I could control how much I let it dictate my life. Which is why when it was finally free of me, it was able to cause so much devastation. It killed people, Peter. I created it and my creation killed people. I will have that on my conscience until the day I die. Something I gave life to took life from others. It's made so many other people feel lonely but I know the blame is not all mine. It never would have been real had it not been for the Guild and all I can do now is make sure I'm ready for the day they show their faces to me again.

For now, Chase and I are happy. Very, in fact. According to him we're surrounded by Happiness constantly. He's become part of me and my life so fast it's as if he's always been here and it becomes almost unbearable when he disappears for too long. I didn't get to see much of it when we were in Plymouth but Chase's smile could light up a small town and I'm so pleased I've been seeing more and more of it as the days go on.

You'll be glad to know that I haven't stopped baking. I don't think I ever will. I don't know when this fight with the Guild will start again, or if it will ever end, but I know we're the good guys. The ones who want to help people are always the good guys – and we do it without electrocuting people, gouging eyes out and removing what makes us human. So we have to keep doing what we do best. We have to keep helping people fight their demons. The good way. The way that allows them to keep being humans with all those gorgeous, glorious feelings and show them that we hurt so much because we care so much. You can't have rainbows without rain. It's true – truer than most people will ever realise but that's why the world has us. That's why the world needs us.

So it can feel.

x

A Letter from Carrie

Hello!

THANK YOU, thank you, *thank you* for reading *All That She Can See*. I really hope you enjoyed it – and if you've read any of my other books, I hope you enjoyed them too!

I can't believe that I have now published three books, and am well underway writing my fourth. It's honestly a dream come true, and something I *never* take for granted. Knowing that people are diving into the worlds I've created and connecting with the characters I love is such a wonderful feeling and one I'm sure I'll never tire of.

One of my favourite things about being an author is meeting and talking to readers – I love going to events and signings and hearing your brilliant insights into my books. So often there's a question or a comment that takes me by surprise! Maybe someone has read something between the lines that I didn't even know was there, or has a unique take on a character or a situation that I've never considered before. That's what I love so much about books, as a writer and as a reader: once they leave the author's brain, they're yours and you can connect with them in a way that's entirely personal to you.

I also love to hear from readers online, so please do get in touch on Twitter and let me know what you think. Or leave a review on Goodreads or elsewhere online and share your thoughts with other readers – it really does mean the world.

Lots of love,

Carrie Hope Fletcher

Carrie xxx

@CarrieHFletcher
#allthatshecansee

Acknowledgements

Oh, I do love this bit! Thanking all the incredible people that helped make this book in your hands a reality.

Firstly, where would I be without my brilliant agent Hannah Ferguson! Your continued support, advice and faith in me is astounding and I can't thank you enough for all you do! My editor, Manpreet Grewal, I honestly don't know how you do it. I send you mad idea after mad idea and you warmly embrace each and every one. I dread the day you tell me I've gone too far! Stephanie Melrose, book flapper extraordinaire, 'come forth' and accept your thanks! Book events and signings can be daunting experiences but I know if you're at the helm, all will go swimmingly. To the designer, Bekki Guyatt, and illustrator, Helen Crawford-White, of this book's cover: you've done it again! Beautiful, as always! To Thalia Proctor, Amy Donegan, Marie Hrynczak and the Sales team, especially Sara Talbot: your work on my work ... works. Thank you SO MUCH for everything you do! Also, to the whole team at Little, Brown, you're the dream team! *Please* never leave my side?!

Secondly, to my incredible, crazy (or incredibly crazy) family. Mum and Dad, I think all my characters have dysfunctional parental relationships because all I've ever known is a brilliant one and so evil mothers and fathers who aren't there for their daughters have only ever been fiction. I love you both so much and you're both responsible for this overactive imagination. I hope you're happy! Tom, Gi, Buzz and Buddy AKA SUPERFAM! You're like a human wall of wonder and a constant source of inspiration and love. Thank you! And, of course, my nan and grandad. I'll be round for cake and tea more often, I promise. <3

Thirdly, to all at Curtis Brown who constantly support my endeavours and indulge my crazy moments where I want to take on everything all at once. You come to every opening night and you're there for hugs, tears and drinks at closing and every single one of you is a gem. Alastair, Helen, Fran, Jess, Emma and Flo. You're the dream team.

Fourthly, to everyone who helped inspire the character and the story within these pages. (This list may be a long one.) This book was written spanning three casts in three different shows, so to the cast of the UK tour of *Chitty Chitty Bang Bang*, you're all marvellous creatures who put up with me turning down nights out in order to sit in bed in my slippers with a cup of tea to finish the next chapter. The *Chitty* lot even threw me a book publication party on a hectic matinee day between two shows and just the thought of it still makes me emotional! Then there's the Dubai cast of *Les Misérables* who kept me sane as I sat in the sun writing, writing, writing, writing, writing whilst you all splashed about in the pool but you also dragged me out of the hotel on days off and made sure I didn't miss any of the incredible city we were in. Then there's my newest family ... The Addams Family! You accepted me and all my bookishness instantly without a moment's hesitation. It was unconditional family love from the start and I hope you all know: it's mutual!

There are a few people in particular that I can't go without mentioning:

Sam Harris, the playwright. You sat with me in many a coffee shop drinking lattes and eating cake as I wrote this book and you adapted *Howard's End* into a play. We kept each other motivated and focused and so much of this book was written under your care. You're utterly brilliant.

Scott Paige, my tour husband. I don't know how many times I've said to you 'I'll just come for one' only to end up stumbling home from a casino at 5 a.m., but you always know just when I need a break and you're always there and happy to provide it! At the same time, you always know when I need to knuckle down and get stuff done which is when you turn up with snacks and drinks from Tesco to keep me going. You're a true friend and I love you with all my heart!

Oliver Ormson, I've not known you long but from the moment I met you in the audition for *The Addams Family* ... I totally stole your face for this book! Thank you for being cool with Chase Masters stealing your looks and thank you for keeping me relaxed on tour when things are getting stressful. What I would do without you? *Who's to know?!*

Mollie Melia Redgrave ... yes, you heard me, REDGRAVE. You're one of the most wonderful women I've ever had the pleasure to meet, let alone call a friend. We're kindred spirits and we knew it right from the off and I hope Cherry does you and your fabulous name proud. Love you.

Pete Bucknall, you watched me write this book, sometimes painstakingly, and I thank you for keeping me going when I felt like I would never reach the end. My workaholism often drove you mad but you stuck by me and my books even so. Thank you.

Also: Paul Wilkins, Anton Zetterholm, Natasha Veselinovic, Alex Banks, Adam Hattan, Gary Caplehorne, Rob Houchen, Jack Howard, Emma Blackery, Louise Jones, Ryan Hutchings, Louise Pentland, Celinde Schoenmaker, Jonny Vickers, Helen Mills, Simon and Nick Loveridge and Jono Bond ... you're all incredible and I have all the love in the world for each and every one of you.

Finally, a HUGE thanks to *you* reading this book. An author is nothing without readers, so thank you for choosing my book to read and I sincerely hope you enjoyed it!

Chocolate Chip Cookies

Makes approximately 25-30 cookies.

Ingredients

80g light brown sugar
80g granulated sugar
150g salted butter, softened
1 large egg
2 tsp vanilla extract

225g plain flour
½ tsp bicarbonate of soda
¼ tsp salt
200g plain chocolate chip
or chunks

Method

1. Line a couple of baking trays with non-stick baking paper, and preheat the oven to 190C/170C fan/gas 5.

2. Toss both sugars and the butter into a bowl and beat until a creamy consistency. Beat in the egg and vanilla extract slowly and then sieve in the flour, bicarbonate and salt over the mixture. Mix everything together and add the chocolate chips once all the ingredients are combined. Stir well.

3. Use a teaspoon to place small amounts of the mixture on the baking trays. Make sure there's plenty of space between them.

4. Place the trays in the oven and bake for 8–10 mins until still slightly soft in the centre and the edges are light brown.

4. Leave the cookies on the tray for 2-3 minutes so they can firm up before transferring to a cooling rack.

Shortbread

Makes approximately 24 pieces of shortbread.

Ingredients

125g butter
55g caster sugar (and little bit extra to finish)
180g plain flour

Method

1. Heat the oven to 190C/375F/Gas 5, and then beat together the butter and the sugar until you have a smooth consistency.

2. Stir in the flour until the consistency is smooth again.

3. Turn the dough out onto a clean work surface and gently roll it out until it's about 1cm thick.

4. Cut the dough into whichever shape you like – rounds or fingers – and then place them carefully onto a baking tray. Dust over the extra caster sugar and then place in the fridge to chill for approx. 20 minutes.

5. Bake in the oven for 15-20 minutes, or until golden brown. Allow them to cool on a wire rack before tucking in.

Classic Victoria Sponge

Makes approximately 8-10 decent-sized slices.

Ingredients

200g caster sugar
200g butter, softened
4 eggs, beaten
200g self-raising flour
1 tsp baking powder
2 tbsp milk

For the filling

100g butter, softened
140g icing sugar, sifted
A drop of vanilla extract
(optional)
170g strawberry jam icing
sugar, to decorate

Method

1. Butter two 20cm round tins and line with non-stick baking paper. Heat oven to 190C/fan 170C/gas 5.

2. Beat all the cake ingredients together in a mixing bowl until you have a lovely smooth batter.

3. Divide the mixture between the tins. Smooth the surfaces so they're flat and then place them in the oven. Bake for approx. 20 mins until golden and the cakes spring up easily when you press them.

4. Turn both cakes out onto a cooling rack and leave to cool.

5. Now for the filling. Beat the butter until it's nice and creamy, and then gradually beat in icing sugar and the vanilla extract (optional).

6. Spread the filling evenly over the bottom of one of the sponges, and then add the jam over it.

7. Place the second sponge on top of the first sponge and filling, and then lightly dust with some icing sugar.

Turn the page for an exclusive sneak peek
at the next bestseller from

Carrie Hope Fletcher

WHEN THE CURTAIN FALLS

A spellbinding, magical and romantic novel

Out July 2018

Available to pre-order now!

Prologue

A certain kind of magic is born when the curtains rises. Intoxicated by the smell of the greasepaint and powered by the glow of the footlights, lovers successfully run away, villains get their just desserts and people die in epic stunts and yet live to tell the tale. Thousands pay to sit and be fooled by illusions and still jump to their feet to applaud despite their gullibility. It's an inexplicable, delicious, addictive power that keeps people entranced and coming back for more, again and again. However, for one theatre on one special night of the year, it's when the curtain falls that a whole different kind of magic takes the stage. Mice scurry through the gaps in the walls, mirror lights flicker in the small hours of the morning and ghosts roam the wings in search of props from productions long past. When the curtain falls in the Southern Cross Theatre, the lonely stage door man wanders the halls checking each door is firmly bolted. All, that is, except one. He turns the key of dressing room four and swings the door open to find the lights already on and a faint scent of tangerine in the air. A high-backed, green velvet armchair faces the mirrors, hiding the woman in the reflection from view. The man doffs his cap to the red-headed lady and her green eyes sparkle at him.

'You're here,' she says.

'Sorry, m'love. I didn't realise you were still here,' he says with a wry smile.

'That's more than alright,' says her reflection. 'I'm always glad of the company. It's rare one finds it these days. Come and sit with me a while, won't you?'

'Always.' He walks to the green armchair and swivels it around, only to find it empty, just as it is every year, on this day, when he comes to dressing room four. He sits down and faces the mirror where he watches the woman pull her pink silk dressing gown tighter around her shoulders.

'You look beautiful.' He smiles, stroking his chin, trying to hide the wrinkles beneath his palm.

'Stop hiding,' she says, reaching out a hand. 'I know what you look like and you know that I like it. Seeing you is such a rarity. I can't bear it when you hide yourself away. It's almost unfair.' Her eyes glisten in the yellow light, and he is afraid her tears will spill over.

'Sorry.' He pulls his hands away and places them on the desk, his fingers splayed apart. 'I know, I know.' Every day of his life builds up to seeing her on this night each year and every year he feels like he lets her down. He's grown older, his skin has wrinkled further, his hair has greyed and yet she's stayed vibrant and sparkling, full of life and full of love for him.

'Please don't hide,' she begs, her fingers pressing up against the glass.

'I won't ever hide from you. Never,' he promises, pressing the tips of his fingers against hers, tricking himself into believing that he can feel the warmth of her skin.

'It's almost time.' Her voice catches in her throat.

'Already?' He checks his watch. 11:45pm. Fifteen minutes.

She nods sadly and stands, her limbs carrying her to the reflection of the door. Her body moves slowly, as if through treacle, every muscle fighting against a force she can't control, a force that is carrying her away from him.

'I'm sorry,' he sobs, a tear trickling down his weathered cheek.

'Don't be. All I ask is that you come earlier next year. Just a few more minutes, that's all I need.'

'I hate letting you go,' he whispers.

'Our time gets so much shorter and shorter and . . . '

'And what?'

'I feel like I'm losing you.' She clutches the door frame, fighting the invisible tide that's crashing against her and forcing her back.

'You will never lose me. Not ever.'

His gaze follows her reflection as she is pulled from the doorway. He gets to his feet and stumbles forward on his aching knees. A line of mirrors, of all different shapes and sizes have been hung in an uneven line along the corridor walls. He catches a glimpse of her hair in one, the hem of her dressing gown in another and then her pleading eyes in the last one. Where he hasn't been able to hang mirrors, he's lined them up on the floor and propped them up against the walls so he can follow her stumbling legs. Some years she takes different routes through the corridors, past different dressing rooms and through different wings, desperately trying to cling to the theatre and the man she loved but ultimately, she is always pulled back to the same fateful place: centre stage. He chases her reflection, sometimes losing her and races backwards, retracing his steps which has become harder and harder every year. So each year he sets up more mirrors in order to keep up with her as her body elegantly bends and bows away from him. It was a dance he had never learnt the right steps to and certainly one he never enjoyed.

She calls his name and her voice echoes through the corridor as he turns the corner to see her silver shoe stepping through the golden frame of a mirror and delicately touching the floor. Despite the click of the shoe against the stone as she pushes her way out of the frame, he can see the end of the corridor through her body. She is transparent and hazy but her green eyes still dazzle him to his very soul and his lips tremble at the sight of her, now in costume, ready for the stage. The train of her burgundy evening gown sweeps along the floor behind her as she is pulled from him once more, her beautifully coiffed, blonde, wigged head twisting reluctantly away. He hobbles after her but with less desperation than before. Now that she is in costume, nothing can stop her and all he can do is watch from the wings just as he has done every year before. She pulls open the double stage doors and a silence falls over the theatre. Mice stop their scurrying and lights cease their humming. His breath catches as he watches her delicately side step props and set pieces, even though were she to come into contact with anything, she would float right through. She turns to face the stage and slowly the warm glow of the lights fades up and he can see the outline of her lovely face. It's all so achingly familiar – the way her cheeks flush at the thought of stepping out in front of an audience, the way she still touches the bridge of her nose even though she isn't wearing her glasses and the way her eyes swim when she turns to him and whispers, 'I'm so sorry.'

'It's me who couldn't save you.' He stumbles forwards, steadying himself against the black painted walls but her smile stills him.

'Oh, but you *did,* my love.'

She takes a deep breath and makes her entrance onto the stage. He doesn't want to watch but the force that had dragged her to this place now has a hold of him too. It gently pulls his body to the spot she had just left. He dodges the props with much less grace but eventually he is manoeuvred into the same position that he takes up every year. Her dress ripples around her young, curved frame and her transparent skin still glows in the light but quickly that light turns blue and cold and the floor becomes slick with a thin layer of dry ice.

'*You were never supposed to find out this way,*' she says, her voice sultry and low, no longer her own.

'*You didn't do well to hide it,*' snarls a snide voice from the shadows. A figure steps into the blue light, tweed clad around his slight figure and smoke billowing from the cigar in his right hand. His thick, waxed moustache twitches against his powdered cheeks as his pale blue eyes drink in her beauty.

'*Leave her be, god damn it.*' Another man appears in a tuxedo, his hair slicked back, jaw chiselled but his eyes are hollow and don't appear to focus on her or the man in tweed. He isn't as present as she is, just a recalled memory, destined to rewind and repeat, year after year. He's on his knees, his lip bleeding. She runs to him and tries to help him up but his body is heavy.

'*Please. Go back inside. Go home. Go anywhere but here.*' She looks behind her and lets her eyes settle on the figure in the wings.

He watches the three of them on stage. This night was meant to have been a night of triumph. A night of life for their love and a night of death for all that stood in their way. The woman he'd met in the dressing room only moments ago had been replaced by the woman from years before and he wishes that he had seen then the signs that something had been so utterly wrong. She, so usually full of light and hope, so young and oblivious, looked like a woman who was carrying the weight of the world on her shoulders. He didn't see it then but he could see it now in this cruel memory. He can see it in the way she's holding herself and the dullness in her eyes. If only he had noticed all those years ago, he may have been able to stop her but his twenty-two year old self had been so blinded by love and the eagerness to escape to a new life with her, he just hadn't seen it.

'*Yes, Larson. Do as she says.*' The man in tweed smiles, taking a long drag on his cigar, the smoke billowing from his lips as he speaks. Larson stays put.

'*Please, Lars. Not here.*'

'*She's not* yours,' Larson hisses through gritted teeth and he mouths the line along with him.

'*Actually, Lars . . . I am.*' She holds up her left hand and reveals a large engagement ring that sends slivers of light dancing on the black stage floor. The ghosts of the audience gasp and a few let out audible sobs.

'*Eliza . . . no.*' Larson whispers. '*NO!*' Larson pulls out a gun from his inside jacket pocket and aims it at the man in tweed. She jumps back, out of the way.

'*Oh, Larson.*' The man in tweed sighs and taps his cigar, ash falling to the floor. '*When will you learn? It doesn't matter how well you scrub up or how many lavish parties you sneak yourself into. It doesn't matter how many of London's finest you rub shoulders with or even how many wealthy women's beds you wheedle your way into. You will* never *be good enough.*'

'*Please don't listen to him, Lars. Just go back inside.*' She is Eliza now, immersed in her role. She puts her hands on Larson's arm and tries to lower the gun but Larson holds strong and steady.

'*Do you love him?*' Larson asks, not daring to glance away from the other man. Eliza looks at Larson, her eyes filling up but her face unchanging. '*Do you?*' he demands again.

'*I fear you'll kill him either way.*'

'*Eliza,*' he breathes. '*If you tell me yes, how could you think that I would kill the man you love and put you through that misery? No, Eliza. Should you say yes, I will turn this gun on myself and the bullet will be destined for me.*'

More sobs erupt from the auditorium.

'*Must we have all this drama? It's terribly dull. We all know you don't have the gall to shoot a rabbit let alone a man. Just put the gun* down, *Larson.*'

'*Do ... you ... love ... him?*'

'I ... ' She hesitates and, back in the wings, he feels every nerve ending fizz. That wasn't her line then and it isn't her line now. He had wondered then if maybe she'd forgotten but she had never forgotten a line in her entire professional life. Was this the moment she was having second thoughts about their plan? He had wondered all those years ago what could possibly have stopped her from saying the line but today he was watching events unfold while knowing exactly what was running through her head. And he was still powerless to stop what was to come.

'I ... ' A tear rolls down her flushed cheek. Her chest

rises and pushes against the fabric of her dress. 'I . . . do not,' she says and what happens next is a blur.

The trigger is pulled, the sound of a gunshot rings out, the lights go out and the gasping audience is plunged into darkness. All of this is as it should have been.

'*Bring up the lights! The lights!*' shouts the man playing Larson. There is panic in is voice. Real panic.

Slowly the lights fade up to reveal her body, centre stage. Her limbs are grotesquely twisted underneath her from where she has fallen and blood is starting to pool and trickle down the stage. The audience erupts into screams and people start to push their way out of the aisles, desperation and fear driving them forward. The crew and actors flood the stage but no one goes to her.

'Get out of here, boy.'

He feels the hot, wet breath of the company manager on the nape of his neck and can smell the cigarette smoke but when he turns his head all he sees is the darkness of the wing.

'Run.'

He looks back to the stage and he knows exactly why no one had rushed to her aid that night. He knows why there was a perfect circle of people around her and not one of them dared to close the distance. It wasn't fear or the amount of blood pouring from her. It was the shock and horror of it all and the simple awful truth that there was no helping her. It was too late. He crouches in the wing, his tears falling onto the dusty floor and he can see that the light and delicious vulnerability that used to live in her eyes, the light that she so happily shared when someone happened to glance her way, was gone.

His muscles relax and she and all of the other ghosts shimmer and fade and the stage is empty and cold once more. His eyes sting and he wills himself to stop crying. He trudges back through the wing, his step heavy, and sighs at the thought of putting all the mirrors away. He has time though, so he walks past the mirrors, leaving them against the walls, useless to him now, and goes to his desk in his small room just inside stage door. Newspaper cuttings cover every wall. Each one contains news and reviews of various productions of *When The Curtain Falls*, collected over the years, and clippings of the headshots of its ever-changing cast. He opens the laptop sitting on his desk and it springs into life and by the time he has managed to sink into the armchair, several emails have already *pinged* into his inbox. He scrolls through but one in particular catches his eye. It's from the production company that owns the Southern Cross Theatre and the subject line reads '*Next In – CURTAIN FALLS*'. His old heart drums against his ribs with more force than he thought it still had and his veins fill with fire. He opens the email with shaking fingers.

I am very pleased to announce that once *Gone With The Wind* closes, April brings with it a brand new revival of *When The Curtain Falls*. An obscure choice, perhaps, but we've discovered this play has a cult following, largely due to an accident that occurred during its last production which also happened to be at the Southern Cross Theatre. We think the combination of this connection and our new star-studded cast will pull in the punters!

We hope you will welcome our new family with open arms, as you always do. Attached is a cast list to help you get acquainted with them all. They start rehearsals in East London at the end of January and will be rehearsing in the theatre from February 12th, ready to open on April 1st.

Sad to say goodbye to such a successful run of *Gone With The Wind* but we're all very excited here about this new production and hope you are too.

Kind Regards,

Susie Quentin

Toast Productions LTD

He sits back in his chair, his breaths coming fast and quick. It's only when his gaze settles on the pair of eyes looking out at him from the photo on his desk that he calms down.

'Oh, darling. I wonder what you'll make of this.' He picks up the frame and looks at the glint of mischief in her eyes. 'You've caused havoc for the shows you do like and pure hell for the ones you don't. What will you do when you're watching someone else play Eliza, *especially* play Eliza and survive each performance?' His desk lamp flickers. 'Come now. You have to play nice. *When The Curtain Falls* is a good show. All casts are family but this one more so because this is *your* show. OK?' His desk lamp flickers again. 'Oh, sweetheart.' He clicks on the attachment in the email and scrolls down to find the face of the actress who is destined to play Eliza.

'Olive Green.' The lamp turns off with a loud clunk. 'I have a feeling you may be sorry you ever said yes.'

When The Curtain Falls

Carrie Hope Fletcher

Coming July 2018

Moulin Rouge **meets** *Phantom of the Opera* **in this spellbinding and magical story of unrequited love and revenge.**

Theatres have a certain kind of magic.
When the curtain rises, we are all enraptured by the
glare of the lights and the smell of the greasepaint but it's
when the curtain falls that the real drama begins ...

In 1952 two young lovers meet, in secret, at the
beautiful Southern Cross theatre in the very heart of London's
West End. Their relationship is made up of clandestine meetings
and stolen moments because there is someone who will make them
suffer if he discovers she is no longer 'his'. But life in the theatre
doesn't always go according to plan and tragedy and heartache
are waiting in the wings for all the players ...

Almost seventy years later, a new production of
When the Curtain Falls arrives at the theatre, bringing with
it Oscar Bright and Olive Green and their budding romance. Very
soon, though, strange things begin to happen and they learn about
the ghost that's haunted the theatre since 1952, a ghost who can
only be seen on one night of the year. Except the ghost is appearing
more often and seems hell bent on sabotaging Oscar and Olive.
The young couple realise they need to right that wrong from
years gone by, but can they save themselves before history
repeats itself and tragedy strikes once more?

Available to pre-order now!